WHEN MY
HEART
SINGS

BETTY LOWREY

Copyright © 2020 by Betty Lowrey.

ISBN   Softcover   978-1-950596-80-5

All rights reserved. No part of this book may be reproduced or transmitted in any form or by any means, electronic or mechanical, including photocopying, recording, or by any information storage and retrieval system without express written permission from the author, except in the case of brief quotations embodied in critical reviews and certain other non-commercial uses permitted by copyright law.

Printed in the United States of America.

To order additional copies of this book, contact:
Bookwhip
1-855-339-3589
www.bookwhip.com

Chapter 1

KANE

IT WAS MORNING. Kane stepped outside the huge glassed door of Alberson Mansion, glancing back as the door slid to a stop, leaving the usual open crack which meant he must always glance back to see if it shut and it never did. Staring out onto the rolling landscape he had to recognize Old Harley was a wonder at keeping everything picture perfect. The mansion sitting on the rolling hills was Kane's home now. It hadn't always been that way. James T had brought his wife here and for a while happiness reigned. He built the spacious home for Andrea, with an extra room for dancing and Andrea named it Alberly, a name few remembered, for when she died young, her husband bundled up the paper work and buried it.

Andrea Alberson had come into James Terrill's life when he was twenty one but she was still a girl. Her parents denied marriage until she was of a suitable age. They knew even then no man could love a woman more. Sadly, their lives together lasted a mere nine years. Andrea died of pneumonia soon after giving birth to their only child Tomas James. After Andrea's death, James T. hired a Nanny for the child and went about his business, gaining acreage, anyway to obtain it, sometimes with ruthless method other times, not. It wasn't that he forgot his son; he neglected him. The child reminded him of Andrea.

From inside, Kane heard his father cough and that would continue until he cleared his lungs, lungs the doctor said couldn't last much longer. Not that Tom smoked, no; his was the curse of receiving it second hand the doctor supposed, "for they are black as a smoker's, that's how it happens." Tom had been slave to his father; perhaps beginning with youth and trying to win his father's attention but that never happened. What Kane remembered was his grandfather barking at his father, "do this-do-that."

In a gentle moment Tom confided, "The only love I have known in life came first from Nanny and then our Rose." He did not say, your mother, at that time, merely "our Rose." She was the light of his life and Kane's; even J.T. did not go against her wishes. Rose held his best interest in her heart, therefore he would not. "Whatever Miss Rose needs," Kane once heard his grandfather tell the gathered group of household and grounds employees. Kane was six years old at the time. Satisfied, hardly listening he heard further, "watch out for the boy, let no harm come to him." Were they speaking of him, or one of the employees sons? Kane wondered but he wouldn't ask, therefore he never felt the old man realized he was around, nor cared. Kane could have been a rock for all J.T. cared.

Perhaps on that he had been wrong. He had established himself in the corporate world, was into his second childless marriage, when J.T. issued the ultimate request, "I need you here. If you have any thought of inheriting what I've managed to build then I'll see you next week, and if you don't come then the town will benefit mightily."

"Mightily." Kane stubbed a toe against a rock he'd been trying for days to remove. When his father sent a hurried message, "Don't buck him, Kane. He'll make your life a living hell," Kane supposed if anyone would know, it would be his father. Gina helped pack, everything was going into two's when he caught on. "What's this about?" In just so many words she said, "I'm going but I'll have my own place, J.T. says. I'm to manage the offices, not particularly the one where the cotton gin is located, but all others."

"You're leaving me?"

She kissed his lips. "Yeah, Sugar, I'm trading you in for an eighty year old with a bank account the size of Texas. What did you think; we were joined at the hip for eternity?"

"Guess not," he'd sighed. He was going home. Gina was going to work for his grandfather. Only one brief minute did he wonder what all that work entailed? He didn't care. Let her go and good riddance. She was high maintenance. He bet he could outshine her. But that was years past, years of making enemies, not friends of the men his age in the community. They feared him; because he did his grandfather's dirty work.

He stumped a toe on the rock, swearing, "I'm fifty four years old and a damn rock defeats me everyday."

Five years since J. T. died. Three years since Hugh Preston died.

Did she ever think of him; Susan of the worried eyes, the question always between them. "Why do you continually watch for me? I know you do. I feel it. If you are around the corner, suddenly I know."

He tried grinning that conversation, actually shaking in his boots he wanted to touch her so bad. "Maybe it's a good thing," he replied. "If you feel something that strong, maybe you should act on it."

That was at the Big Store where everyone went for groceries. She hurried to her truck. The winters following Hugh's death she had led in organizing the Cotton Boll Ball and he with the other men were part of the work force that turned an ordinary unattractive community center into an ethereal mystical old time plantation. Using donated shingles one wall became the imposing front, the columns intact. It was a believable replica complete with long strands of Spanish moss the women sprinkled with glitter to make shine.

He tried to mind his manners that first year when they were thrown together. No doubt, she felt as he did they were forced to attend, both representatives of the community. Not only was she head of the Farmer's Wives Club but the board asked if she would serve out Hugh's time on the school board. On several occasions Hugh found himself taking the last empty chair by Susan Preston. If anyone questioned his doing so, no one said. The second year she was coming out of the deep grief and looking well, her tan from working in the fields was attractive and she was lean of figure. He wouldn't have cared if she was as heavy as Bailey's hog.

Man. He headed back inside. He had to work harder not to let anyone know he cared for her. As usual the door liked a crack's width closing; just enough a snake could crawl through. A thought crossed his mind, maybe Old Harley could fix it. But then again, he had a lot of ground to mow. For a man stingy with others, J.T. had cut a great landscape out of good farmland. The grass was always greener on J.T.'s side. Kane's phone buzzed as he was giving himself one last glance in the mirror. He read the message, *hey, it's Faith, just want to remind you there's a reception for Ware Ward's kid that did the deal on old man Johnson, you know saved him, the breathing bit. You said remind you. See you there 7:00. Faith.* Great. School board members probably should attend.

Faith had a thing for him, but not only was she too young she was one of the customer's daughters. He could be her Uncle. The eyes that stared back mocked the fact he was getting older; more than half a century. That age girl would have starry eyes for a huge wedding and then before you knew it wanting a baby. Lord, help us all. He sighed. His mind did wander toward his and Emily's son; Susan's son in law.

Where the heck were his keys? He found them where they'd fallen into an open drawer, lying beside the picture of Susan that Sherry had taken during the Wives tea at the mansion. For a minute he studied the picture; Susan in the evening dress, not as flashy as the other wives, not imbibing either but beautiful, yes, she took the crown that evening if they had one. Clearing his throat, Kane placed the picture back inside the drawer, pocketed his keys and headed out the door, closing it firmly.

What could he do to show her he had changed? Surely she noticed the office procedures were different and he hadn't pursued his grandfather's underhanded ways in adding acreage at the hand of one already encountering hardship. He had faced his father the day after J.T. was buried.

He found Tom T. sitting at his desk, surrounded by a heap of papers but it was the one he held in his hand that mattered.

"Realtors left this for you. Looks like Sam and Larson Engle have put their farm up for sale. They thought you might want to look into it. They think it will go for a lark. What do you want to do?"

"I won't take ground from these men when they're hurting. I was mean spirited when I came back to the farm, just out of my and Gina's sham of a marriage and I didn't flinch when he said go take that man's land, but I won't do it anymore. Tell me now, what you expect, so I decide whether I leave or stay." Kane wondered was his father so out of it the day of J.T.'s burial he forgot what he told him.

A spasm of panic registered in Tom's eyes. "He left this to you. It's your decision from now on, not mine." Tom's hand trembled as he sat there thinking. "My father never allowed me one decision, I wouldn't know how to make one, now."

Kane stepped closer to lay a hand on his father's shoulder. "If that's settled, then, let's you and I make decisions together. We may not turn the fact around that a lot of harm was done but together we can, in time, make a difference… from here on out."

"Gina informed me she is in charge of the other offices."

"That takes work off of you, Dad. Gina's smart. At the same time I'm going to push J.T.'s lawyer hard to see if there's anything on paper puts Gina in the driver's seat, because…knowing Gina the day will come she will think she can take over. If there are no papers, she doesn't have a leg to stand on."

"You need a wife."

Kane laughed. "Out of the blue, you tell me I need a wife…when I've been through Gina and she's still here."

"A man shouldn't live alone," Tom sighed. "I miss your mother something terrible."

"At least you have a friend in Mrs. Preston."

"Lotta good that does me, now that we're both old." Tom coughed. "And *that* family thinks the Alberson's were spawned by the devil."

"Been told that a few times myself," Kane agreed. "I've an errand to run over to Brighton, need anything?"

Tom pulled a prescription paper from the pile. "They don't keep this here; see if you can find it in Brighton. I rest better nights when I take it."

Kane gave the piece of paper a hurried glance and placed it in his shirt pocket. "I'll not be back for a while." His eyes were on his father's face, pale, almost gray. "Dad, are you all right?"

"Just melancholy," Tom replied. "A day like this…all a man remembers is how it was when he was happy."

Kane grinned, "Then I guess I don't have a worry."

Tom watched his son leave and then muttered to himself, "either you were or you weren't. Ever."

The Engle place wasn't far out of the way, Kane turned on the inner road and slowed, it was good soil. A man could feel proud owning acreage out here. Just ahead he saw the brother's, one on a tractor, the other walking the turn row, ready to hook an irrigation pump to the back of the tractor. Larson, seeing Kane waved him in.

"What are you doing out here, circling like an old hawk, waiting for the kill?"

Kane stiffened behind the wheel. "I just heard, Larson."

"Sure you did. And you couldn't wait to come out and pick up the dregs, could you?"

Kane crawled out of the truck as Sam climbed down from the tractor. "What's goin' on?" Sam asked.

"Your brother thinks I came out to scour the land."

"Did you?"

"I was just driving by."

"Sure you were." Larson leaned to one side, his arm resting on his hip. "Like there's anywhere to go out here, down this road to a ditch bank, and either way nothing for a mile. So you're lyin."

"Whoa," Kane's eyes drew to a squint. "You might have to eat those words, Larson."

"Let me guess," Larson smirked. "You went to the Café, had a cup of coffee. Barrington came in and sit down by you. All arranged. Right?" Larson snapped his finger. "Just like that we lose our funding and what do I bet, you get the first bid on our family home not to mention what you're after, the acreage."

"What do you mean you lost your funding?"

"Does that surprise you? Silverline Bank has been doing that for years."

"Doing what?" Kane demanded an answer. "Look, you brought this out into the open. What do you mean? Were you unable to pay off your loan?"

"Not all of it," Sam replied, his voice cold, his eyes holding on Kane. "You know how that works. They take everything you've got as collateral, then when you hit a bad year and can't pay they close you down and you got nothing to stand behind your loss but an old worn out plug truck you need."

Larson interrupted, "But you knew didn't you? You've been doing this stuff for years. You ain't nothing like our Pap said your granddaddy was before he lost Mis Andrea."

"I'm not happy about my past, Larson, but no, I didn't know what was behind the rumor." He recognized Sam was the stable one, Larson allowed his mind to wander and his tongue to blame. "How much?" He spoke directly to Sam." Sam had a shop on the side, but he couldn't farm and do both.

"What does it matter? For the amount we don't have, they can take a place a hundred times the worth."

Kane had known something was amiss. He'd heard Silverline employees were locked out of meetings, according to what was gossiped the big bosses had come in, parked their shiny black cars in front of Sam's shop and were digging in the dirt outside town as though it were liquid gold. He'd joined them way back when but now, they were reluctant to trust him. He was Paul from the bible, they were wary.

"How much?" Kane set his jaw, let them wonder all they wanted, he was tired holding this rigid stance.

"Hell," Larson gave a quick glance his brother's way. "Ain't none of his business it's us what sinks."

"If he helped us, it's me that's got five kids." Sam thundered. "Get that in your mule head." Turning aside from his brother, he asked, "What you got in mind? You don't do nothin' less there's something in it for you. You ain't changed." Sam spit in the dirt. "Let's hear it."

"This land's been in your family three generations. Right?" Sam nodded. "If you aren't beholdin' to any other than Silverline, then you are actually a free agent to do as you please." Again, Sam nodded. "So you didn't make too good a bean crop?"

"No, we didn't," Sam replied, trying to spit again, his mouth was as dry as cotton.

"So, if I'd loan you the money to keep Silverline at bay, would you be willing to grow cotton next year and bring the cotton to Alberson Gin?"

"I said I'd never do that." Sam's chin came up, eyes squinted he stared at Kane. "Ain't never grown cotton."

"I have," Kane replied. "You'll learn. You'll have to sign papers, the cotton comes to Alberson."

"You'll have to give guidance." Sam stubbed his old leather toed boot in the dirt. "You think they'll give us a loan after we finish off this year's debt?" Kane nodded. "Can't wait to see their faces," Sam said.

"Can't believe you're doing this," Larson began as Kane turned toward his truck.

"Gin. Seven tomorrow morning," Kane shut the truck door and started the engine. "Don't be late."

"Didn't I hear you say you'd like to grow cotton?" Sam's eyes rolled as he stared hard at Larson. "Then shut up. IF he loans us money they ain't getting our Daddy's farm." Sam waited for Larson's eyes to drop. "That's better," he said. "Don't know why Mam and Pap left you for me to raise."

Susan

Through the window the sun was trying to shine. Turning, the sheet caught her body as she rolled on her side to touch his pillow, to run her hand along the place where he lay; Five years and still upon waking he was ever on her mind. Pulling her body into fetal position she remembered. A tear sliding down her cheek, she remembered. Where are you, why did you leave me behind? I'm alone. Hugh, my mind cries out, I can't forget your breath on my neck, when I lay in the hollow of your body, when we made love in the morning hours. My day began blessed ; did you say goodbye?

The first year the dreams…the dreams…how they come to haunt her day and night. The rooms of the house seemed to press down on her as the hours were dark and empty. Why? She cried on the pillow, remembering Hugh by her side but now the world had become cold, you took everything with you, she mourned, what am I to do, where do I go to find rest? Many the time she stumbled from the bed, down the hall to check each room knowing the children were in their own homes; she was alone. Where did you go? In her robe she found the keys, left the house, and drove the mile to her parent's home.

Star heard the lock turn as she rose from the bed to meet her child. In the dark of the living room, her arms opened to hold Susan as she cried, no word necessary only the balm of a mother's love closed tight, hands rough with age soothing, knowing when to turn loose as she listened for all the years between happy times turned sad; Susan's voice a mere whisper, "Mom, I didn't get to say goodbye. Mom, do you understand?" The tears had not lessened, this one that seemed strong to the world, cried her heart ache in her mother's arms and Star worried.

"I understand, if I could do something to ease your pain, I would. But my love, you must turn loose; Hugh could not stand to see you in such despair. You must have this talk with him and listen with your heart…for the children you must go on…this grieving does not celebrate the love you knew, a soft sweet smile will carry you through their heartache but this sadness is killing you and perhaps a part of them, too."

"But Mom he's gone. Just when we thought we could have more time together to do things," the sobs muffled in her mother's arms shook Susan's body. "Why, Mom, why?" And no one knew Susan Preston drove the mile to her parent's home, the days building to months that became years. To the world Star's brave daughter wore a mask as she carried life farther on her own, the life she thought she and Hugh would live. Star prayed God would send peace and calm before she lost her only child. "Don't ever leave me, Mom," the tears finally stopped, her child finally pulled away. "Thank you, Mom." Susan left as quietly as she came.

Star slipped back into bed, trying to settle as Anson put his arm around her. "She'll be all right?" Star's tear fell on his hand as she replied, "I pray to God she will, before we lose her." Anson's voice was gentle. "She'll be fine; it's just taking longer because they loved better than most…God's watching. She will be just fine, Star…turn it over to him." With that, Anson's breathing become quieter and he went back to sleep while Star prayed, Lord, bring back love. Lord, you will have to send someone. She won't let go. Lord, if you took Hugh, then I know you have a plan for her. She has so much love to give…please Lord, before I lose my child give her someone to love, someone to hold her."

The second and then the third year Star began to see a release in Susan, she wasn't coming in the middle of the night and then it was four years. Now it was five when Susan came to sit with her. "Mom, it wasn't that I thought Hugh would return. I'm a believer and I know death in this world takes us to another. It was just that he left so sudden, of all nights after our son's wedding…" Susan paused to think what impact that had on Barkley. "Barkley had to find a way to turn it into something other than tragedy… it took a while. But Mom, you said I have to let go…you don't mean the memories, now I've seen what you're saying, I have to let go the terrible sadness because it's dragging me down. I thought I was doing good, and then last night that terrible sadness brought me back."

"Yes, dear," Star nodded. "But I couldn't give it to you, you had to find what it takes to heal."

"I've gone through the motions of so many things, Mom, but I was up most of the night and there's a glimmer, I feel, maybe to find my way, the one I shared with Hugh, it's over, isn't it but I have to figure it out now, don't I?" Star agreed her eyes on her daughter. "Just want you to know how much I appreciate you. You never scolded my waking you up in the middle of the night. How did you know, Mom? I could have been a burglar." Susan almost giggled, but the act ended in a sob. "I could have been a burglar breaking into your home."

Star had to consider all the nights, the endless gatherings when Susan's children suspected but allowed their mother the benefit of the doubt hoping that she was getting over the fact their father was gone. "You knew when Caroline was sick? But I'll have to say when there was such a spell in there you didn't come I thought well, she is accepting the pain, now there's healing and then last night?" Star gave a shudder as her eyes went wide. "I said to myself, that has to be Susan. Please Lord, Susan."

Yes, Mom." Susan thought about Caroline. "Thank God, she's been well since her daddy died or I'd really be a mess."

"You're going to be all right now, right?"

"I'm going to try." Susan rose up from the sofa. "Thanks, Mom. I better head out now."

Weary, Susan remembered, she had driven to her parents. What would she do when they were gone? Never in a hundred years would she have known grief would happen so strong it took her to her knees, it's hold claiming her while she tried to pray but she could not pray for herself; but for the children she ask God's grace in a thousand ways, "And don't let them see me like this."

She glanced at the clock. She had to drive over to Brighton. Life went on in spite of how she felt. Even now she heard the drip of the shower head, just another item on the list she must purchase. She applied makeup, dressed in gray denims and a long pink shirt and remembering her words to Star clasp a silver chain around her neck and earrings to match. "not flashy, just an accessory," she said aloud, nodding at their being the right accent, not large, just right. Stepping into gray wedged boots, she glanced at Hugh's picture. "How do I look? Just remember, I love you, should some tall handsome stranger take a liking to me, I love you." A sad smile dawned in her eyes knowing he would say, "woman, I said I'll never share you."

Chapter 2

MILES HAD PILED up on the Surburban. One of the salesmen had driven it before her; fifteen thousand miles when she purchased, now one hundred thirty in the years since Hugh was gone. Lately she noticed the steering seemed a bit off but she hadn't found the problem. Miles would do that and she traveled many picking up parts, delivering suppers and the occasional trip to Caroline Dawn's to see her grandchildren. For that she thanked the Lord; Caroline Dawn was still in remission. Sophia Raine lived nearby and her little tow–headed boy was coming along beautifully. Almost unbelievable, Sophia's child played the piano as Caroline Dawn had when they were young and his mother had no interest but now she sat on the bench by his side adding to her natural talent. Grinning like the nymph she was, Sophia Raine asked, "Who knew, Mom? I like it."

Pulling into the Dealership, Susan viewed the parked cars, hoping to find a good used Suburban and not have to pay the sticker price. A salesman was quick to join her, walking briskly alongside the Suburban when she noticed him. "I didn't mean to bother anyone," she said. "I'm just looking."

"Well, Ma'am, I think its your lucky day to be looking, looks to me like you've got a wheel about to come off, how's it been driving?" He paused, "By the way, my name's Dan."

She was trying to open the door to follow him and see for herself. "I don't know how I missed that at home." She was studying why the door wouldn't open.

"It could have just reached this point." He was stooping down examining the wheel. "Why don't you drive up to that long door over there and I'll have Jimmy come out and tell us what it needs."

Following instructions, Susan parked where the new guy pointed and then waited a short while inside until Jimmy gave her the bad news. "If you can leave it over-night we'll get 'er fixed right up." He said, as he and the salesman were giving each other some kind of message that apparently was not in her favor. "Ma'am, you didn't purchase here, we have a new owner and a new program, if a customer didn't buy here we can't supply a loaner but we can run you home if that will help. Ma'am, there's a problem with the door on the driver's side. I almost couldn't open it to get in or to get back out."

"Let's talk about the vehicle first, what is the extent of the damage if I drive it?"

"Ma'am, don't you have a second vehicle at home you can drive? You could damage it further if you…"

"Hello, Susan. Dan." She turned. She knew that voice. "I believe I owe my neighbor a ride home. She stopped and picked me up one hot summer day about five years back, when my wheel ran off….no relax you weren't responsible, I was up in Illinois where some ya-hoo claimed to fix it and didn't."

Kane didn't let up. He had his hand on her elbow escorting her back to the Surburban, "just in case she forgot something and then we'll lock it since you have the keys. All right? He flashed his beguiling smile Jimmy and Dan's direction and then led Susan to a shiny new Pick up truck. "My new wheels," he said. "What do you think?" Perfect gentleman he gave her a hand up and went around to the driver's side. "I know, black will pick up the dust and look bad when weather is making mud, but it looks good today. Now, what have you been up to, Susan?"

"Why are you acting as though we are friends and you stop to chit-chat every day of the year?"

"No hissing, now Susan." Kane grinned. "If I didn't do it this way, you know you wouldn't give me the time of day. Now, sit back and relax. Are there any places you need to go? I'm supposed to pick up a prescription for Tom. Do you mind if I stop at the Pharmacy?"

"Of course not," she snapped. "I can't believe I'm doing this. I came here for a reason."

"I'm very glad you did." He was suddenly all serious. "When wheels run off a vehicle a person is not always on a country road as I was and the vehicle in a worse case doesn't always stay upright."

She faltered, anger settling. "I meant, I had no idea this turn of events and me sitting in your truck."

"How do you like it?" He glanced her way. "Would you have chosen another color?"

"It's nice, Kane and black is a good business choice. It suits you."

"Am I reading something into those last words?" She wouldn't meet his eyes. "Do you really think I'm that bad?" He stared at her. "I hoped with five years in between perhaps you and I could at least talk."

She took a deep breath. "What do you want to talk about Kane?"

"Nothing in particular, just…you know…talk, maybe as neighbors, how's the weather type thing."

Hadn't she decided things would be different? Susan sat there, hating where they were now. It wasn't planned. She hadn't added Kane Alberson into the list, only that she would try harder at being a normal person instead of a shut off widow, because that's what Hugh made her, what she had allowed herself to become.

"I don't want a boyfriend, Kane. I'm not interested in any of that, so why would you have any interest in me?"

A pained expression crossed his face. "Must you always put me in my place, Susan?" He turned in the seat to face her. "Have I ever once kept my feelings from you? I find you intriguing, interesting, and completely alluring. I want to know you." He gave a comical eye lift, purposely trying to break the mood and hoping she would relax. "What about all that threatens you?"

"Do you mind pulling away from the number one place in town where people are likely to see me sitting in a vehicle with you?"

"Sure," he agreed, putting the truck in reverse to pull into the mainstream of Brighton traffic. "Shall I go on through town or do you think the stop lights will be taking our pictures?"

"Now you are being facetious."

"I don't even know what that means. Silly?" He questioned. "Sorry you think so." He drew another deep breath. "Let me think this out…you don't want to be seen with me…so I assume you are ready to go home?" She nodded. "And, I question whether you would like to ride back to Brighton with me, when they are finished with your vehicle. I'll let you work that one out. I'll call you before I leave in the morning."

"There's a real reason you will be coming back, not some made up excuse just to help me?"

"Yep, a real reason, like new tags for the truck and paying the sales tax. Is that good enough?" She relaxed a little until out of the blue he said, "I've never seen Sophia and Thorn's little boy?"

"Why would you want to?" She asked too abrupt. The fact was Kane's birth son was her son in law.

"If Barkley had a child with another woman, other than his Betsey, wouldn't you want to know about the child, and if possible see him?"

She thought for a minute. "You are bound to see him."

"My shame causes me to avoid any encounter." He paused, glancing away, "I do find opportunity to watch him from afar but I won't bring shame to my boy."

Softly, studying his face as she spoke, she said, "Thorn considers himself Sam's boy. Sam's son."

Kane flinched as though a pain ran through his body. "I know." He replied softly.

"I didn't say that to hurt you…but its late to try any sort of…" Her words ebbed into silence. "I can't imagine your thoughts. My kids are everything to me, they're …."

"As they should be." He was quiet for a spell, but finally admitted, "It was all my fault, never Emily's."

"Why didn't you marry her? She loved you or she would never have given herself to you. Women don't do that…good women…"

He studied her, beautiful as ever, age had not taken anything away, perhaps added and what he heard in her voice was hard earned wisdom. He suspected there were times life was worse than others, but she had made it this far and she would go farther. As a young man, how had he missed knowing she was there?

"How was the wedding?"

"Really, Kane, are you serious or baiting me for some…fluke of the brain to make me talk when you aren't one bit interested in Thorn, you are biding time to put me in my place…"

"I have always believed, Susan, there's not a mean bone in your body…I was young, there were extenuating circumstances…"

"It wasn't your parents," she countered. "I," she stressed the word, "I always heard you had good, have good parents. You told me how close you and your mother were…." She let the sentence drop.

"In the end, it was my fault. By the time sense came in to my head, Emily had married Sam." He sighed. "Are we having a disagreement, Susan?" He heard her stomach rumble. "I take it you haven't eaten, either. No, no, don't start floundering and making excuses why we shouldn't have dinner together. It's mid-day for heaven's sake, Susan. I'm not going to harm you and we are right here by a good place."

She was experiencing so many emotions, she could barely lash out at him when her stomach was rolling like a ship at sea. Taking a deep breath, "All right," she agreed. "I'll do my best." He was pulling into the drive of what appeared to be a shack, but there were a dozen or so cars parked near the entrance.

They were seated when he said, "Something you said back there, reverberates in my head…"

"What's that?"

"That your kids are everything to you…I've always wondered what it's like to love someone that much. I gave up my opportunity to love Thorn and even though I've been married twice, I haven't…" They were being served and Kane dropped the conversation.

That night, preparing for bed, Susan recalled his words. What kind of man married two women and said he had never loved that much? So much the person became his world? She was exhausted as she climbed into bed. Reaching to turn off the lamp her eyes came to rest on Hugh's picture. "But we did, didn't we, love?" Sighing she turned the switch and the room went dark. "Hugh…." She whispered and slept. There were no nightmares, no need to go to Star and Anson's house in the middle of the night.

He couldn't sleep. His mind was barraged with a thousand thoughts, all coming to rest on the fact Susan had settled down and they had enjoyed a dinner of sorts, together. He recognized her being uncomfortable in the beginning but not recognizing anyone she eased into enjoying the food.

"How did you find this place?"

He smiled. "You don't recognize the chef? Take another look. Andrew used to work at the gin company. He was always on hand when we had an occasional lunch with various company reps stopping in and when we were told he was an excellent cook we gave him a chance to shine… of course that led to someone saying you should have your own place."

"And now he does." She folded her napkin, "I don't know why I do that, you are supposed to leave it undone. That shows you are finished and I can't eat another bite."

"I guess mother forgot to tell me that." He opened the leather tab book the waitress had left. "She said they have a melt In your mouth chocolate pie. Interested?"

"No, I'm sure it's delicious but I can't." As by magic the waitress appeared for the book.

"Maybe next time," he replied without looking up and to ward off her denying that he said, "I bet you cook. What kind of pie do you make?"

"Well," she smiled for the first time, "Caroline Dawn prefers coconut, Sophia asks for Cherry and Barkley is actually a chocolate pie or cake."

"I'm with him," Kane agreed, rising as the waitress handed back the book for him to retrieve his card.

That night as she prepared for bed, Susan remembered Kane's words. A man who was married twice had never experienced love that meant everything to his life? She climbed into bed, reaching to turn out the light and her eyes caught on Hugh's picture, "but we did, didn't we, love?" she whispered. The room went dark and Susan began her prayers but fell asleep. The Lord willing, she would waken in the morning and be ready by ten o'clock. There was no trip to Star and Anson's house that night.

Kane was restless, standing outside peering across the rolling landscape of the slight hills where his grandfather built the mansion, his father asleep down the hall, while he recounted every word of the evening. Was there hope? She was such a lovely woman, still caught in the web of grief he supposed.

He found himself at the piano as the clock struck midnight, his fingers trailing across the keys, first the songs his mother insisted he learn, those of the masters, she said fit any mood he would ever experience. A slight smile formed as he heard her voice. "Someday you will meet a girl and then these will make sense."

His fingers trickled across the keys, as enticing as though a summer breeze guided each finger and he was studying her lips as he bent his head and she tilt hers and they kissed and it was right, not heated and sexy but soft and gentle and full of promise. The sound stopped as suddenly as he had made it happen. There was no girl, no Susan, no kiss, he was caught up in a dream of his own making. Disgusted with himself he arose and trailed down the hall. Once years ago, he had felt this way over Emily but not enough…he had not pursued her and when she came to him, worried and crying he rejected her.

If there was the slightest doubt he was not serious over Susan Preston, he must stop now. She had been hurt enough. Lest he add to that hurt, the Lord above wipe him from the face of the earth. She was golden, her honor unblemished. He shook his head in frustration, was he as vulnerable as a school boy? Better that than the evil of the man he used to be.

If he slept at all it was because tomorrow he would return to her house to drive her back to Brighton for her vehicle. Surely God was in this, otherwise she would not give him the time of day. Maybe he should return to church. It did seem these days God was setting things up in his favor. He did not deserve it.

She heard the wheels of Kane's truck crunching on the graveled drive, hurriedly glancing around to check everything was in order to leave and finding it so picked up her purse as she slid an arm into the green denim jacket with it's embroidered design trailing front and back and to the elbow of the sleeves; Hunter green, an accent to her medium blonde hair. When a few gray strands crept in she decided to go lighter instead of the dark hair she was born with. Hugh wasn't there to tell her if it was becoming or not and Barkley hadn't noticed. Near Caroline Dawn's color she thought it appropriate. It was Sophia laid a hand on each shoulder studying her astutely, "Why, Mother, I like it. But where is my mother with hair the color of mine? Am I an orphan?" They laughed together, Sophia did not change.

He watched her lock the door and slid from the seat to open the truck door. She was waving him back. "I'm your neighbor, remember? Isn't that what you told the guy named Dan? You don't need to do this." Inside she heard the strains of music on the radio; he did seem to like music.

"I want to," was all he said, returning to slide back under the steering wheel. "Have they called you?"

She shook her head. "Do they usually? This is a different dealer for me. You noticed if you don't purchase your vehicle there they don't loan you anything to drive." She sighed. "Thank you for the ride."

"My pleasure."

She turned, studying him. "What? Are you sick? You are usually talking."

"I believe I got the impression you didn't like my talking too much, so I decided to honor…"

"I never implied such…but just so you aren't ill."

"Never felt better," he quipped. "So just sit back and enjoy the undulating hillside between here and Brighton. I could give you a travel talk, you know a speech if you like, otherwise I'll just drive and soak up your presence."

Quite unexpectedly Susan laughed. "There's not much to say about the countryside this time of year. It's gray but come spring, when everything turns green," she sighed. "I long for busier days."

"Winter is a time of monotony? Not much to do?"

"Something like that. My Mom calls it the doldrums," she replied. "Used to, Hugh worked the winter months in the shop with the men making repairs and I don't recall this feeling that almost borders on despair, I guess because he was in and out or I'd go out to the shop…but no one works out there these days…" she let the words drop. In the silence the words to the song played, *living without you* …

"You miss him, specifically. I can understand that."

"What happened to Sherry? It's been five years and she hasn't returned for any of our Cotton meetings."

"Sherry married," he gave a soft laugh. "I was as surprised as anyone. She always said she wasn't the marrying kind and those terrible baggy flannel pajamas she wore to bed…I never." He grinned, "Well, I told her she would have to do better than that."

"So you and Sherry were bed partners." She glanced out the window. "I'm shocked I'd say that."

"No, we were never bed partners. What we were was comfortable friends who could each lay on our own side of the bed and talk things over. She was a wealth of information on the cotton industry."

"So she married a cotton farmer?" The music played on; *not knowing what to do…*

"No, Sherry married Mr. Cotton himself when his wife died from lung cancer. They waited six months or so, and went down to the courthouse and made things legal. She is happy as a hog in a mud hole."

"I doubt she lives in anything compared to a mud hole."

"Does that matter if you're happy?" His gaze rest on her, a serious expression waiting for her answer.

"Money makes life easier but if you love someone you can be happy in a one room shack. As long as you are together that's what counts." They listened to the words of the music, each lost in their own thought. *I was without hope but you knew, you saw through….and when I'm in despair….you're there….*

"You love music."

"Yeah," he said. "It calms the savage beast."

Chapter 3

DAN MET THEM at the door, ushering both in to a little side room. "I know you were headed to the service department, Mrs. Preston, and Jim, who is the head mechanic ask me to talk to you as he left for a dentist appointment, said he was up all night with a tooth hurting," Dan was apologetic, "Anyway, he has a part ordered and it should be here, tomorrow." He cleared his throat before proceeding, "I know you need your vehicle but they said to tell you the problem with the door handle requires a few hours."

She wanted to throw up her hands in despair. "Well, I have to be able to use that door and the other part does sound as though you can repair where needed." She took a deep breath to stomach the problems. "So I guess we're finished here, for the day."

"Ma'am, the price to repair both the door and putting the wheel back on takes a bit of time." Dan stepped closer. "I'd be really remiss if I didn't tell you a price like that could be better attached to the vehicle you use in your business, assuming you use it more often."

"I think you are implying I should put the cost on a new vehicle. I tell you what, Dan, if Kane has the time, I'll see what's out there. How's that?" Dan beamed but Kane looked disappointed. "What, Kane?"

"It sound as though you were dismissing me, I'm going with you to look at the vehicles. How's that?"

The walk across the dealership's lot was tiring but Susan had to admit she would never have considered the questions Kane ask. Once, he turned to her and said, "It is not my intention to get into your business, Susan, but you need to know these things. By the way, would you prefer Barkley walk through this with you?"

"Barkley and Betsey are at a seed conference, Kane. That's why I didn't have anyone to pick me up, with the girls living in Memphis." Tilting her head as she studied the black Suburban she continued, "I don't particularly want black since I travel the fields of the farm, but I guess if one has to there are always car washes."

"I have one other to show you," Dan said. "It's one of the owner's and approximately five thousand miles on it and it's white." He paused a moment before asking, "Are you interested at all in a used vehicle?"

"Yes, according to the miles and five thousand should be enough that if there was something wrong; the problem would have been found."

"Exactly," Dan agreed. "It's in the shop. Mr. Creed's wife drove it and it was always in the garage." He motioned they follow him. "It's loaded, but you know drive one off the lot and the new price tag drops considerably." He opened the door, motioned for Susan to get into the driver's seat. "You all take this little jewel for a ride and see what you think." He waited for Kane to cross around to the other side. But Kane didn't move until Susan spoke.

"Kane, what are you waiting for?"

Dan grinned. "He's waiting to hear the motor purr, and this one will purr."

Once they were out of the drive Susan glanced at Kane. "What was that about?"

"Well, the way you keep me in my place I wasn't sure you wanted me along."

"Think of yourself as a technician," she replied, "I like this vehicle. It looks new, it's loaded and the sticker price has dropped, so how about you help me figure this out."

"Using me, huh?" He sat back, the grin on his face, pleased. "I could get used to that."

Susan's eyes narrowed. "I'm not sure how you mean that, but I think this proves we are going to be running into each other and I don't want to be mean spirited and people noticing."

"Yeah," he reached across to turn on the radio. Music poured out of the speakers. "My station," he said. She didn't answer, she wasn't listening to him. "You don't want me around you and I want us running into each other." He glanced to see if she was listening and she had to think what he said.

"I said I'm beginning to accept that." *As you melt this heart of stone, take my hand and lead me home…* Susan was listening to the music, hadn't she heard the song when they were having lunch the other day? She was vaguely aware he was talking but he could be a thousand miles away for all she was thinking. Would she ever lose sight of the fact, every song made her think of Hugh.

"I want people to know, to talk about us. I want to take you to the best restaurants, dancing…"

"Oh, Kane, I'm sorry. I was listening to the song and had you completely tuned out."

"Story of my life with you," he admitted. "It wasn't important, to anyone but me."

They returned to the dealership, Dan was waiting but he wasn't alone. Before she saw who stood behind him, Susan registered the worried expression on the salesman's face.

"It's lovely," she said. "I need to sleep on this, though, before I make a decision." Then her heart gave a leap of surprise as happiness registered on her face. "Barkley, when did you get back?" She reached out to touch him, but he moved and then she saw his face; his eyes were anything but friendly. For a moment, she did a recoil. What was wrong with her son? "Barkley, are you ill?"

"Why is he…"Barkley's words were thick with anger, "Why are you with him?"

Taken back, Susan felt the color wash out of her face. "What do you mean? I'm not with anyone. I'm here, your mother, looking at another vehicle and why would you question me?"

Barkley wasn't bending. His eyes held on Kane and he did not flinch. "I'll take you home, Mother." He gave the salesman a rude glance as though it were all his fault. "For what he has done to us, you don't have to ride any where with him."

"Barkley, your manners." Her voice faltered. "He came along at the time my vehicle wouldn't run."

"I'm here now. So he can leave." Turning to Kane, he repeated, "We don't need you. Stay away from my mother."

"Barkley." Susan's thoughts were in a whir, what did Barkley think they had been doing? "Son?"

"Betsey's out front, Mother. Go join her."

Trying for dignity, Susan started to speak to the salesman but he turned away. Kane was staring at her son and then his eyes were on her; sad eyes, she thought and for a moment felt his pain.

Barkley's hands were clenched tight. "I mean it Mother. I'll leave the farm and never come back."

"Barkley." She was aghast, that the situation escalated to this. "There's nothing that serious…"

"All right, you want me out of the way?" Barkley's eyes were blazing though his lips trembled. "I'll go."

Susan turned to follow her son, quickly as the door swung between them.

The last Kane saw was her hand on Barkley's arm and the boy leaving her almost to fall as he jerked his body away. She hurried the remaining distance to the truck and climbed unaided into the back seat. Barkley left the car lot the wheels of his truck spinning dark spots on the concrete before it shot forward.

Kane was on his way out when the salesman caught up with him. "I don't suppose you know if she liked the truck?"

For one moment, Kane stopped, stared at the man until he turned away. "I guess not," he said.

Kane stood outside, mindful of the cold air but uncaring. Could the Preston kid hate him that much? He began a back log of history between the families, mostly his and Hugh's relationship. He couldn't remember the two of them having words, but maybe they had. God knew he had done some wicked things at J.T.'s bidding. He had become the devil's spawn while J.T. with all his benevolent deeds appeared the community's benefactor. He pushed at the rock. Immovable, as always, while the toe of his boot appeared scarred. Like my heart, he admitted taking a deep breath.

It hadn't mattered she ignored him, experiencing the fineness of the vehicle she was driving compared to the problems with the one she owned, tuning him out as she heard words to a song that he figured made her think of her dead husband. Dead. Her husband had died but she had not. What was it she did she not understand that life could go on? But not with him, it was obvious Hugh Preston's son would never allow her peace if she so much as spoke to him.

He returned to his room, shutting the door firmly against the cold air and shuddering as he thought of the nights he simply crawled in the truck and drove to the nearest bar and drank until he couldn't think, but that was behind him, God willing he felt the need to change his life, but how to make it through the lonely hours, no one to talk with, no one laughing and sharing life. He thought of Sherry, happily married and Gina…probably locked in her closet counting the money J.T. left her. Yeah, he knew about that and he didn't care. Gina was a cold fish. He left his room, ambling down the hall toward the piano.

The furnace kicked on and the thaw appeared in his body. He sit down at the piano. *You give your hand to me…and then you say hello…and I can hardly speak my heart is beating so…*.Michael Buble, he thought you knew your lyrics, wish I'd written that song but then who cares what Kane Alberson writes? He sat at the piano for over an hour. His dad came in to the room carrying two glasses of orange juice.

"You want to talk about it? Your mother said even as a little boy when something hurt or someone hurt you, you played the piano." Kane shook his head as he took the glass Tom offered. "That bad, huh?" Tom sat in the chair opposite the piano. "We're supposed to be so calcified we can take anything, Kane."

"Calcified objects break into little pieces, Dad."

"Yeah, I know. I've been lying awake thinking how to handle our newest problem."

"What's that?"

"Gina wants control of the business. She says J.T. promised he left it to her."

"Then Gina has to present papers and deeds and J.T.'s promise to her in writing, doesn't she?"

"She says she has it."

"Then we better find a hand writing expert, hadn't we?" Kane swung around from the piano bench and stared at his father. "She is as black hearted as J. T., no scruples whatever. Next to her, I look like a choir boy." Rising he sit the empty glass on the table next to his father. "Go to bed, we'll worry this one over tomorrow."

"What in the world did she do to make an old man that age sign over his legacy?"

"Whatever it took," Kane replied. "Whatever it took." He was walking away, "Good night, Dad."

"Good night, Son."

The rains came beating on the roof, streaming down the window panes and then the cold. The weatherman said it was their coldest winter since nineteen ninety two. Susan shuddered. Staring out onto the frozen ground, she could not feel at peace. Barkley still was not speaking to her, whether his shame or thinking there was guilt laid on her shoulders which she denied hotly.

That day when they were alone, she berated him as a mother should. Betsey had never seen the two so troubled as on the ride home. So deep was Barkley's anger he had dismissed her as though she were no one in particular, a fact Susan hated to see. "I need to talk to Mother alone," he said and Betsey simply left the two of them sitting in the truck at Susan's home.

"She cannot get in, Barkley. That was terribly rude." With that, Susan in her haste had practically fallen from the truck and followed Betsey. "I'm so sorry," she said upon catching the girl. "I have absolutely no idea what has gotten into your husband, my son." Unlocking the door, she motioned Betsey inside, only then seeing the tears in the girl's eyes. "Is there more, Betsey?" She asked, taking her son's wife into the living room where they both sit down on the sofa.

Betsey was twisting her hands together. "He loves you so much, Mrs. Preston."

"Susan," she corrected her daughter in law. "When did I become Mrs. Preston?"

Tears slid down Betsey's face. "It was terrible, Su-san." She was trying hard not to sob out loud. "We entered the building happily expecting to see you but when Barkley glanced toward outside and saw you and then Mr. Alberson it was like he came unglued. "Go to the truck," he said, and I was so shocked I glanced around to see who he was speaking to and he meant me." Now her voice broke and she couldn't control the sobbing. "He has never talked to me that way."

"And he shouldn't again." Susan glanced up as the door slammed and Barkley stood before her.

"If I ever see you with that man again," he threatened, "I will pack up and move." His eyes rest on Betsy. "And if you think to help her in this…this…I am helpless as to what it is, I will leave you behind."

Susan stood to her full height. "I thought at first you had the wrong impression, Barkley James Preston, but now I realize you are wrong in so many things the first impression has nothing to do with your rudeness to me, your own mother, and especially to your wife. I expect you to apologize to her and you don't have to worry about leaving the farm, you ever speak to me with disrespect again and you will not be part of this operation. I cannot stomach the thought of working under such conditions when you have jumped to conclusion and not once said to me, Mother what was the reason he was standing there."

Barkley gave a ridiculous laugh, his eyes as fiendish as Old Moon when the dog was run over by a neighbor and his pain was so terrible he would not let them care for him. Hugh had put the dog down but you didn't do that to a human, especially a child you loved. Still, Barkley needed discipline all the while she realized he needed love at this very moment. She went to him.

"Son, this is a terrible misunderstanding. Can we forget it?"

Barkley stiffened, holding his hands at bay and replied, "No, we will never forget this." In a terse voice he asked, "Betsey you going home with me?"

The second week after their differences, Caroline Dawn's family came for the weekend and attending church services together found only Betsy in the usual pew. "Where's Bub?" Caroline asked. Betsy shook her head, looking to Susan for an answer. Oliver, ever the peace maker filled in the gap, jostling the children around and handing Betsy the baby. They were all lost in her funny little antics.

Dinner was not as happy as usual. Betsey felt the need to return home after church services and it was several hours until Caroline's family would leave.

"Mom, do you want to tell me?" She studied her mother with those serious eyes that reminded Susan so much of Hugh. "No, it's not what you want to share, I can tell, so I'll leave you alone. Things that run deep hurt too much to discuss." She smiled, placing an arm around Susan's shoulder. "Come over here and let me show you what I'm ordering for Easter for the rug rats."

But the next week when Sophia Raine came, Thorn driving and a back seat filled with her child's keyboard and books; there was no evading the subject. She waded right in. "Mother, Caroline tells me Bub didn't make a showing and Betsy went home after church, so you just as well tell me because I'm ready to barge right in and give him a piece of my mind. We are his sisters and we have done nothing. I expect to see him. So what did he do, or you?" She paused for breath. "Phew, that was a mouthful, wasn't it?"

"I did nothing, Sophia, but in some strange mixed up manner your brother thinks I did."

"What did you do?" Sophia flopped on the sofa, patting the cushion for Susan to join her.

"You know I've changed vehicles? Before I did, I was at the dealership needing a ride home and the person that came along was Kane Alberson. Barkley and Betsy were on a trip, the dealership didn't supply a loaner and Kane Alberson brought me home. He offered and I didn't want to bother you."

"Is that all?"

"No. The next morning he was going back in to Brighton and picked me up to return to the dealership." She sighed heavily. "That's where Barkley saw me and after that…nothing but frozen silence."

"So, Barkley feels threatened?" Sophia became quiet for a while. "I'll give him time and then I'll talk to him."

"I don't know what to think, Sophia. I thought Barkley and I could talk over anything but on that day he didn't give me a chance. He said if I saw the man again, he would leave the farm operation."

"What did you say, in return?" Sophia listened intently. "Mother, Barkley has always had a fear of losing you."

Tears sprang to Susan's eyes. "I miss him but he won't even talk to me. Bert is the go between. Give our boy time, he says." She sat next to Sophia, "I just need to know someone cares, Sophia. I'm so lonely missing your Dad and now Barkley has left me and I don't know how he's treating Betsy, she seems a bit distant. Is that my fault, too?"

"I don't mean to worry you but I do sense something is wrong in their marriage. Maybe Bub…well, really, I don't know what's going on." She pulled her mother to her side. "It may take a while, but our family's strong, we'll get through this. Has Mr. Alberson been back by or called?"

"Why no, why should he?" Susan's voice took on an indignant tone. "I certainly don't expect him to call." She leaned away to look into her daughter's face. "Honey, we have a crop to make. It's our livelihood; if Barkley left I'm not sure I could manage. I've grown so use to his taking the lead."

"Try not to worry, Mom," she slipped into the endearing tone, "Barkley's always been stable, set in his way with a head full of all kind of statistics the rest of us could care less about, but he's a good person."

But Sophia felt the concern and when her husband brought their son in and gave her a worried look, she felt the undercurrent. He waited until they were in the car headed home to tell her. "I don't think your straight arrow brother is that straight anymore."

Her heart lurched. "What do you mean? He's never wandered the beaten path."

"I thought I'd drop by to see him. We may be brother In law's now but we've been friends longer. Even that short spell I worked in Memphis we stayed in touch but several months ago he began to avoid me."

"What did your sister tell you?"

"It's what Betsey isn't saying concerns me." Thorn shook his head, staring straight ahead. "She wouldn't say, except made me promise not to tell Mother there's a problem."

"Do I need to talk to him?" Sophia glanced back at their son, happy in the back seat, an I-pad in one hand, ear buds in his ears. Sometimes she couldn't decide if he resembled Thorn or Bub more. It pleased her to know her father's blood came through, because Bub was his father's image at that age.

"Betsy begged we not interfere. I don't know if your mother told you what started this whole thing?"

Sophia nodded. "Mr. Alberson gave her a ride home the weekend Betsy and Bub were on a trip and coming home early, they saw her at the dealership but seeing Mr. Alberson, Barkley jumped to conclusions and Mother said Barkley lost it." She gave him a sharp glance. "Is that what you mean?"

"Yeah, but it goes back farther than that, your mother has no idea how far."

"What has Betsy told you?"

"It's what she isn't saying concerns me. Barkley has not touched my sister in months. She is wondering if she should leave before he asks her to."

"But they went on a trip together. I thought that meant something."

Thorn's jaw set firm. "It should have but she said the way he put it was, you can go or you can stay."

"I feel terrible over this. When Betsy became emotional, I thought perhaps she was pregnant."

"She is."

Sophia's mouth dropped. "But you said he hasn't touched her in months."

"She is four months pregnant, Sophia, and only if you know would you notice the change in her body. She's losing weight. She said her hair is thinning and her nerves are on edge. She doesn't want my mother or yours to know. Much less, Dad."

"Sam wouldn't beat sense into Bub's head, would he?" She sighed heavily. "I mean, yes he does need it and if Dad were alive…but Sam? He doesn't seem the type." Sophia stared down the road. "I don't know what to make of this. He was always so protective of mother, then Betsy, I mean, he loves them both so what would make him behave so…so… unlike himself?"

"Are they financially sound, Sophia?" Thorn waited for Sophia to process the question. "I mean if the bank turned down their loan that might be ground for a man to go off the deep end."

"Is that what it is, the deep end?" Now Sophia was running her hands through her hair, twisting that one strand around her finger as she did when a little girl. "He's not into drugs, is he? We'd know. Right?"

"The usual signs are missing but how would I know? He doesn't gamble, does he?"

"Where would Barkley gamble?" The idea seemed preposterous. "If there's no money, that's a problem, anyway."

"Remember the casino is less than fifty miles away and Betsy said some nights Barkley leaves home."

"Is he drinking?" The fact her brother was behaving strangely was making her own nerves stand on end. "And worse coming to worse is she thinking there's another woman? I think she would know…"

"Betsey is so tore up she doesn't know what to think and it worries me. One thing for certain, she has to see a doctor."

"I take it she hasn't told Bub?" Sophia knew she wouldn't have, false pride would've reared up.

"No, she hasn't." He gave her a puzzling glance. "You would be just like her."

"After I followed you and figured out what you were doing and maybe did a bit of surgical repair on you if I found you with another woman." Her eyes were snapping.

Thorn laughed. "You do have a colorful imagination." Still, he reached across to squeeze her hand.

"I think you and I will outlast this kind of fracas." He gave her a smoldering look. "Yeah, we will."

Chapter 4

S USAN HEARD THE door bell. There stood Mattie. "Girl, what are you doing out in this weather?" Susan pulled her into the family room where she'd moved her books to be near the fireplace.

"You weren't at church yesterday. We missed you." Mattie grinned. "I missed you. I had to lead singing and without you at the piano it was pitiful but I'll have to say Corrine beat the daylights out of that thing."

They chuckled together. "Eighty if she's a day," Mattie was saying. "Can't hear a thing and Lord help us all. She doesn't follow the music she's so busy putting In those extra chords."

Susan was pulling the chairs closer together. "How about hot chocolate, or would you rather have something cold?"

"Well, I don't want to take you from your work." She glanced at the papers strewn across the table.

"Ha, like if I'm making any sense of this, anyway. I need Barkley in here to add his brilliance."

"What's going on with Barkley?" Mattie was removing the heavy wool scarf from around her neck. "Did you hear we're supposed to have a good six inch snow? So don't let me stay long. And yeah, let's go fix hot chocolate before we settle, got any of that instant kind?"

In the kitchen Susan took down two mugs, Mattie emptied the packets into the cups and Susan poured the milk. By using the microwave they were back in the family room in minutes settled before the fire.

"So what's going on? Betsey was at church, alone. You were absent and I know there's a reason."

"Well, you ask about Barkley…" Susan's troubled eyes rest on her friend. "I wish I knew what's going on in my son. Right now he's not speaking to me but I am surprised he isn't attending church with Betsey,"

"What's it been? Five, six years?" Mattie paused the cup midair before taking a sip. "Missing his Dad, Susan and he doesn't even know what's happening. I'd bet on it. Barkley's too good a boy to be doing anything wrong."

"No, it's wrong if he treats people who love him this way, Mattie. We've done nothing to deserve it."

Mattie studied Susan. "Why do I sense there's more? Are you holding out on me?" She sit down the cup and waited. "How long have we been friends? If we can't trust each other then no one can."

She told Mattie the whole mess. "I certainly had no further thought of seeing Kane Alberson and I haven't. That was over a month.." Susan did a mental count and recollection, "A month and a half."

"This explains Kane asking me if I'd seen you lately and how you are doing," Mattie stated.

"That's a bit strange. Why would he do that, Mattie? That could get people talking."

"I just said you were fine and staying in as far as I knew." Mattie sighed. "I sense Kane's trying to change." She grinned, "But I did wonder why he asked about you. He'll always love lady companions, in that he will never change. His mother taught him to appreciate a woman's mind."

"Not my opinion, exactly," Susan replied. "So don't ever let anyone connect my name to his."

"He could change in that regard, Susan if he met a woman and fell in love."

"What would I know about that?" Susan's face was filled with indignation. Amused, Mattie chuckled.

"I've known him since first grade, Susan. Kane's got quite a legacy besides that what I saw the other day was a very lonely man."

"Why is this the first time I've heard that?"

"Well," Mattie rose up to cross the room and look out the window. "Let's face it; he wasn't always the most popular person to discuss in friendly meetings, was he? But I have always known him, but my Frank doesn't like Kane's ways, says he feels entitled. At this time in life I don't feel that way about Kane."

"What do you mean? I'm not following you. I can see you're going to leave me wondering about this."

"Well, just as we have grown older and hope we've accumulated some bits and pieces of wisdom, I think Kane is having to look back on the things he did wrong and …" Mattie paused to gather her thoughts; what she'd seen was someone searching for understanding. "I'm serious, the man is truly lonely."

"Don't look at me when you say that." Susan's voice rose in despair. "I've already suffered because of him. In all fairness I'll have to say it wasn't his fault Barkley had such a fit, and he was trying to help."

Mattie was getting into her coat. "Don't be surprised, Susan, if Kane Alberson takes you on as his latest project. Who else is there around Alberson to soak up his needs but little old Corrine? Huh?" Mattie began to laugh and in spite of herself Susan couldn't help but join her.

"Mattie, Mattie," Susan hugged her friend. "You bring sunshine on a cloudy day."

"You're keeping too much to yourself, Susan." Both hands on Susan's shoulders, Mattie stared into her eyes. "I think there's a remedy for that. I've signed Frank and myself up for dance classes over in Brighton and we are going to swing by and pick you up. No, don't give me that…it will be good for all of us."

"Dance classes, Mattie? Whatever for? Once they're over there's no place to use them."

"Good grief, you are a party pooper. So we open up a class in the center, soon the whole community will be in there tying one on." Mattie's infectious laugh carried her out the door and to the car. Susan returned to the fireplace and slumped into her chair. She needed a dance class like another hole in the head. What was Mattie thinking? Her thoughts went full circle, wishing Barkly would come by.

"Dance classes?" She sighed, a deep hopeless act, wishing Hugh were there to sit opposite her in the chair Mattie had just left. Somehow, she knew Mattie would finagle until she said yes and went along.

Two weeks later, a honk of the horn told her they had arrived. She hurried out. Frank was standing with the door open. "I'll say, Frank, I don't know what I've gotten myself in to."

Frank laughed. "You'll like it. We've done this for years."

"You and your wife, that one up there driving are a surprise. Why didn't I know this?"

Clearing the drive, Mattie pulled out onto the highway. "You, my friend, were so wrapped up in that handsome husband of yours; you two had your own symphony going on and didn't need outside entertainment. Frankie Boy and I, we needed exercise…so we took these classes in the winter."

"This is what you called *the exercise class*?"

Mattie was laughing, "Yeah. Sounds more like something we need doesn't it?"

Frank chuckled, "Most of the fellows I know think I'm too fat to dance, they see me as the guy sitting in the recliner with the remote in one hand and a plate full of food in the other."

"You do that," Mattie yelped."But my boy, here, is a very good dancer, Susan. He's slick."

"Trust in the Lord with all thine heart; and lean not unto thine own understanding. In all thy ways acknowledge him, and He shall direct thy paths. Proverbs 3:5" Kane studied the scripture that had come through the mail, mysteriously unsigned., the flap of the envelope unsealed but tucked inside where it read, Your appointment is seven o'clock Friday night in Brighton at number seven Laurel.

He had been shaking his head over the piece of mail all week, wondering how it arrived at his home instead of at the office. For some reason he couldn't keep from re-reading it these five days and trying to pull from his mind something to verify an appointment, but for the life of himself there was nothing in his memory to say he was to go to Brighton that night but he did circling the busy section until he found number seven laurel. He was early. It was six o'clock and he backed his truck behind the sprawling branches of a cedar tree, knowing it was going to shed on the hood and the roof while it gave a medium of concealment. IF this was some kind of lark, he did not want to face embarrassment.

Inside he found a young girl who quickly told him it was not time and he asked her what kind of meeting would be held. "Oh, no, Sir," she replied, "this is where people come to learn how to dance." She shrugged, "But a lot of them already know how and come anyway."

"Do they have partners?" She nodded. "And do you have a list of who might be attending this dance?" He was removing his wallet from hip pocket. Her eyes lit up. "May I see the list and you tell me the ones who do not have a partner?" She was practically taking his hand to lead him to the tall counter. She handed him the book. "This one," he said, putting a finger by a name, "has a partner?" She shook her head. He handed her a hundred dollar bill as he glanced at her nametag. "Leslie, please do all you can to see I dance with this person and that hundred dollar bill won't have to be returned." Leslie quickly wrote on the clip board. "Yes, Sir. I have laryngitis and they said I can't talk I might spread germs."

"Now, Susan," Mattie locked the car, handed the keys to Frank and took Susan's arm. "You may have to dance with another woman, or me, or Frank, but think of it this way, you are out of the house, there will be people here to talk with and…da da da da…da da, you will be dancing. Good for your spirit and your body."

"Woo-hoo!" Susan threw her arm up in the air as though roping a calf and let it spin. "Woo-hoo."

"Frank, did that sound like a sarcastic woo-hoo to you?" Mattie was laughing and Frank joined in.

They entered the building. Music makes the heart glad was written in huge letters on a banner suspended from the ceiling. Of course there was music, too, Susan was thinking as the girl behind the counter took their coats, asking did she want to keep her scarf. Susan nodded and the girl gave her an armband to wear around her arm. Puzzled she glanced to Mattie for an explanation. Mattie showed her the two she and Frank were given.

"Our armbands match," Mattie explained. "You look for the person with numbers matching yours and that will be your dance partner." In the background she saw the people who played the music enter.

"I don't get to choose?" A bit of a worried frown creased Susan's brow. "Mat-tie," more of a groan than a complaint she called her friend's name. "I haven't danced in years. What if I get some perfectionist that wants to throw me out in the cold?" Aware of the musicians she said, "I could just sit and listen."

Laughing, as usual, Mattie replied, "take my coat if they throw you out in the cold. It's heavier than yours." She hugged Susan. "It's not going to happen. There are no finalist to America's Got Talent in this group. Honey, relax and have a bit of fun. You barely go out of the house except to see after that farm. True?" The laughter had eased into a gentle smile and worry was in Mattie's eyes. "True? Five years?"

"True." Susan conceded. "But do I really need this?" The musicians were setting up.

"Yes, you do." She turned to find Frank, seeing a man was at her elbow making his way to Susan.

"It's a waltz," the gentleman said to Susan. "Would you care to take a spin around the floor?"

Susan found herself in the arms of a colonel Sanders replica except he was tall and thin and a very good dancer. "Thank you," he said when the song ended. "I'm kind of the spare tire around here." They bowed to each other and Susan had to chuckle as Mattie reclaimed her. "It wasn't bad?"

"Not bad, but I should have checked this scarf with my coat, I'm going to lay it on the table."

No, it wasn't bad but she found herself the belle of the ball; the second dance a crew cut guy wearing a muscle shirt that showed off his tattoo sleeve came to ask for a dance and the third was almost her undoing, if he was a day less than four hundred pounds was anyone's guess but he could move, his feet were like greased lightning and they were still doing pieces she thought related to the waltz or possibly a two-step and here she had this dynamo spinning and jerking and only the Lord knew what else and she was feeling foolish standing in the center of the dance floor wondering if he had forgotten her. No doubt the intimidation of the precarious moment shone on her face because someone came to her rescue, taping her on the shoulder, speaking in her ear, "May I have this dance?" as she turned to face him.

Her eyes wide with surprise, she was lost to his taking her away from the gyrating figure of her former partner. "He will never realize you have moved on," he said. "So how have you been?"

Relief, surprise and dismay, were equally at play as she gazed that close into Kane Alberson's eyes. She detected a hint of humor, maybe decorum of a gentleman's ways all the while he held firm to the reason they were on a dance floor, in front of a dozen couples that came as far as they knew, from ten buck too.

"Kane."

"Susan."

"I'm surprised to see you here."

He tilt his head, eyebrows raised as he considered her words. "Me, too," He finally said. "And you."

"You are surprised to see me here?" She asked.

"Yes, is that hard to believe? I've not seen you in months and certainly we have not spoken." When she remained silent he asked further, "How is Barkley? Did he settle down and allow you to explain?"

The music ended and they walked toward the empty chairs, farthest back in order to hear each other. "As a matter of fact, Barkley still wishes not to speak to me and Bert is our go-between."

"It will be difficult putting in a crop without discussion." He brought the chairs near the one empty table.

"Believe me, I do realize that but there's little I can do to correct this if he won't listen."

"Barkley married Thorn's sister."

"Yes," She studied him wondering where this was going. "Betsey is Thorn's sister."

"How are they, Sophia and Thorn?" He leaned across the table. "I just want to hear, Susan. And the little boy, what is his name?"

Susan smiled. "He is a dear little boy. His name is Shane." Something crossed her mind but she would not encourage Kane's interest and she could not have Sophia angry with her, too."

"Shane." His smile was content but a sadness had come into his eyes. "My grandson that I will never hold, doubtless, who will never hear my voice…" He rose up. "Would you care to dance again, Susan?"

She glanced around and then pointed to the number on her armband. "Thanks, Kane, but I was told I'm supposed to meet up with someone with a matching number."

As though reminded Kane searched his coat pocket and pulled out a matching arm band, turning it to find the number. They matched. He held out his hand. "For tonight, Susan, could we be friends?"

She left the scarf at the table and they danced, speaking of his grandfather's absence and the landholdings of J.T's life work going on. "No one's indispensable, I guess," Kane offered, "But it was a huge undertaking, not without complications."

"What looms the largest in a holding as large as your grandfather's?" She asked.

"If you refer to the gossip fed by my ex-wife, that's it, ownership and control; Gina claimed ownership immediately, but my father worked in the business his whole life. The problem was, J.T., didn't share the most significant aspects of the business with my Dad or me." He grimaced, "Somehow, though, I can't see him bringing Gina into confidence. He regarded no one as worthy to his private business."

"I have heard very little, so how does one resolve such?"

"Oh, there's lawyers involved to the hilt. The question is, does she have the papers she claims are in her possession where he signed everything over to her. If so, my father and I are out of a job, a home and will probably be the laughing stock of the community."

"Does that bother you?"

"Of course. Would you have me answer that any other way?" The band began a second offering with the tempo greatly increased as the dancers on the floor adjusted, laughter sounding over the music, a few whistles and cat calls were offered as they became serious in their efforts. "How about we sit this one out?" She nodded. "So let's turn this around," Kane was saying. "What if Barkly took control and you thought you might have to leave the home that you have put your energy into all these years?"

"I would not like it one bit and while I don't think that will ever happen I know in other situations it has."

"If it all hinges on papers," Kane finished, "then whoever has them will be the victor and I have no earthly idea where they might be. We thought the bank box, after they were not in his personal vault."

"Why are they hidden?"

Kane grinned. "Are you the only person in Alberson that does not know? J.T. trusted no one."

"I don't think the community would be laughing over the matter, Kane."

"No?" He saw Leslie across the room and motioned her over. "What would you like to drink, Susan?"

"How about a coke?" Kane nodded and ordered two. They sat in silence until the girl returned. "Thank you," Susan said, her eyes on Mattie and Frank across the room. Mattie was right, Frank was a dancer.

"So you and Mattie are friends?"

"She told you I ask about you, didn't she?" He considered what to say. "Yeah, we go back to the beginning of school, I guess. You know… people don't really change…Mattie was kind then and she still is. Now that husband of hers," Kane grinned, closing his eyes for a moment, then holding gaze with Susan. "Mattie's husband doesn't seem to think I'm worth much salt…I know that by the off-hand way he ignores me if we ever run into each other and Mattie and I talk. He almost rolls his eyes."

Susan found herself chuckling. "Would Frank do that? He's the epitome of kindness to me."

"Believe me, he would. Frank is his own man."

"Aren't you?"

"I'm trying," Kane replied. "I have a lot to live down but I've hoped the difference in the way the holdings are operating since J.T.'s death is transparent and people will notice things have changed."

Susan yawned and apologized. "I'm afraid it's past my bedtime. I usually don't get out at night. There's really no reason I can't get my errands run in the daylight hours and used to I had a lot of time on my hands but now I stay busy."

"There are a number of social events I attend, strange as it is Gina doesn't like being shoved into a room filled with talky men on subjects such as trade and farm bill. You get the picture? She's a city girl, turned right hand man to J.T., in hopes it would be handed to her on a silver platter…she doesn't particularly like people… which always puzzles me that her life dream is to get rich and go to Italy. Italy is people."

"How in the world did the two of you find each other, I mean, usually it's similarities that attract a couple, but what will she do if the lawsuit ends in her favor and there's all these yammering farmers vying for her attention over the land?" Susan shook her head. "I'd like to be a spider on the shelf watching." She shook her head. "I have to ask, is Italy your dream?"

"No, to both," he sighed. "You wouldn't. You have a gentle side. Gina doesn't. She has a tricky side that makes you think she does and then she lowers the boom. We met under the guise of that tricky side."

"What ties up your hours when you don't have to attend those functions?"

"I find myself wandering to the piano and I sit there playing for hours."

"You are a musician." She realized she delivered her question with punch. An hour earlier she wanted to ask, when they discussed little Shane's name, if anyone on Kane's side of the family was musically inclined, but fearing an aftermath should she ever mention it to Sophia, she did not ask. Little Shane was born to music. If he was not playing an instrument he was studying something to do with one.

Kane was standing and with relief she saw Mattie and Frank approaching the table.

Mattie gave Kane a pat on the arm and the two men shook hands. "Mind if we sit with you a minute?" Mattie gave Susan a weird little smile as if to say, I told you. Susan ignored her, her hands in her lap, and eyes studying the mottled top of the table. "So you only do slow danced?" Mattie addressed Kane. Susan won't break if you catch her in the middle of a fast one. As I recall she and Hugh entered a contest one year."

"Mattie, we were in twelveth grade. I can't believe you'd bring that up. I promise you I've certainly lost my agility."

"Even I remember that, what were you, a hundred pounds dripping wet, Susan? And Hugh this big old gangly boy…but y'all could dance." Frank reached for Mattie's hand. "This old girl was just showin me the ropes. Talk about my Daddy getting worked up. He caught us practicing moves on the old barn floor and he had a fit."

Mattie started laughing. "Frank, please, make it clear those were dance moves on the barn floor." She turned to Kane, "you might remember that old barn had a wooden floor and those planks were pretty well oiled from moving things across them and to top it all off, his Daddy gave permission for the school to have its Barn Dance out there."

"Why was his dad upset?"

"Don't you remember? Frank's dad was a minister and sorely against dancing of any kind and Frank…well he took to it like water to a duck's back. You saw those feet moving? Didn't you?"

"So, he gives permission even though he's against dancing?"

"That's where the plot thickens. His daddy thought it was a sit down and be nice type share your box supper and don't do anything that rings of fun." She and Frank were obviously warming to the story. "I am telling you it was a far cry from anything we're used to but it was outstanding."

"And Dad got the barn cleaned out for free." Frank leaned over to kiss Mattie. "Come to find out the person calling said the Box Sisters would be there to sing and Dad thought they said it was a Box Supper," He grinned at Mattie, "But you said that, didn't you?" Frank had warmed to the telling of the story. "That dance was my first time to kiss this gal and I'm telling you I've never forgotten."

"I think he kissed every girl that was there." Mattie looked at Susan. "Did he kiss you?"

"No, as he said, he was smitten with you and I probably wasn't at that party. My folks would've said I might get in trouble."

"Why?" Mattie was confused on that. "Well, like Frank said, it was in a barn, but it was chaperoned?"

"Don't look at me," Kane held his hands up in self-defense. "I think that must have been when I went away for a year. But if you ever have another one of those, I want in. Let's have a dance practice tho."

Frank was rising from his chair. "You girls ready to go? You know it has been snowing while we're here."

"I can bet there's something the man wants to see on television. Right Hon?" Frank only grinned.

Kane stood, his eyes on Susan. "Thanks for the dance and the conversation, Susan." He followed the three to Mattie's car and opened the door for Susan.

They were safely out the drive before Susan spoke. "Mattie, I hardly know how to take the fact Kane was there. Did you all set that up?"

Frank glanced back. "That's something I would not do, Susan. I've always had my guard up as for as Kane ALberson's concerned, but I'll have to say he behaved as a gentleman tonight."

"Does that mean you would reconsider how you feel about him, Honey?" Mattie asked her husband.

"Let's just say I'd prefer to go slow, if you don't mind on that one." Frank turned and winked at Susan. "How about you, Susan?"

"Mattie didn't answer; did you set us up, tonight, Mattie?" Their eyes met by way of the visor mirror.

Mattie gave a deep sigh. "No, Susan."

"Well, Barkley would leave the county if he knew. I don't know how I'd handle that."

Susan hurried inside, hanging up her coat, going to the fireplace and stoking the fire. She had plenty of wood in case the power went off but there was something about a fire in a fireplace cried out for companionship. Oh, Hugh, she whispered. In spite of my heartache the years are passing. I never thought I could make it without you. But I am and I am so lonely, sometimes I think I'll die.

She wasn't in the mood for television or the weather, she found music to fit her mood on the i-pad and sit down in front of the fire. Sometimes she hated going to bed alone and this was one of those nights. She must have drowsed off, awakening to a tap tap tap. It sounded like the kitchen window…but that little project had been turned around. Knowing Jewel, she wanted in. She was on it, her cheeks red and her mouth pouty. Tap tap tap. "Jewel, what's wrong?" Jewel, the cat was never permitted inside but she still persist. Tap tap tap. Jewel was quite the classy diva and tonight she really wanted in. Tap tap tap.

Leaving her shoes, Susan hurried through the rooms, stopping at the refrigerator, "I'm not letting you in," she said, "But here's a piece of bacon for you." She opened the door, glancing down, to find a pair of men's shoes in view. Her eyes slid up.

"Didn't your Momma ever teach you not to open a door before you knew who was on the other side? Confused and giving an embarrassed laugh, Susan was rooted to the spot. "May I step inside?" He asked.

"Oh, yes," she was almost speechless. "I was …"

"You were not expecting me." Kane smiled. "I know. You left your scarf. I guess it's a scarf. It's pretty long. Maybe a shawl?" He held it out and they both studied the scarf. "May I shut the door?"

"Yes, please do." Immediately, she had an uncomfortable thought. "Was there a reason you are using the back door? I thought you were our kitty."

First his eyes held a serious glint and then she saw the grin taking over. "I don't mean to be dramatic, but I was trying to avoid anyone's prying eyes, especially if Barkley came to check on you. I didn't want him finding me in your front yard."

"So you walked here?"

"No, I parked at the back. The way it's snowing, any ruts will fill in quickly." He did that funny tilt of his head that she had seen in Shane when he was thinking a deep thought. "For myself, it doesn't matter but if I can prevent bringing pain to your doorstep….well…"

"Come on in. There's a nice fire and it's warmer than in here." He was noticing her bare feet.

"I'll slip my shoes off, it was pretty wet coming in." In seconds he was following her, when she turned suddenly.

"Did I just hear your stomach roar?"

He grinned. "Can I plead the fifth?"

"Did you go to the dance without eating, Kane?" She turned back toward the kitchen. "Come with me, I can scramble eggs and fix bacon in a jiffy and I'll just be honest…I haven't eaten anything, either."

His stomach growled again. "Sounds wonderful," he said. "What can I do to help?"

She pointed to the Keurig, "Coffee, tea or O.J., your choice. Your department. I'll have O.J."

In ten minutes they were sitting in front of the fireplace, the piano bench had become their table.

"Best meal I've had in ages," he said. "Thank you. Scrambled eggs could not have taste this good at home."

She laughed. "The bacon was a little thin, but it has the taste even if it is pre-cooked."

"Can I take the dishes to the kitchen?" She was rising, stacking the plates and silverware.

"No, it will only take a minute and I'll start the dish washer. Just me, it takes a week to fill."

He placed the piano bench back where it belonged and sit down at the piano. He began with Skater's Waltz, progressed into Maple Leaf Rag and then into the old standard of pianist everywhere, Summer Place. She returned to stand by his side. "There's such melody in that, isn't there? I see you play by ear."

"I used to think everyone did," he replied. "My mother insisted I learn by note, but I always revert back." He moved left on the bench. "Shall we?" He began an easy rendition of Dancing in the Dark.

"Oh, no," she protested, scooting off the bench. "Get up. I'll have to have the music." She rustled through a few sheets of music, placed several on the piano and then sit back down. "Here we go. I'll follow your lead."

"Thanks for a fun evening," he said upon leaving. "I hope this means we can be friends and please call me if you need anything while the snow is on." He hesitated. "Or anytime, Susan."

She glanced at the clock as she heard him drive away. It was eleven fifteen. "Oh, my," she said out loud.

Chapter 5

SHE SLEPT LIKE a rock but woke up worrying that she had the next morning. Why must she feel guilty over every action in her life? Barkley would never come home if he knew Kane had been in his father's house the night before. Hugh's house. Her house. She lay there, worrying. The house phone rang. From the bed she reached across and answered.

"Good morning." As she turned, the bed squeaked.

"Good morning, to you. Is that morning husk I hear in your voice? I didn't mean to waken you. I have this feeling you are still in bed."

"Now why would you think that?" She sat up quickly and the bed squeaked again. She didn't remember the bed ever doing that. What was it with her world? "Excuse that petulant voice, I haven't talked to anyone yet this morning."

"Been up ages, have you? Feed the chickens, milked the cows and all that stuff farmers do, right?"

"I'm embarrassed. But I do believe I detect a smile in your words. I can see you laughing at me."

"No, no, never at you, but maybe with you? How are you?"

"Fine." She sounded carpy. "Last night was a night of music and dancing. I'm good."

"If I knew you better, I'd say you are sounding a bit sarcastic, there, Mrs. Preston." He chuckled. He was that happy. "I'm calling as your local ginner association. There's a four day trip coming up to California, sponsored by one of the seed dealers and I was wondering if you would be interested in going. Mattie and Frank have agreed, reluctantly on his part but whole heartedly on Mattie's; they will be part of the group, then there's the Kelso family from Newton will be with us."

It was simply too early to be doing business, so she would nip it right in the bud. "Thank you, but I don't believe that interest me."

"The Golden Gate Bridge, Disney World and the Grandest Movie Conglomerate in the states doesn't interest you, not to mention the newest technology will be shared for our cotton industry and a lot of freebies, starting with a number of free products and seed. That's just to mention a few." She heard him say, "hmmm. I thought as a lady farmer you would want to be first on the learning curve."

Those were fighting words but she was not rising to the bait. "Thank you," she said, demurely, "I'm not interested," and hung up.

At first, Kane was startled, and then he laughed. He had not been this happy in a long time. His happiness was short lived when Gina walked in.

"I'll be taking this office," she said. "Next, I'll be moving into the mansion, but then again maybe I'll build my own and watch to see how long it takes that mausoleum you live in go down."

"You won't have any part of the Mansion nor my office," he countered.

Gina's smile was more a smirk than anything pleasant. "Why would you say that knowing your grandfather left everything to me?"

Kane presented the papers the lawyer had copied. "This house was built for my grandmother by J.T. himself, she had full ownership and deed and saw that it was legally recorded and left to the female members of the family to follow and to the first son. That would be my father and me. For that matter, the first ginning company had her name on it and for whatever reason he let it carry on down. So I'm not sure you can touch that. Now, what were you saying, Gina."

She flipped a finger his way and replied, "You win some and you lose some. It was worth a try. But you need to get used to the idea you are going to be replaced as overseer of the land. The lawyer's are working on the transition and when they're finished I'm cashing in and moving to Italy."

"Would that be the lawyers J.T. used, Gina, because if it is, they know where their bread is buttered and it is definitely not by you." He gave her a smirky grin. "You might forget Italy, it ain't gonna happen."

"No, darling, that would be the hot shot lawyers I hired out of New York. The best, sweetheart. They worked on the last President's case against one of his cohort's that tried to upseat him before he was even sworn in."

"Remember one thing, Gina, don't be spending Alberson money just because your name is on the account. Should you fail to prove J.T. left everything to you, you could be brought up on embezzlement charges and guess where you would spend eternity? Not in Alberson mansion. Maybe not even where good folks go…to Italy, you hope." He was able to give the old sarcastic laugh he knew she hated.

She stomped out of the office, calling over her shoulder. "Rot in hell, Kane. I'll get rid of you, yet."

When he knew she was far enough away, he slumped down into the chair at his desk. She always took the wind out of his sails but he could never let her know it. He hoped she didn't pounce on Tom. His father was too gentle and easily defeated. J.T. was of the narcissistic bent, but Tom wasn't and he loved his father, regardless. He'd never known any different. Sometimes a man was imprisoned by his own fears and J.T. and the world outside fenced Tom Alberson in. He wished Susan could talk with Tom, she had a way of lifting a person's spirits and right now he was concerned over Tom. Maybe Gina had already tried her voo-doo on him.

Funny thing about depression; you never knew who it would strike, whether of one's own doings or caused by a situation one had no way of controlling. His mind sped on to the talk he had with Mattie. It was the same day he asked Mattie how Susan was doing and she looked him square in the eye and asked why do you want to know?

"Because I like her," he replied. "I've always had a great respect for the woman, Mattie, is there something wrong with that?"

"I'll tell you right now, Kane Alberton, you don't mess with Susan. She's my friend." Then she surprised him further, "Have you messed with her son's business?" Mattie's piercing eyes looked right through him.

"Just tell me what you're getting at, if you're such a good friend of the Alberson's why are you asking me?"

"I'm asking because I don't know what's going on but there's bad blood between you and Barkley."

"That's all on his part, Mattie. I've always admired the boy's spunk. You were there, years ago, at the ball game the time he tripped me, tore my knee up...I had pain for months until it healed. I'd witnessed J.T.'s attempt to run Hugh off his land, the boy only knew his dad was in turmoil and he decided I was the culprit and went after me."

"Don't white wash it, Kane. You know you had a hand in it. They didn't bring their kids up to fight their battles. It was more like let sleeping dogs lie with Hugh, but Barkley had this strong sense of loyalty. I guess he thought you deserved it."

"Sounds like you think so too, Mattie."

"It didn't concern me one way or another. Frank says we will benefit by keeping out of other people's business."

Kane laughed. "Except your friends. Ah, Mattie, I used to be your friend."

"Friends don't hurt other friends, Kane, and that's where I drew the line. Hugh and Susan were and are good people. You set him up. I think Hugh lost two years of his life because of you."

Kane remembered her words as though she said them again, this minute. They cut through his heart.

"I'm trying hard to amend things, Mattie. J.T. was behind the ugliness but you're right I was his henchman."

"How could one old man be so mean?" Mattie asked.

"I have wondered if losing his wife early in life he may have been angry with God."

"Susan lost Hugh and I haven't seen her out chastising those who persecuted her."

Kane shook his head. What exactly did Mattie say in regard to Susan? He blew out a breath of hot air. Seemed like his every thought was of Susan; conversation always came around to her. What was he going to do? He could turn loose of the thought of Susan going on the trip to California.

The joy he'd felt first of the morning left a dull thud in his heart. He had to get out of there. He locked the door behind him, found his way to the truck and headed down the road. He didn't know where he was going but he had to go somewhere.

Susan received papers from the Cotton Grower's Association. The trip was a lucrative deal for those elected to go. She called Barkley and asked him and Betsey to stop in to discuss it. A stoic Barkley and a nervous Betsey came but they turned down her offer to take them to dinner.

"I'd rather cook for you and us sit down and have a nice meal together," she said when they arrived.

"You don't need to worry yourself for us," Barkley replied. "We wouldn't stay."

"Is there a reason, Son?" Susan slipped into the familiar name Hugh had used when he and Barkley talked business.

Barkley's face turned red and she saw the spark of anger in his eyes. After a moment he replied. "You don't need to soften our conversation by calling me Son. That was Dad's word. It will never be yours,"

"Well, Barkley, you are my son and always will be whether you want to or not. So sit down and let's discuss these papers that came in the mail." She hand a copy she had made to each of them. "This would be a good trip for the two of you and it reads like it would benefit our farm. You know the price of a bag of cotton seed."

Barkley reached the end of the page where it was listed those invited on the trip. "I'll not be a part of the trip," he said, rising and ripped the papers in to halves. "Let's go, Betsy."

Betsey's eyes pleaded for understanding. "I couldn't go, anyway, Mrs. Preston," she whispered.

Barkley was already out the door, slamming it shut behind him. "You haven't told him?" Susan asked.

No, Ma'am," Betsy replied. "I can't keep it secret much longer but if things get any worse at home I'm going to leave, anyway."

Susan was horrified. "Betsy, is Barkley abusive. Has he physically hurt you?"

"No, Ma'am, but he throws things around and it gets on my nerves. I get really upset and I don't know what to do. I'm afraid my cryin and being nervous like that will affect the baby."

"I'm so sorry, Betsy." Susan reached for the girl and wrapped her in her arms, just for a moment. They both knew it wouldn't do for Barkley to return. "I'm praying for both of you. I hope you don't have to leave, Betsy, but if you do I'll understand."

Out in his truck, Barkley laid on the horn and didn't let up.

"Here," Susan thrust a pie into Betsy's hands. "Tell him we were getting the pie ready. It's his favorite."

"He won't eat it, Mrs. Preston."

"It doesn't matter. Perhaps it will keep him from being angry with you for not following him right out."

She shut the door behind Betsy and watched the girl walk down the path. Barkley did not open the door for his wife and it was only second after she was settled into her seat, Susan saw the window roll down on Barkley's side and the pie thrown, dish and all into the yard. Glancing quickly to Betsy she saw the girl's hands go to her face. She knew there were tears.

Susan walked through the rooms. What's happened to our home, Hugh, without one of you it's sad but without two at times it's almost unbearable. You are not here to hold me anymore. Barkley's sweet voice doesn't ring in my ears. What am I going to do, Hugh? You never had to face this. You left me to deal with a boy that grew into a good man and then something went terribly wrong. Help me, Hugh. If God allows it, give me a sign that it's going to be all right.

She tried to study Hugh's picture. She thumbed through their last Christmas pictures. But the Barkley she saw in the photos was not the one who slammed the door today. What is wrong? What is he not telling me? What is Betsy going to do? If she goes home to Emily and Sam, Sam is going to be on guard against our boy. Barkley won't be allowed the privilege of visiting her. And she knew in her heart that was a father's way of protecting his daughter. Hugh would have done the same.

How was Barkley missing the fact Betsy was pregnant and would it make a difference?

She paced the floor until barely conscious of the fact she had picked up the keys and was in the surburban driving. She didn't know where she was going, only that the vehicle was moving and the landscape was sliding alongside of the vehicle. She registered nothing, taking a backroad to arrive at the shack she'd seen once before but her mind was numbed by now and she went in and sat down.

"Hey, Missus, Welcome. You ready to order or you waitin' on somebody."

She tried to smile. "Waiting. But I'll order a sweet tea, Please."

"Coming right up." Andrew hurried to the kitchen. "Anna Ruth," he said to his wife, "Look out there and tell me is that a troubled woman and is she not or she is the one our Mr. Kane brought here before?"

"Shore do believe you're right," Anna Ruth replied. "She cryin, now but she don't want no one to see."

"Take a glass of tea out to her, Honey. I got something to do."

Kane was a mile out of Brighton when the call came through. "Andrew? Why, this is a surprise." He listened, his heart skipping a beat. "Is she all right? I'll be right there. No, no, believe it or not, I'm about five minutes or four miles away, whichever you call it." He sighed. "Thanks, Andrew." He stepped on the accelerator.

He parked his truck around back with Andrew's. He walked in, giving a slight nod to Andrew as he went straight to Susan's table. "Susan, are you hungry?" She shook her head. He reached for her hand. "Then come with me, let's take a ride."

She followed, not sure what to do but not wanting to make a scene. Once outside, he said, "Give me your keys, we will take your vehicle. Mine parked here won't raise any eyebrows." She handed them over as a young boy ran out and pressed a large package into Kane's hand. Kane placed the item behind the seat, started the suburban, drove a short distance and took another back road. "Now, don't worry. I have a hunting cabin. Not far, and it is a place we can talk or not talk, whatever you decide. I can tell something's wrong." His voice turned gentler. "You're too far gone to protest, aren't you? It must be pretty bad."

"How did you know?" She shuddered as fresh tears slid down her face. "I didn't know where I was going."

"Andrew called me. He said, Mr. Kane, that lady you brought once is here and she looks sad."

"But you couldn't get here that fast."

"No, I couldn't if I was home but I was at Brighton and Andrew's shack in the woods is not far."

"Oh." She was shivering. As if understanding, Kane pushed a logo on the dash and her seat began to warm. She leaned forward, her face in her hands but before it was over she was threading her hair. Once her mother seeing Sophia doing the same mentioned, "You did that as a child, Susan, when you were upset," and Star smiled. "I guess with Hugh you don't have to do that, do you? That's good."

She heard the door shut and realized Kane had turned off the motor, and was on her side waiting to open the door. He took her hand and then instead of helping her to the ground, gathered her into his arms and carried her to the door. Bending he caught the knob and with his knee opened the door.

She was speechless and still shivering. He removed his jacket, placed it over her and she watched as he made a fire in the stone wall enclosure, a stack of wood obvious in the side compartment and a box of kindling in a bronze pot on the other. When the blaze grew, he placed one larger log on top the others and came to sit by her. Now he simply took her hand and held it as they stared into the fire.

There was no clock but she suspected they had sit there an hour when he finally spoke. "Was it bad?"

"Yes. I ran away, for the first time since Hugh died, I just ran. How would you know?"

"I ran today, too. Sometimes things can't be shrugged off; they nearly choke you to death."

"I didn't know men run. I mean as in having to get away from things the mind won't turn loose of."

"Yeah, we do. I had such anxiety in myself I didn't know what to do so I headed to the truck hoping I wasn't headed for a bar because I've tried to quit that and I thought I had it conquered, but maybe not."

"But you didn't," she said, quietly. "That's encouraging."

"I don't know, maybe I was on a one way street to destruction of all these months I've been sober."

"Maybe all these months I've thought I was praying myself through troubled times and I've failed."

"You aren't the kind to fail, Susan. You just had a lapse. Something happened you don't understand."

"How do you know?"

"I feel it. With you, that's all it can be. You're a strong woman, Susan."

"Not today." She yawned. The heat of the room was making her sleepy and she'd worn herself out with all the crying. "Today, I wondered if God had forgotten me, I couldn't pray anymore, I just walked through the rooms."

He was surprised she'd share that about herself. "How does praying work for you?"

"Normally, it calms me, but today I was so filled with loneliness and despair…" She grew quiet.

He sat there letting her words soak in. He was settling down, the heat was comforting. When he finally glanced her way, she was asleep. He eased an arm behind her shoulder and pulled her to his body and that was his undoing, he drifted off liking the feel of her in his arms. His mind was too drugged by the warmth of the room to consider the consequences.

He woke up first to stare down at Susan. She was wearing a peaceful expression if one could explain it that way after what Andrew must have seen. "She done gone sad, Mr. Kane. Something terribly wrong has made your woman grieve. You love her, you come take her for a drive cause she sufferin." He shifted as easy as possible afraid he'd wake her. What had caused her to be that upset? She was still breathing hard as they drove toward the cabin but he dared not mention it. There past was so precarious he didn't know what he could say or shouldn't.

Just as he'd seen the peaceful expression, now he saw the sadness, her face had softened with the smile but now it was drawn in pain. He moved his arm, slowly, to pull her close again. Her breath on his cheek made his throat tighten. He never envisioned this, hadn't he told himself just hours ago, she will never consider me and she will never go on the trip?

He tried staring into the fire, the flame had ebbed to a dance of blue across the half burned log and he was glad he'd added the last one; otherwise the fire would have gone out. "Kane?" He was startled by her voice, thinking it was his imagination he looked down. "You thought about kissing me?"

"How did you know?" He wondered if his eyes were as slack in the warmth of the moment as hers. "Your eyes are liquid pools, did you rest good?"

"For the first time, no I take that back I slept good the night I rode with Mattie and Frank to the dance."

"I was there, remember?" He smiled and she returned the smile. "What would you say if I kissed you?"

"I'd have to think about it first, this is one of those kind of warm and hazy peaceful moments we don't get very often."

"Are you thinking?" He was feeling things he hadn't felt in a long time, anticipation, maybe even…She leaned in …he kissed her. And she did not pull away. For once, she allowed him to look into her eyes as she placed her arms around his neck and he pulled her against the front of him, their bodies soft and pliable, fitting each to the conforms of the other and she lay her head on his shoulder. "Are we friends?" He asked, hearing her ruffled breathing and then a slight chuckle.

"More like the troubled damsel and the conquering hero."

"Today, I'm your hero?" He whispered, barely able to speak, happy within his soul.

"I was very distraught. There's something about the comfort of a human body…"

"A male body, I hope."

"Yes."

"Are you using me? There's nothing more but that one word I think keeps surfacing between us, comforting?"

"Yes," she whispered. "I felt I had no one. Are you sorry?"

"No, much as it pains me, I can wait." He gave a ravaged groan. "It does cause me pain, but I will wait.

"What if what you are waiting for never happens?"

"Then I will savor today…as an old man, bent and out of shape I will go to my grave remembering this hour." His stomach rumbled. Hers replied. They laughed together. "I would bet my bottom dollar Andrew sent food." He looked down at her sitting so close in the bend of his elbow. "If I get up and go after the food are we going to lose this magical moment?"

"We might." She yawned and stretched. "I would never have seen this coming."

He was standing ready to see what was in Andrew's package. "I'll be right back."

"Ah, a bottle of wine, bread, brisket, lettuce, and condiments." He grinned, "there are two mint patties. My man was thinkin', wasn't he?"

"You have dishes?" He was holding up fancy paper plates, napkins and two paper cups.

"Your man truly does think of everything. I could not have done better."

They ate in silence, enjoying the food Andrew had packed. He finished before her, going to stoke the fire and close the screen. By then she was sacking up the paper ware and they were ready to leave.

He studied her with troubled eyes. She was more chipper now, herself. He suspected what happened was a once in a decade happening and he had been privileged to see her let down her guard. She turned, sensing his eyes on her.

"What?" She smiled, a smile of gratitude, he suspected.

"I'm wondering, where do we go from here, back to hardly knowing each other, or will we be secret friends that can talk now and then in the quiet of night, perhaps when no one is listening?"

"How about the latter. We've kind of crossed the line today, anyway I did and I apologize."

He held up a hand. "If you don't mind, don't apologize, I needed this as much as you."

"Truly?" She wasn't sure and now that they were leaving she felt embarrassed. "I just don't let people see this private part of me, Kane."

"I know." He opened his arms. "One last hug?"

Her expression turned sad as she walked into his arms. "Thank you for putting bygones away, today, and holding me." She raised her head to look into his eyes and that's when he tilt his head and their lips met. His arms tightened around her as he lift her up on tiptoe and she didn't mind, she felt the first tingling sensation slide over her body. She had not forgotten how nice it was to be held by Hugh, she had set it aside because it made her sad, and now overwhelmed that Kane was the one holding her, she let her lashes fold down over her eyes, felt the last of their kiss and pulled away.

"I feel like you are saying goodbye, Susan." He stepped back, putting his hands in his pockets.

"I don't know," her voice was hardly above whisper. "Give me time. Okay?"

"Okay." He locked the door behind them and opened her door to the suburban. "When we arrive at the Shack, just come around and take the driver's side and head on home. I'll look and if necessary fend off anyone that might know you."

"Thank you," she said, reaching across to hold his hand. He cared for her, now she knew, before she considered perhaps he thought of her as another prize he won from Hugh, making him a better man, but it wasn't that way. He had not pressured her and for that…she was grateful.

She drove the speed limit, her mind on review of the afternoon. It had all began with Barkley's anger. What was the reason? When her nerves were on edge and her sorrow at its deepest she had spent the afternoon with the very man Barkley thought he hated. How could that be? She found it unbelievable. Barkley would find it reason to hate her. Overwhelmed, admitting her own need, she accepted what she had done. While she was glad no one knew, there was a peace inside now, where before had been turmoil. The warmth not only of human touch but caring of another heart had pulled her through. For that she was thankful. Would it happen again? She did not know.

Two weeks passed. Another month and they would be into starting the new crop. It would take most of those days for the ground to dry out. The heavy rains had kept the drainage ditches full. Susan made a Saturday foray down the gravel roads they traveled to reach the fields they farmed. Mentally, she began to check off what they must do. Five years had taught her a lot. She knew enough to cause trouble, she often told Bert. Dear old Bert. He was the go between her and Barkley, keeping life on an even keel.

There was a field needed a bit of shoveling to reach the ditch across the field that carried excess water away. She found a shovel in the back and put on the rubber boots she kept there. She was almost finished with the shoveling when she heard a truck on the graveled road. Barkley came to meet her, not saying a word as she shoveled the last cut through the field's small drainage ditch that would allow the water to drain out of the hole and carry on out to the main ditch.

His eyes weren't friendly as he took the shovel and started toward her vehicle. She watched as he put the shovel back and climbed into his truck, leaving her half stuck in the mud wondering if she should slip out of the boots and make it back to the suburban barefoot. "Well," she said, looking up to the heavens, "I guess that's a first. You do work in mysterious ways."

"I wonder if he knows about the baby?"

Mattie was sitting in the front porch swing when she pulled into the drive.

"Hey, you know where the key is why didn't you go in? You could've called me?"

"Ah, I've always liked this old swing. I thought I'd give it a few and maybe you'd show up."

Susan spun around, none too easy in the rubber boots. "And here I am." She slipped out of the boots and found room in the swing by Mattie. "Hugh and the girls did their daddy-daughter bonding here."

"Tomorrow night is the night for more dancing over in Brighton, do you want to go?"

"Is that why you're here?" Susan wrinkled her nose. "Nah, not this time. I'll skip out." She reached over to hug Mattie. "I am very glad to see you but if you drove all the way out just for that, you could have called."

"Actually, I'm here for another reason."

"What's that?" Susan felt fear rush her veins, but she had just seen Barkley and the girls hadn't called.

"Don't sound threatened," Mattie frowned. "My goodness, is the problem not over with Barkley?"

"No, but why are you here? I'm curious, and by the way did you see the doctor?"

"It's the California trip. Sherry from the Hosting Company called. It seems she is now in charge from the main office and she thought of you and hopes you will go but she hasn't been able to reach you."

Susan shrugged. "She's probably using the house phone. It doesn't work. Needs a new line they say."

"Sherry called Barkley, and he told her to get lost." Mattie shook her head. "That's not our Barkley."

"No, it isn't." She was waiting for Mattie to continue. "I've already turned down that trip."

"But that was Kane asking, right? This is a nice young woman. Do you want to discuss the trip with her?"

Susan peered into her friend's face. "Why do you want me to go? I'm a bit dull these days. I won't be good company, besides you will have Frank with you."

"Yes, and they have all kind of things men love on the ship. I want you to go to be with me during those times."

"And then, I'll be alone when Frank's with you."

"I need you, Susan. I did have that appointment and I do have a problem. They found a lump."

"There's more. I can tell. What is it?"

"Because we had this trip planned, they rushed the procedure and I had a lumpectomy. Last week."

"Oh, I would have gone with you."

"I was already there, when they closed down the clinic and the Dr. was all gowned up and Frank came. I think I was in shock and couldn't remember your name."

"Oh, Mattie, I'm so sorry. I wish I had known."

"Well, you know now, and I want to know you are with us. Frank doesn't know what to do with me when I get emotional…" Suddenly Mattie laughed. "I was hurting so bad where they removed the lympnodes and he was wringing his hands and said, "hon, I just don't know how to do this, what do you need to settle you down?" I clenched my teeth and said, "You can pray." And I tell you, he dropped to the floor and started doing business with the Lord and I tell you Susan, it was serious and it wasn't and I just fell on the bed in a laughing heap…" Mattie sobered in the telling. "Well, I hurt his feelings bad."

Susan sat there taking in Mattie's story. "It does hurt where they remove the lympnodes. I understand."

"Do you understand I'll feel better if you are along?"

"Mattie, they will try pairing me off with whatever loose male is in the group. I can't take it." She waited for Mattie to accept her refusal. Mattie didn't protest. She began to cry. "Why are you crying?"

"I don't know." Mattie began to mop her cheeks with a wadded tissue. Susan glanced around for Mattie's purse and not finding it hurried inside and was back in a minute. "I've been crying all week. Frank's about had it with me. He asked me did I think you'd go and I said I'd come see."

"Oh, Mattie, please don't put pressure on me. I love both of you dearly but I have this feeling I shouldn't go, something might happen I can't handle."

"Kane wouldn't allow that, Susan."

Susan closed her eyes as she shook her head, "That's what I'm afraid of; I can't be linked with him."

"For Barkley's sake?" Mattie tried to understand, "But he won't be there, you said he refused to go."

"Mattie I can't be seen within ten feet of him. Barkley would leave and we have a crop to plant."

"Then we won't let that happen. Think about it, Susan and let's go and have a good time."

Mattie rose to leave. "I've blessed you with my tears and promised to protect you from problems; the next decision is up to you. I'm going Susan. I feel so much better just seeing you. Thank you my dear."

Mattie's emotional outburst left her tired. She poured a glass of milk, spread peanut butter on a slice of bread and called it supper. Once she showered she was ready for bed. She must have drift off to sleep immediately because when the phone rang she woke with a startled thought that something was wrong,

"Hello."

"Oh, I've wakened you, again."

"No."

"But there's that same quality of voice, I think it's your sleepy voice. Go back to sleep."

"Kane, what's wrong?"

"I didn't think you would be in bed this early. It isn't even eight, Susan. I apologize."

"When there's no one here to talk with, what should I be doing, Kane?"

He chuckled. "You are asking me?"

She closed that subject quickly. "You wouldn't call unless something's wrong. What is it?

"Frank was in today. He's worried about Mattie. He ask my advice whether they should go on the trip or not."

"Why shouldn't they?"

"I think he's worried if you aren't going, maybe they shouldn't." Kane paused.

"I hear you thinking, just spit it out. Please."

"He's worried over Mattie. Have you seen her? It's not good, whatever she had removed, cancer-wise."

She waited. She wouldn't tell him she had seen Mattie today. "Wasn't it a lumpectomy?"

"It's stage four, Susan." Kane coughed. "They let her think it's a lumpectomy."

"That's not fair to Mattie. She can handle it." Tears were coming into her voice. Not Mattie.

"I just told you Frank's opinion. I don't have one." He waited for her to reply and when she didn't, he asked, "How are you Susan?"

"I was good." Her voice caught. "Don't be kind to me, I'll cry."

"I'll come hold you." Time caught between them. "Wrong answer?"

She tried to laugh. "How are you, Kane?"

"Lonely. Biding time until a certain lady says I can see her. She leads a reclusive life….."

"Yeah? This woman, what do you see in her?"

"I think I've fallen for her. She's beautiful and kind and I think she is lonely, too."

"I wasn't expecting that. I think I should hang up."

"I held her once, and I can't get her out of my mind. I remember the feel of her skin. I can't forget her."

"Goodnight, Kane." Susan placed the phone back on the cradle as she curled into the fetal position and wept, whether for Mattie or herself, she did not know. Had they put Mattie through the radiation for nothing?

The next day she called Frank to find out the truth.

Chapter 6

IT WAS THE following Monday Barkley broke silence long enough to say, "I think you should go on the trip to California. Bert's wife cleaned at the Alberson's this week and Kane sent home papers for Bert to read. The winner on the cotton seed alone, should it be you, is enough to sweeten the pot on our loan for seed. Which means if you win, we can use that amount of money in another area where its needed."

She studied her son, wondering what changed his mind. "Betsy and I can't go because she shouldn't travel that far and be on the plane for that length of time." So that was it. Stunned that he was breaking the silence all she could think to say was, "and if I don't win?" Barkley didn't realize she was trying hard to connect the dots whether this was real or some figment of her imagination. "Chalk it up to you tried but you have to take the trip to enter to win."

As though some master hand was lining up the stars, Kane called that night. He was sitting at the piano. "Susan?" He let his fingers slide into a gentle rendition of Hello Dolly. He heard her breath, thinking she wasn't impressed. "Susan?" He slowed the tempo to match the low volume.

"Yes." She felt herself almost holding her breath waiting for the next mesmerizing note.

His chuckle was warm and accepting. "I waited, hoping to catch you already retired for the evening to hear that sleepy time voice. You are in bed, aren't you?"

"I'm not sure that is proper for you to know, Kane, but yes, I am." Still she heard the trickle of the keys.

"This is the last time I'll ask if you would reconsider taking the trip to California."

"Yes, I'll go. Thank you for calling. Goodnight, Kane." She knew he was stunned. She heard him chuckle.

"You think my answer is funny?"

"Ah, don't hang up, Susan. No, I was surprised and relieved, that was a smile you heard. I'm glad."

"I'll need an agenda." He gave a rousing increase to the volume of the song and suddenly stopped.

"Actually, it is in those papers I sent by Bert." He was hesitant. "What changed your mind?"

"The prize award is worth the trip and my heart breaks for my friend. Mattie wants this trip."

"I see." His words were drawn out. "So it is as Frank said? They just sewed her up for treatment?"

"Stage four. How does that happen, one day a person thinks they are healthy, the next find out…"

"They are not," he finished. "I'll have papers to you in the next few days. You are in." He heard the click and the line went dead. He smiled and his smile widened as his hands were on the piano keys. "I'm acting like a school boy," he said out loud. "Maybe there's hope" And then he thought of Mattie.

The phone rang early Tuesday morning. "Mom?" Sophia's voice came over the line. "Could you keep Shane today? Caroline wants me to drive down to Memphis and go with her for her annual doctor visit."

"Is she expecting bad news, Sophia? Normally she would get a sitter."

"She says all the sitters are on some kind of mission trip through the church. I don't think I should add Shane to the fracas. Her two will be enough."

"I'm surprised she didn't call me."

"I don't know Mom." Sophia's voice dropped low. "I wonder if she's pregnant and wants a bit of support while she finds out."

"I don't know whether to laugh or cry," Susan replied. "The doctor told her she needed to enjoy the two she has and not put her health at risk, otherwise. But of course, I would love to keep Shane."

"Mom," Susan envisioned Sophia curling a lock of hair around her finger. "Mom, it's those other wises we sometimes can't control. Things happen." Susan had a mother's intuition they were no longer speaking concerning Caroline Dawn.

"Sophia, are you pregnant?"

"Yes, Mom, I am."

Susan began to laugh. "Congratulations. Shane will love a little sibling."

"It's a girl, Mom. We are going to name her Emily Sue, is that close enough?"

"Sounds good to me."

"We tried Susan Emily or Emily Susan, seems like Emily Sue sounds better. What do you think?"

"Sweetheart, since Johnny Cash sang that song about Sue, I've not been really gung-ho on the name." Sophia was quiet. "But if that's what you want."

"No, Mom, we didn't want to hurt your feelings by leaving you out."

"You won't hurt my feelings but did you try my middle name after Star's mother?"

"Emily Elise?" Sophia chuckled. "We didn't even think of that."

Smiling, Susan hung up the phone; A little girl and she forgot to ask Sophia the due date. She glanced at Hugh's picture. "Oh, my darling, how happy you would be and proud of your daughters."

Shane arrived early the next morning. His school was observing Spring Break. By afternoon, they had made cookies, painted a picture and were sitting at the piano when the doorbell rang. "I'll be right back, go ahead and find another piece you want to play." She left him riffling through sheet music.

She opened the door to Kane. "Step in," she said, not thinking, "The wind certainly has a cold breath, doesn't it?"

"I brought your papers." His attention was drawn to the music coming from the next room. "Susan?" He caught her expression as she realized her error asking him in. "Is there something wrong?"

"No. Everything's fine."

"May I ask who is playing the piano? That's a favorite of mine. Are your girls home?"

It was then the music stopped and Shane came to see why his grandmother delayed.

"This is a neighbor, Shane," and to Kane she said, "This is Sophia and Thorn's son, Shane."

Kane dropped down to Shane's level, extended his hand and said, "I am very glad to meet you. I heard you playing and you do an excellent job."

"Do you know the song?"

"I do, it's one of my favorites."

"Would you play it with me?" Shane's eyes lit up with anticipation but quickly dimmed.. "But not everyone plays piano, do you?"

"Actually, I do." Shane was motioning for him to follow to the piano and Kane was hesitant, begging Susan's understanding. "What are you thinking?"

"I think it would make less impression if you do as he asks," and there were no further words.

She listened, marveling at their grandson's skill and filed the hour they were together away to think over in the years to come because she knew she would. Kane seemed acutely aware of the passing of time as he rose up from the piano bench, shook hands with Shane and thanked him for a "most enjoyable hour of music we have made together," and at the door bent to kiss Susan on the cheek, saying absolutely nothing as he left but she had seen the emotion at play on his face.

"Nana," Shane said to her, "that man is the first person ever to play by ear like me and we knew the same songs. Don't you think that is remarkable?"

"Yes, remarkable." She could spend the rest of their time together wringing her hands and worrying or she could celebrate something that ended up feeling quite right. She chose the latter wondering how she would handle Shane's telling his parents. "Please Lord; just let us have a case of forgetfulness here." The prayer was intended to cover tracks and avoid dissention in the family; she seemed to be getting good at that.

In the week of preparation for the trip, Susan found life's little surprises were not all bad. Barkley stopped by to discuss their plans for the New Year without once hurting her feelings or making her defend her way of thinking. During his absence when he went to his truck for a platt book to all the farms she asked Betsy, "what's this all about, Betsy, the change in Barkley?" For, Betsey had set to one side listening to the two and Susan felt certain her daughter in law had a hand in the difference in her son.

Dropping her eyes to study her folded hands, Betsy finally met Susan's serious gaze. "I told him, Mrs. Preston, we have a baby on the way. I know this is something you want, but I will not have my child raised in a home where his father has no regard for his own mother. My child will learn respect from us or I will leave today, Barkley Preston, so decide now if you want to help raise this baby."

"Evidently it worked, Betsy. Thank you. In all honesty, dear, I wish it was of his doings, but I'll take what you have given me and maybe in time, the old Barkley will return. I'm glad he's standing by you." She turned back to the papers they had been studying. "I have to ask, Betsy, would you have left?"

Tears came to the girl's eyes. "It would have hurt, Mrs. Preston, but yes, I was prepared to leave."

Suddenly Susan laughed, taking in Hugh's picture on the mantle. "Hugh," she said, as though he were still alive. "Do you realize we are going to have three babies added to our family this year? How do you like that?" Sheepish, she turned to stare at Barkley's wife. "I know, that seems ridiculous, I still talk to him. Do you suppose he hears a word?"

Betsy was grinning. "I don't know, Mrs. Preston, but I'm glad to see you have humor. It's time."

"I'm glad you and my son have cleared the air."

"Not completely," Mrs. Preston. "I have agreed to stay but the intimate part between Barkley and I will not happen until this baby arrives and I know why he treated me as he did." She met Susan's gaze. "A man does not do that to someone he loves."

"I won't interfere. That is between the two of you."

"Mrs. Preston?"

"Yes?"

"Barkley refuses to attend church with me. Is it all right if I sit by you on Sundays?"

Susan hugged her daughter in law. "Yes. Yes. Are you sure you couldn't go on this trip with me?"

"I could, but Barkley made the rules, rules I suspect to hurt you previously. But now it's too late." Betsey drew a deep breath. "I want our marriage to work, Mrs. Preston. I love Barkley but you know the circumstance of my mother and Dad's marriage. My brother, Thorn, isn't Dad's son biologically but that doesn't enter in to being raised with my Dad as his father, because no one would ever know the difference where love is concerned. If I had to leave, I could only hope either Barkley would be a father to this child or if someone else came along that he would love my child as his own. I had these thoughts when Barkley was going through having nothing at all to do with me except his rude ways."

"You are a strong woman, Betsy. I don't know what got into my son and I make no excuses for him."

"I don't want you to, but I want to be honest with you. There's still things Barkley has to make right."

Susan waited for the other shoe to drop. Shane had evidently forgotten playing piano with Kane. She knew Sophia would have been on the phone, nothing flat! She felt herself getting excited over getting away with Mattie and Frank. They were riding with her to the airport, even sick Mattie was fun.

The phone rang early the next day. "Susan?"

She recognized Kane's voice as she answered. "Yes, Kane?"

He smiled, so she knew his voice. That pleased him. "Susan, I'm not sure how you will take this but I've received word for some unknown reason the resort where we will be staying has been closed."

"Oh." She was quiet for a moment. "That means the trip is canceled. Thanks, Kane."

"No, not quite. Don't hang up." He waited to be sure she didn't. "They have changed it to Orange Beach. Thinking most people's bags were packed, they said the weather is good and this time of year the resorts are ready to go, because Spring Break is coming up. How do you feel about the change?"

She thought for a minute. "Well, I was hoping to see the Golden Gate Bridge and Fisherman's Wharf, but if its changed I'm still in. As you know, selfish as it might seem, you said this trip could be quite beneficial. I guess the seed still stands?"

He chuckled. "Always the farmer, Susan? Yes, it still stands. Only the destination has changed. I'm glad you aren't finding the change a problem. I'll see you in three days. By the way, I've contacted Barkley and his wife, in the event they could attend since last we spoke and Barkley has agreed. I hope this is satisfactory to you."

she was so shocked she couldn't reply. She just hung up the phone. What in the world made Barkley change his mind? The location? It wasn't as if he hadn't been there. Was she glad he changed his mind? But then the time on the plane was cut in half. Shocked was the only word she could muster, but yes, the trip would be good for them and she certainly wouldn't get in the way. Mattie and Frank were her companions. The thought did pass her mind, had Barkley reconsidered in order to see if she and Kane were sociable? She would ask them if they wanted to ride to the airport with her.

There was a storm that night that took out the power and for two days there was no internet or television for the news but she was busy and didn't mind, but she was relieved when utility trucks arrived the night before leaving and began work on the problem of a broken pole that had pulled down the lines. Two of the men attend church with her family and they assured her she could relax all would be in working order before she left on the trip. If there was another storm they knew she was away and would check on her place and they informed her a crew was working on the cell tower near her home.

Unable to call Barkley and Betsy the morning of leaving arrived and she dropped by to pick up Mattie and Frank. Mattie had done her best but Susan saw the loose garment. Mattie was losing weight something she'd always found difficult and she was walking with a cane, waving it in the air at Susan as she explained, "I can go faster with this." Susan smiled and nodded although she felt sadness that Mattie was weak and needed the cane for support. Frank had his hands full with two suitcases and a carry on bag as Susan popped the trunk.

"I hear Barkley and Betsy are going?" He said. "What changed their mind?"

"Heaven only knows, I haven't seen them since I heard."

"Hmmm," was all he said as he helped Mattie into the back seat and climbed in the other side."

"Hey, you two, what am I, your chauffeur?"

"Looks like it," Mattie replied. "Onward, James." They all laughed.

Susan parked and they were getting their suitcases out when Barkley and Betsy arrived. Barkley was his usual reserved self but Betsy hugged each one, her smile as brilliant as the sun. Susan recognized happiness in her daughter in law that she hadn't seen in a while. "I'm so glad you changed your mind," she whispered to Betsy.

"I didn't, he did but I'm so happy to go." Betsy whispered the first and then added. "I've never ridden in an air plane."

"Let's hope you don't get sick," was Barkley's comment and to Susan, he nodded. "Mother."

A group was forming on the upper landing of the building where the steps were ready to raise for admittance to the airplane. "They've just recently set this up for passengers in our area," one man was saying. "Before that we had to drive to Memphis or take a flight out of St. Louis but they can't handle the big planes here. I don't mind the smaller one though, it's usually good service."

"Oh, don't say usually," Mattie whispered to Susan. "He should just say it's always good service."

"Not too late to back out," Frank countered. "If you got the least doubt, it won't set down for you if you change your mind mid-air, you know." He made a face at Mattie. "Whatta you say?"

"I'm not backing out." She met Susan's gaze. "He's not either. They have a group there that's in training for the big league. Baseball. We've been there and he loves to watch them play. You know."

"You mean like Florida?" Susan didn't know.

"Yeah, Florida can't handle them all, too many leagues and the Cardinal's rule. But here, they get good training and advice and then go on to do some famous plays." Frank nodded, firmly. "Then they go on to train with the Cardinals in Florida. By then they've rooted out the wannabees' that can't make the mark."

"I guess there's struggle in everything, isn't there?" Mattie saw the group on the platform make way for Kane. "I think we better move in, don't you?"

Kane was taking a head count. "Everyone's here. How did that happen?" Everyone laughed. He nodded in passing Susan, but lingered a moment to say to Betsy, "I'm glad you two could make it." Betsy smiled brightly but Barkley was busy studying a paper he had picked up on the history of the airplane.

"This is one of those that had the different motor put in, isn't it, Barkley?" Frank was reading the same brochure. "It says in order to better understand the change made in our planes we take this opportunity to preview their history." Frank laughed. "That makes me feel better, doesn't it make you feel better, Barkley?" For the first time Barkley grinned. It was hard not to smile with Frank being the man he was, always caring about the other person. Everyone was listening to the revving up of the plane and then they were loading.

Susan relaxed, if anyone could loosen up her son, it would be Frank. Too, she was thankful Kane passed by without so much as a blink of the eye. A second brochure revealed the hours they would meet with the Company funding their trip; a Brunch session at ten o'clock and a list of side trips for enjoyment.

"It's more like a vacation than a farm meeting, isn't it?" Mattie whispered and Susan nodded. Everyone was settling into their seats and fastening seat belts. The engines revved again and the plane lift off.

Susan noticed Mattie's face was flushed. "Are you okay, Mattie?"

"Just a little problem with breathing for a minute; I think I got a bit anxious over the plane going up." She grinned as Frank reached for her hand. "I'm fine now. Doesn't it affect you at all, Susan?"

Susan laughed. "I don't know, my mind was on you."

"Don't worry," Frank whispered, "We'll be there in about an hour and a half, double that if we'd gone to California. I think as the bird flies it's around five hundred miles."

Mattie stared at her husband. "Are you saying we are traveling five hundred miles an hour?"

Frank did a mock wipe of his forehead. "Woman, you are killing me."

Susan watched the landscape below. It could have been a colorful quilt where the land was offset by roads and ditches and her mind traveled to time past going places with Hugh. Laying her head back on the tall backed seat she closed her eyes. Once she heard the stewardess say, "Sir, you will have to sit here. We are experiencing a bit of turbulence due to the crosswinds." Susan knew there was a body settling into the seat beside her but she was in the middle of a dream with Hugh laughing and showing her a field. "I have missed you," he said and Susan smiled.

Kane saw the smile and wondered why she appeared so fierce awake but sleeping docile and appealing. They had moved him from the front seats near the cockpit. In the turbulence the stewardess stayed near the captain. He didn't mind, except Barkley being in the group he didn't want to appear too familiar with the boy's mother. There his thoughts stopped, Barkley was no longer a boy to reckon with, he was a young man married and his wife expecting a baby, but still protective of his mother. Barkley's presence on the trip made him a bit nervous. He rubbed his knee remembering the boy's capabilities.

Chapter 7

SUSAN STOOD ON the balcony breathing in the fresh air. The view was spectacular. There was the swish of a sliding door and Mattie and Frank stood on the balcony next door. "Is this awesome, or what?" She asked. "But I am wondering why there's no one on the beach. It's beautiful and normally people hang out until dark."

"Did you bring a suit, Susan?"

"No, did you?" They laughed together. "I came for the seed, remember? I think Frank did too."

"Let's go walk up an appetite. I hear they're feeding us an Ocean Surprise tonight," Frank suggested.

"I'd guess shrimp and fish with all the fixings," Mattie guessed. "Now where did you hear that?"

"The guy who brought up the luggage said we don't want to miss it. So let's go walk, girlies."

They met Kane as they stepped off the elevator. "We're going for a walk on the beach, you want to join us?" Mattie, ever welcoming offered and Susan saw the offer was hard for Kane to decline. She smiled. What else could she do, she knew he was waiting to see what she thought. He fell into step. But once they ran out of concrete sidewalk Mattie was unable to navigate with or without her cane.

Frank said, "Mattie, my love, I believe I'm too out of shape to walk in the sand, how about you and I sit on that bench out on the edge and let these two go on at their pace. No need us holding them back."

They were a distance away when Kane commented. "She's getting weaker. Is it the treatment or the cancer?"

"I don't know. We've been friends so many years my heart aches seeing her struggle but she's so stubborn she won't say no to anything, gotta keep trudging on if it kills her." Susan's voice caught in a sadness she hadn't meant to reveal.

"Stubborn, huh?" Kane tried to lighten the moment. "I'd say you could give her a run for the money?"

"What? I mean why, would you say that?" She stopped for a minute, studying his expression.

"You hung up on me the other morning."

"Did I?" Momentarily confused, so much had happened, the power out, Barkley coming on the trip, and now Mattie growing weaker by the day. She studied the sand wishing she had slipped off her shoes and stalling she bent to do that now. He was still waiting for her reply as she raised to find his eyes on her, his own shining with humor.

"You know you did and the time before that."

"When was that?"

"The night I called and you had already gone to bed." He grinned. "I like that husky voice."

"That's not husky; it is someone who has been a sleep."

"Ah, yes, your very dignified sleepy time voice. What does it matter if I like that voice?"

"You embarrass me." She tucked her arms to her sides as if for protection.

"I suppose if I turned to you, took you in my arms and kissed you right here on the beach, that would embarrass you?"

"You wouldn't dare." She didn't say Barkley might be looking and it would make my life hell.

He scuffed a toe in the sand, then bent to take off his shoes, tying the strings together to sling them across his shoulder. "Nah, I know it could raise all kinds of problems, but I wish I could. Give me credit, that day in the shack I didn't take advantage of that situation."

"You were a gentleman."

"Yes, I am."

She laughed and threw a shoe at him. It bounced off his shoulder and raised up to nick his chin. A thin line of blood rose along the cut. "Oh, my goodness, Kane, I'm so sorry. I didn't mean to do that."

"Yes, you did." He wiped his hand across the place that hurt. "Wow, you brought blood. I'd hate to see you with a real weapon."

She was mortified. "I am so sorry. Please, forgive me." He was picking up her shoe, handing it to her.

"Forget it, Susan. I'll try not to ask again if I might kiss you." With that he turned back the direction they'd left Mattie and Frank. "Come along, Wonder Woman so our friends won't see there's a rift."

"Is there a rift?" She hurried to catch up. "I notice you don't wear socks. Did you forget them?" He ignored her and kept walking. "Well, did you?" She hollered. He didn't stop until they reached Mattie and Frank.

"What in the world, Kane?" Mattie was curious. "What happened? You are bleeding."

Kane pointed a finger at Susan. "She threw her shoe at me."

"Susan?" Mattie glanced at one then the other. Frank was trying to contain laughter. "Susan wouldn't."

"I did," Susan replied, miserable. "It was an accident."

"We won't even ask why," Frank said, rising. "Come on, my love, let's go back to the room before dinner." To Kane, he asked, "Is this dress up?" He pointed to Mattie. "She will want to know."

Kane nodded, "Jacket. Wear a tie only if you want to. And," sarcastically he added, "Socks, is up to you."

Confused, Frank asked, "Are you wearing socks, Buddy?"

"No, I forgot to pack any." A fresh supply of blood surfaced. "I'll see you all at dinner." Kane headed toward the room.

"Well, so much for that." Susan examined the flat she held in her hand, "I see what happened. That little metal do-dad embellishment has come loose and it's sharp. "Okay, I'll see you at dinner."

"I can't help asking. Were you two fighting?" Mattie paused in her walk but Susan was already gone.

The next morning, the group under Kane's supervision settled around two of the round tables. A representative of the company was making his way to each group asking if the accommodations were suitable, did they eat enough breakfast and did they have their day planned? "We'll be out of her around eleven thirty and it is your free time until eight tonight when we gather for dinner. How's that?"

Susan sat across the table from Barkley. She noticed Betsy seemed a bit subdued, the brilliant smile hadn't shone once and that concerned her. Either the two were fighting or Betsy didn't feel well. She did a silent count how far along Betsy was and came up with five months. The morning sickness should have ceased and usually from that point on pregnancy was easy but there was something going on.

The first drawing brought twenty bags of seed to a man at the next table named Rob and then the second drawing claimed Jim, one of Kane's group. "Twenty bags," their host cried out. "Not bad. Remember each day the amount of bags increases. By that, I mean tomorrow it will be twenty and thirty."

"Is that fair?" The first to draw, Rob, asked.

"Well, let's see," their host said. "You keep what you have drawn no matter what the outcome will be while we put your name in this basket with nothing but blank slips of paper and we'll draw a slip, if it has your name good, but if we draw a blank slip you will see what could have happened. All right? If it draws a blank slip that means you could have gotten nothing. Agreed?" The man nodded.

Everyone feared the slip coming up blank. Their host read it a sad expression on his face and handed it over. Number one, read it and burst out laughing. "It says thirty bags of seed."

"It's yours," the host said. "Now how do you feel about the draw?"

Number one draw came to Kane's group and held out a hand to Jim whose name was drawn after his, also receiving twenty bags. "I'll split it with you," he said and everyone in the room clapped.

"That's not bad," Mattie whispered to Susan, "Is it? Thirty bags each?" She turned to Frank, "You'd take thirty bags wouldn't you, hon?" Frank reached across to put a kiss on Mattie's cheek.

"You bet," he said. "That guy was lucky; it could've been a blank. A freebie is nothing lost, a lot gained."

Susan considered Frank's words. Somehow she wasn't thinking of bags of seed at the moment with Kane's eyes on her. Why was he staring? That bothered her and the band aid just above his lip bothered her more. She was drawn to someone calling her name.

But then the meeting was called to business session and clip boards were handed around as the host explained they were going to have a bit of fun on paper as the video was played and a little knowledge was shared. "You will learn about the new product while drawing on your own experience and wisdom," he said and everyone chuckled over his choice words. "Farming is a gamble, isn't it? He asked. The session did seem to fly by and their host was an excellent instructor. "Now, you are free to spend your time as you wish. Dinner tonight will be served at seven instead of last night's hour of eight."

Mattie laid a hand on her arm. "Susan. You were a million miles away. Did you see Barkley leaving with Betsy?" Susan searched the hall they would be taking to get to their room.

"No, but I did notice that Betsy was pale and she wasn't smiling. Did you?"

"I think, dear that he wanted to talk to you but he is just too stubborn. He's worried about something. Do you think they are fighting?" Mattie put a hand to her mouth. "I shouldn't have said that. It just seemed something was wrong."

"Yes, I just hope Betsy is not ill, but she seemed fine on the flight, didn't she? Excited even?"

"Yes, she did. A child-like enthusiasm. Even Frank noticed. He said there's a fine young couple."

Susan was dialing her son's room. Betsy answered. "Betsy, are you ill?" She listened, nodding. "That's probably best. I'm glad you have some with you." Breathing a sigh of relief, she tucked the phone back into the small purse she was carrying. "She said she has indigestion and they were going to stay in a while as she has taken medication the doctor prescribed and usually if she rests a bit, then everything resolves and it doesn't last all day."

"Thank goodness," Mattie sank back down into the chair. ""I'll just sit until Frank finishes talking to the men. You go on to your room, Susan. Did you have anything in particular you wanted to do today?" A fine bead of sweat had broken on Mattie's upper lip. "I honestly believe I should stay in and Frank wants to watch the boys play ball."

"Are you sick?"

"No, just weak. Sometimes it takes a while to get my bearings." She turned doleful ey

"Why don't you let me help you to your room and Frank can talk as long as he wants?"

"I didn't want to impose. You didn't come on this trip to babysit me."

"Mattie, are we best friends for how many years?"

"A lifetime?" Mattie was trying to rise out of the chair. Frank turned to help her. "Susan's going to help me to the room. You take your time. All right?" He smiled, sadly and nodded to her and then Susan.

They were opening Mattie's door when she reached to clasp Susan's hand. "If I die would you look after Frank for a while until he gets on his feet? Because he's going to miss me, Susan."

Trying to make light of Mattie's sudden request and the grip on her hand, she asked, "I don't have to marry him, do I? Because that would be…sacrilegious you and me being best friends." Then she hugged Mattie tightly. "You are not going to die, not for at least ten more years, hopefully twenty."

"But if I do, it's important to me to know…will you check on him?"

"Yes, I would do that for you but I'm telling you, what you are sayin' it ain't gonna happen. Promise."

Susan went to her room. It was a beautiful day, too pretty to be locked in a room when the beach was right outside the door or take the trolley to the center if one wanted to browse the shops. The brochure said not your ordinary shops. There was one Simply Shells, where she could imagine all kinds of exotic jewelry, and decorative objects, another called the Croc, she wasn't certain if that would be filled with real life looking alligators and crocodiles or if it would be a shoe shop. She changed into a pair of white knee length shorts and a coral top with crossed straps front and back which showed off her olive skin as though she had been religiously tanning. Picking up her purse she went down to the lobby to wait for the trolley.

Most of the people were in pairs. She noticed they by passed her as though she were invisible as they found seats. By the time everyone was on, her seat was the only one with space left when the driver stopped to let on another passenger. Kane stood in the aisle, asking, "May I sit here?" He was wearing that aloof face again. "Or, I can stand in the aisle. It isn't far."

She gave him a dirty look. "Why are you doing this?"

He shrugged. "I thought, possibly, you like your space all to yourself, today."

"You are being childish. Petulant. I apologized. What more can I say?"

"That I can sit down?" Obviously the other passengers had been watching and listening. They were clapping their hands amid a few whistles. She rolled her eyes as he beat on his chest for their benefit. "Where you going?"

"To the Center."

"That's obvious, as that is this trolley's destination."

"Maybe to the Simply Shell shop or the Croc?" She glanced his way, her eyes half-lidded, trying to study the band aid area without his noticing.

"Oh, you cut me, all right." He nodded. "I can read your mind. You're wondering if there is a cut beneath the band aid and there is. I never knew a girl before that had razor blades in the toe of her shoe."

For a minute she chuckled. "You are crazy. It was a pure accident."

"I figure you owe me and I aim to collect."

"You want money, Mister?" She unzipped the purse and brought out a ten dollar bill. "Will this do?"

"Fraid not." He crossed his leg. Tan leg, she noticed as he was wearing khaki shorts and a white polo.

"I see you're still not wearing socks."

"Forgot to pack them." He finally grinned. "Isn't this just too cozy? Me and you on the trolley."

The trolley stopped and everyone got off. "You two have fun," an elderly man said as he passed by.

"Sure thing, I plan to follow her everywhere she goes." He placed his hand on her elbow as she started down the steps. "Now, which shop first? Oh, yes, the SImply Shell. Seas shells by the sea."

He wasn't jesting. As she wandered around the shop, collecting necklaces for Sophia and Caroline and even one for Betsy in case she wasn't up to shopping, and necklaces that looked like flowers for the little girls, he was always close by. "What about the boy?" He asked.

"Not here," she said. "If the Croc has little fake crocodiles, that's good."

"I was thinking a drum. They have them, they're made out of native wood with a rubber top stretched tightly across and the sound isn't bad, at all. What do you think, since he's musically inclined?"

"Hmmm." She was finding it very hard to keep from smiling. "Your enthusiasm is very catching."

"I've never done this before and he was such a trooper. I think that was one of my most fun times in life." He watched while she chose a pillow for the sofa at home. "Better get two," he suggested.

"You are referring to the two of you playing piano?"

"Of course, It was completely unexpected and I enjoyed it. Thank you for that day,"

"You are welcome. I think if you remember I had very little to do with it. Shane was in charge."

Kane's expression changed, as visible as a cloud covering the sun Susan was thinking. "I don't suppose it will happen again. He's very good, you know."

"He was born to it." She replied, "I'll check out and we can go to the next shop." He stood back while she paid and then took the larger sack.

"My mother used to say that to me," he said. She glanced at him, puzzled. "That I was born to playing the piano. My mother said that." He opened the door for her to the Croc. "Ah, yes, drums. See?"

Some time later, they were on the trolley and back to the hotel. "Would you join me on a walk on the beach?" He held out a hand as she came down the steps, turning loose as she stepped onto the sidewalk.

"Kane, there are any number of women would take a walk on the beach with you."

"I ask you."

"Why?" She stopped at the nearest bench and sit down. "It's futile, Kane. You know how Barkley feels about you and he's barely speaking to me and with a baby in the future, I can't risk more problems." She remembered something and smiled all of a sudden. "Sophia and Thorn are expecting, too." She had thought to lighten the moment but she had done the reverse. He appeared sad.

He waved her away as he turned to stare out onto the water. "Just go," he said. "I get it. It is futile."

She wandered back to the hotel, thinking he would catch up. He had the package with Shane's drum in it. Strange how excited he seemed to be buying the drum, but now she felt she had caused his remorse and she fret that he was left holding the bag. It was all right, he would bring it the day they departed.

Whether the trek up town or sparring with Kane, she was tired. She slipped out of her clothes, showered and dressed for dinner, for now substituting the dress she would wear for a silk robe. She had things to think over before dinner and the game for seed was being played tonight. She needed a few minutes to think, but when she closed her eyes, she did none of the thinking through of a few problems, she slept.

Was that a knock at the door? She listened again. There it was a slight tap, so reminiscent of Barkley's childhood knock. She gave up, slid from the bed and answered the door. Kane stood in the hall holding the bag with Shane's drum in it. He gave her a gentle smile. "Sorry, I forgot about this."

"Oh, I bet you've been trying out the drum. So? Does it have a good sound?"

"I think so." He was hesitant, "Are you ready to go down?"

"Five minutes," she smiled. "You can wait here, or I'll see you down stairs."

"Are you sure?" She held the door open and he walked in as she removed her dress from the only chair.

"Five minutes." Disappearing into the bath area, she closed the door firmly behind. He smiled, waiting for the lock to click but it didn't. Maybe…that meant a smidgen of trust.

Susan peered into the mirror, checking her make-up and then slid out of the robe and the dress onto her body. She was having a bit of a problem with the zipper, midway of her back. She finished putting the pearls in her ears and the single drop around her neck but she couldn't move the zipper and she couldn't get the dress off. She opened the door, "Kane?" He was sitting his back to her, as she walked out. "Kane? Could you do me a favor, I think my zipper is caught in material as it slid up, do you mind?"

He rose up, coming behind her to chuckle at the zipper caught on one side of the material. He tried sliding it down, but it wouldn't go, and then up but the zipper didn't move. "Hmmm. Were you in a hurry? Because you've got it stuck in those tiny little teeth, too."

"Well, I did say five minutes, but I was just doing my usual thing. Try pulling the material to one side."

"I thought of that but it may tear the material."

"Oh. I wore this dress one time, to Barkley and Betsy's wedding." She thought for a second, "Well, I can't help if it tears. I can't wear it the rest of the trip, so go ahead and try."

"Do you have tweezers?"

"I might." She hurried into the bathroom to rumble through her cosmetic bag. "Yes, here's a pair." She returned to hand them to him.

In a matter of seconds he had the material out of the zipper pull, and zipped it on to the top. "I don't think anyone will notice the tiny threads, probably when you press it next time, or whatever you do it will be fine."

"Thank you." She laughed, relieved, "I never thought what a person would do if they had no one to help. Wear the outfit until it fell off or cut it free, I guess. Thank you." She stood tip toe to kiss his cheek, but he turned just so that it landed on his lips.

Surprised, his arms went around her pulling her close, as her head went naturally to his shoulder and he held her. He felt her body soften, she was a warm mound against him and he treasured the moment. "I told you I would collect. How do you feel about that? Just loosen up, Susan, you don't have to run the world with all those strict rules you've made for yourself. He tilt her head just so and kissed her. "Now, isn't this nice? I'm just holding you."

He was right, it was nice and the sound of his voice, gentle, barely above a whisper, was mesmerizing. She was tired, not physically but tired of doing everything alone; Tired of trying to be both parents by encouraging her children in an effort for all to go on. It was as though they were trying to meet the challenge, reach the goal since Hugh was gone. But what was the goal? Yes, she was tired and there was no one to hold her and say everything's going to be all right. No one to turn to and say, 'what do you think?' She had not sought out Kane…but then she came to her senses and pulled away…

"I'm sorry, Kane, it seems I lean on you when things are heavy on my mind." She gave him a sad smile. "Don't let me use and abuse you, Kane. I'm lonely and your attention confuses me."

"What would it take, Susan, for you to let me into your world?"

"I think I have, Kane, but it is not fair to you because there can never be anything between us…."

"You said that before." He rubbed his chin, thinking. "Is it really the children or it it you?"

She sat on the edge of the bed facing him. "Don't you see? Barkley can't forget his dad's frustration from all those years…."

"And the girls?"

"I don't know." She sat there twisting a strand of hair between her fingers. "I am their mother and they loved their father dearly. Sophia for all her brash ways might…but Caroline was her father's daughter."

"There has to be more." He sat there trying to figure it out. "You can't be that …."

"Self-serving?" She sighed. "Maybe I am, putting you through this again, when it is hopeless."

"You are the least of self-serving people I know. You gave your all for Hugh and now the children, where do you fit in, Susan?"

"I don't know, maybe I'm vulnerable at this point…trying to figure things out."

"We could have twenty years together, Susan." His voice was soft, but it compelled her to look at him, "Twenty years of not being alone, of travel, sharing the children's lives. I don't think I'll have an opportunity to enjoy grandchildren." Now he sighed, a soul wrenching sigh, "not the way you do."

For the first time she laughed. "Kane Alberson, there's any number of women that would gladly take you for a husband, a companion…" She saw a grin twist his lips.

"Yeah, I can think of a few, but I want to be the one who chooses, Susan, and you have been on my radar for years."

"We live two different life styles, Kane."

"I don't understand that, our little community hardly has any social life."

"You step between two worlds, Kane. You, of all people travel outside, you have a life."

"I do what's necessary, Susan. It looks like I have a life. In reality, I spend a lot of time playing the piano." They laughed together. "So what else is a problem for you, where am I lacking?"

True to who she really was, Susan considered here they sit in a hotel room, two unlikely persons together and there was something she had wondered. Hugh had been such a devout Christian man. Did she dare ask Kane if he was a believer? Some inner voice questioned, *is it important to you?*

She cleared her throat. "Are you a believer, Kane?"

"Are you changing the subject, Susan?"

"Well, maybe, but I don't think so, it's important. It just came to my mind."

"I'll have to think on that."

"You should know immediately." She had the answer. Glancing at the clock on the side table she said, "It is almost time for dinner to be served, Kane. I think we should go and thank you for fixing the zipper."

He stood, "thanks for letting me in." He took a deep breath shaking his head as he did, "I guess we're back on first base, aren't we?"

She smiled as she picked up her purse and turned to the door. "Kane," she said softly, "at least we are friends, in spite of the past and present."

He managed a sad smile. "That was not what I had in mind, Susan. I would give you my heart."

Chapter 8

BARKLEY WAS ALONE when he came down for dinner. Their host was already at the podium, setting the rules for winning seed tonight. "If you've won already, that means you're out." There were a few groans and one or two verbal complaints. "Ah, come on guys," he protest, "hasn't this been a nice trip? Aren't you having fun yet?" Reply to his statement was a general clapping of hands. "All right, now," he was smiling. "We are passing the basket. Beside your plate there's a piece of paper and a pencil, write your name on it and drop it in the box for the drawing."

Kane was not eligible as a seller but both Susan and Barkley were. As the box made the rounds, the first course of dinner was served and the second and third. By the time they finished eating, their host was having one of the waiters draw names. "Draw number one goes to," he fumbled, dropped the paper, retrieved it and called out, "Barkley J. Preston." Waiting for the applause to slow, he said, "Ten bags."

Barkley went to the front to take the certificate promising seed. When he returned, Susan bade him pause. "Barkley, where is Betsy, is she all right?" The second draw was being called. "Twenty bags." And as Barkley replied, Susan heard her name. "Susan Preston, forty bags of Perfect New number P-N 300, our best prize yet, with an outstanding worth of over… well I'll let you do the numbers. Way to go, Susan." There were whistles and cat calls as everyone waited for Susan to claim her prize.

Kane was expecting a jubilant Susan; instead he watched her rise, evidently to leave with Barkley. He hastily tossed his napkin onto the plate, went forward to accept Susan's certificate and followed the two. They were getting on the elevator when he caught up. "Is something wrong?" Barkley ignored him. Susan replied, "Betsy wasn't feeling well, the reason she didn't join us for dinner and now…while we were at the table she called and thinks she is running a fever and she has been throwing up." The elevator stopped and Barkley with card ready to open the door, hurried to his and Betsy's room.

Kane waited in the open door but Betsy was lying on the bed, pale and wan, a wastepaper can beside the bed and the room smelled foul. Susan's hand was on Betsy's forehead and her troubled expression conveyed a problem. "Kane," she called and he stepped inside. "On the chair, there in my purse, is the card to my room, would you please go to number 312 and on the table by the bedside there's a small zippered purse that actually has a fever thermometer, and if you would bring that back, please?"

He was walking down the hall when he realized he was going to her room, like a person someone knew they could trust, and he smiled. She was beginning to trust him. You didn't let just anyone into your room and the funny thing was even Barkley in his worried state of mind had not questioned her asking him. He almost laughed out loud when he remembered she was so intent on Betsy she forgot he'd been there before and told him the number but he didn't laugh. He was not alone.

Within minutes he was handing Susan the small thermometer, encased, she removed it from the shield and coaxed Betsy into opening her mouth. He saw Susan had damp wash cloths on Betsy's forehead, which meant she already knew Betsy had a fever, she just didn't know how much. "One hundred three," she said. "Barkley, we have to call a doctor. Now."

Kane saw Barkley's confusion, and before the words out of his mouth were completed, Kane had taken control. "Barkley, I'll go down stairs and see what they do under these circumstances, if they have a house doctor on staff or know who to call. You can stay here with Betsy, is that all right?' Numbly, Barkley nodded from his positon on the side of the bed, holding Betsy's hand.

"No, Sir, the girl at the desk replied, "We don't have one on staff, but it being weekend I'm not sure we can find one that will come to the resort. Is your daughter too sick to travel to ER?"

Never mind the mistake, Kane was thinking, when an elderly white haired gentleman tapped him on the shoulder. Kane had noticed him sitting in one of the chairs reading a paper and he was certain the man could hear their conversation but at this point it didn't matter.

"Young man, I'm a GI, doctor, tf I can help you; Retired but still knowledgeable." He was aware of Kane's puzzled expression. "That's a Gastroenterologist, one who specializes in treating disorders of the digestive system, and that's what caught my attention, I overheard you say she's pregnant and she is definitely vomiting even though she hasn't eaten. I'm glad to see her, if you wish."

The girl was getting off the phone. "I've called five offices and all I get is a recording saying go to ER."

"Thanks," he said to the girl and to the white haired gentleman, "Come with me." On the way he found the man was Dr. Miller and he and his wife were celebrating fifty years of marriage. "That's my age," Kane replied, "plus two. But who's counting?" The elevator stopped. "Thank you for agreeing to see Betsy," he said. "My name is Kane Alberson and those you will meet are Betsy and Barkley Preston and Barkley's mother, Susan Preston."

"And where is it you fit in?"

Kane felt in flux for a minute and then he laughed, "In general, friend to the family, sometimes foe."

Dr. Miller smiled. "Perfectly normal, you'd fit right in to my patient list." They waited for someone to hear Kane's knock and quickly footsteps sounded as Susan opened the door, beckoning the doctor to the bed.

"Hello, Young lady. I'm Doctor Miller. I have just a few questions to ask you." He glanced up at the others. "If you all don't mind, just back off over there to the sitting area and lets let our little mother have a bit of privacy." To Betsy he asked," how far into the pregnancy are you?"

After that, the three in the sitting area heard very little. When Dr. Miller returned to stand with them, he asked, "Have you folks been listening to any of the news?" They shook their head no. "Well, I believe our world is about to be in a heap of trouble, but what do I know? There's a virus running rampant overseas and what I'm wondering if it has reached us by way of people who travel outside our country."

"Does Betsy have a virus?" Barkley asked. "If she does, I bet she got it from her group of friends." He saw the doctor was waiting for further information. "They planned this trip when they were in high school, came by, but Betsy decided she shouldn't go being pregnant, but a couple weeks back returning from a week in Rome, they came to see Betsy and tell her all about it."

Dr. Miller was listening intently. When Barkley finished he said, "Now, let me get this straight, your wife's friends came by to see her upon their return from Italy, did you say?" He seemed to chew his inner lip while he considered the information. "Would there be a way you could call at least one of the friends to see if all are well?"

"Betsy, do you have their numbers in your phone?" Her reply was a mere whisper, as though she didn't have the strength to manage more. Barkley was searching Betsy's purse for her phone. "Here it is, now to find their names. Would Judith be the one most likely to know?" Betsy nodded and Barkley stepped away to make the call.

There was very little the three waiting could do until he rejoined them and when he did they could tell by his expression something was wrong. "I spoke with Judith's mother. She is there taking care of Judith who is seriously ill. They don't know what the problem is, since the other girls have it, too, they are thinking a bad case of food poisoning from food served on the airplane."

"At this point, I don't know either. I can give Betsy something for the fever but we need to know what's causing it. I've learned from Mr. Alberson you folks are away from home. I should be advising you to take your wife to the nearest Emergency room, but I don't think you want to be in a hospital here instead of at home. The nearest one here is in transition stage of new ownership and not at its best." He was hesitant to continue. "If I were you I would get a flight out of here first thing in the morning, or tonight."

"You are scaring me, Dr. Miller." Susan was grasping the situation pretty quick. "Are you afraid this problem will affect the baby?"

"First," he said, kindly, "We don't know what it is without blood work and secondly, with any pregnancy there's a margin of concern as to what will affect the baby, but in this case it's the little mother we are concerned over. We can't know what harm could happen until we know the cause."

Susan and Barkley were staring hard at each other. "Our flight is scheduled the third morning from now."

"That is too long a wait," Dr. Miller cautioned. "I'll work on getting the prescription for your wife, young man, and you work on getting a flight back as quickly as possible."

Barkley was caught between a rock and a hard place. How could he appear assuring to his young wife when his whole being was in shock at this turn of events? A doctor didn't make rash opinions, especially one well into his seventies who seemed competent as Dr. Miller. He had been a complete ass to his wife and his mother, gone against his upbringing in the way his father taught him to treat a woman because he wanted to put a stop to his mother seeing Kane Alberson. All this washed through his system as he was trying to think how to handle the next step.

He had to let that issue go. Was Dr. Miller trying to tell him Betsy's life was hanging in the balance or the baby's? Both ways it was heartbreaking and how to get Betsy back home and taken care of was in his hands. He realized the doctor was speaking to his mother and Kane as he stepped to the far corner again and found a number to the nearest Air service. No flights expected for two days. He asked would the lady please call other services to find their schedules. This is a medical issue, he relayed. Her reply was as devastating as the first information. He turned to face Betsy but she was curled into a fetal position, her eyes closed and the sheet hiding most of her face. She couldn't deal with even discussing the problem. He glanced his mother's direction.

Susan met him, her hand out as she saw he was trying to control his own upset in order to find a way to take Betsy home. She was hesitant to lay her hand on his arm thinking as usual he would shrug away but he didn't. He took her hand and held on so tight it hurt, but she felt such relief she didn't dare remove it.

"Mother, there are no flights out until day after tomorrow."

"Barkley, it's more serious than we realized. While we've been here enjoying being away from home, the news has been warning people of a new virus. I won't go into what Dr. Miller is telling us, but we have to all go together, because our being around Betsy means we could also have it but it isn't in full force, yet, or it may not affect us, he doesn't know, it's that new."

Kane stepped forward, "Any luck?" Barkley ignored him but Susan replied.

"Nothing going out for two days."

"My next question is what about Mattie and Frank?"

"What about them?" Susan was puzzled. "I don't understand."

"Has Betsy been around either of them?"

"I don't know."

Barkley shook his head as if trying to get a hold on the reason behind the question. "She and Mattie were together yesterday, I went with Frank to watch the team play ball and she and Mattie watched some kind of craft workshop put on for the ladies, I think according to Betsy, mother went shopping for her grands,."

Susan was nodding. "So, yes, we have all been together."

"Barkley, is it all right if I try to find a way to get us home tonight?"

Emotion played over Barkley's face but he knew he had to get his wife home. "Yes, sir, I'd appreciate it."

"Six of us," Kane replied. "According to Dr. Miller we all need to be quarantined for around two weeks."

"Can you leave the rest of the group?"

"I'll have to, but it's up to the new company to see them off, day of departure, so I'm mostly relieved of that duty. This is what we have to do, anyway. About the quarantine, that I don't know, it is out of my hands." He started to leave, but paused to explain. "I'd say pack your bags and be ready. I think I know someone that will take us home."

Susan didn't ask, she started collecting their personal items. "Barkley, get the suitcases out of the closet and if Betsy has something easy to slip on, clothes wise, you do that while I take care of this and then I'll go get my own things together, and as an afterthought she said, "I must call Mattie and Frank."

Kane was half way down the hall, headed toward his room when he realized he'd taken on the responsibility of six people and whether his friend would return a favor and deliver them home, was an unknown…he stepped into his room and dialed the number of his friend who now lived in Orange Beach. Kane shook his head wondering how that could be just when he needed someone.

"Hey, I'm not here. Leave a message and if I'm still kicking, I'll get back to you…sometime."

Kane stared at the cell, wasn't that just like Jack Bellows? A crop duster turned city slicker he called himself when his wealthy mother passed and left him a fortune. Now Jack owned his own little passenger plane. He mostly used the plane for his own pleasure but when Kane's mother was ill, Jack had called and offered his service if she needed to be flown anywhere to see a specialist. Kane hadn't forgotten the kindness but truth was before Jack's mother passed Kane had bailed Jack out many times. Kane left the message, telling Jack the facts in as few words as he knew how, "it may be life or death."

He packed his suitcase and left a twenty dollar bill laying on one of the pillows as the phone buzzed. Jack went into his usual banter, "what's an old coot like you doin hangin out with sick folk. I figure you down South would be livin' it up and havin' a ball but that ain't what your message says. How can I help? You need a ride back home? Then here's the deal, have someone drive you to the address I'll send to your phone as soon as we hang up. That's where my plane's housed and we'll take off from there. You decide where we're going to put down. Hell, if it's a country road, you know I'm used to that." Jack's laughter reminded Kane of a few episodes but there wasn't time to go there.

Jack was quiet for a minute. "I tell you what, I got this fellow needing cash, I'll send him in my Suburban to pick you all up and bring you out. Does that sound all right to you? That's the least I can do for you, Bud, I don't forget what you've done for me in the past. I'll have him there in the next hour and he'll be early."

Kane stopped by the front desk, ask to leave his suitcase and explained they were checking out and if there were any additional charges he would take care of them now but there were none. The attendant wearing a badge that showed her name to be Lola, replied, "they only ask for one service and that was when everyone was gone except that sweet little girl, she was not well and ask for ice as she couldn't leave her room for it being down the hall and I did that myself." The attendant beamed. "She was nice as could be and pregnant…I remember those days."

Kane asked for Mattie and Frank's bill, but there were no charges. "We are good to go, aren't we?"

"Yes, Sir. I'm sorry that you are leaving early but that's life, just don't forget to come back to see us." She was checking their names, when she glanced up to say, "Your little miss is not the only one not feeling well, we had two other couples checked out. They said if they were going to be sick, they'd feel better in their own home and sleeping in their own bed." She covered a yawn. "That was yesterday."

"If you have a back entrance that would keep our little party of six from having to parade in front of your guests, it would certainly be more convenient for us."

Lola thought a minute and then smiled. "I will have to be with you but we can use the door next to the kitchen where all the supplies are delivered. You just come get me and I'll see you out."

Kane thanked Lola and called up to Barkley and Betsy's room and Susan answered. "We'll have someone here within the hour to drive us to our plane," he said.

Susan was overwhelmed with gratitude. "Thank you Kane. Barkley is worried because Betsy's never ill, though she did have the morning sickness. I'll let them and Mattie and Frank know and I'll be down."

His cell vibrated and Kane saw it was Dr. Miller. After the customary greeting, Dr. Miller ask for the group's general well-being and when Kane told him about Betsy, Dr. Miller replied, "I need to give you some instructions, Mr. Alberson, according to what I'm told." Kane listened, growing more concerned for those he was in attendance, minute by minute, as the doctor told him what might happen in the days ahead.

Kane kept watch for a suburban fitting Jack's description and when he saw it pull into the drive he went out to direct the driver to the back entrance. The elevator was opening as he arrived back inside to find Barkley under strain as he carried Betsy in his arms. Behind him stood a worried group, Mattie seeming to have aged through the night and Frank sweating under the burden of suitcases he was trying to corral. Then there was Susan, the mother, were his thoughts as she worried over each one. Barkley and Betsy took the first seats, Mattie and Frank the center and that left Susan in the back while Kane waited until Jack bade him take the seat by Susan and buckle up.

"I came prepared," Jack's driver said. "I won't shake your hands and if you don't feel insulted I won't remove the mask. If you've been listening to the news we could be in the throes of some new kind of virus attack and I suspect that's what your little darlin's got." He shift into gear and the vehicle shot forward. "Jack's got the plane ready to go. Good thing it was serviced yesterday. Old Jack said, you never know someone might have an emergency and we can help them out. Isn't that just like him?"

Within fifteen minutes of leaving the resort, they were at the airstrip where Jack was waiting. He helped Barkley out of the seat, an arm under Barkley's arm for support and stayed with him as he went up the steps and found a seat in the plane. And then Jack became his own boisterous self, "but we've been advised not to shake hands or do hugs, though I don't think I need to hug ole Kane. It's an effort to not spread the virus germ to anyone."

"I feel so ashamed for not keeping up with what's been going on," Susan admitted once everyone was seated and Jack was revving the plane engine. "It wasn't that I was that busy, I just enjoyed the difference of the weather, I suppose. Back home we'll be in cold and the effects of the thaw on the snow. It won't be easy compared to the beautiful days we just experienced."

"There's something we need to discuss," Kane said quietly.

"I saw something was bothering you, anyway you are quite serious and I hoped it was only the fact you were able to work this miracle of a way home for all of us." She sighed. "Is there more?"

"Dr. Miller called me. He ask what kind of setting we come from, meaning rural area or city populated and I told him we have a sleepy little town. He said we must not take whatever Betsy has to the people."

"It's that bad?" Shock registered on Susan's face. "I had no idea. If that's the case, Betsy didn't get this from her friends, did she?" Even now as she glanced Barkley's way he was applying a damp cloth to Betsy's brow. If her temperature kept increasing Susan feared she would go into spasms.

"I don't know, but let me finish. The doctor said we must quarantine ourselves, Betsy and Barkley for sure don't need to go wandering around and if there's medication to help with this, he wasn't certain. He said treat it as the flu and we'd probably be all right. Now, what do we need to do?"

"Well, if he will, Barkley and Betsy should stay with me, Frank and Mattie will want to go home." She turned to him, her eyes wide with fright, "What if Mattie gets it, will Frank be able to care for her?"

"I don't know." Kane glanced to where the two were sitting. "I thought he looked pretty weary and it made me wonder what's going on in him?" He shook his head. "Dr. Miller said if a person can make it at home that's better than going into a hospital where you are shut off from everyone and family can't see you."

"I didn't know that. I'm in the dark on all this. I've got to study up on this. I don't know how I'm so…"

He interrupted. "I don't think anyone has much information, but I'd say it will soon be a daily thing. We have six hours to think on this for all concerned. I'll just go home but Mattie and Frank, I don't know."

They were a subdued group, Barkley holding Betsy close, Frank and Mattie weary with their heads resting close together and Susan and Kane upright and worrying. Susan was aware Kane slipped her hand into his and held it and she, too scared to remove it, held tightly as she wondered what lay ahead.

When Jack announced they were within fifteen minutes of the airport, Susan knew she must speak, her mind was made up. "Barkley, Dr. Miller said we must quarantine ourselves and if possible at all to make it home, not to go to the hospital. Possibly, you would not be able to stay with Betsy, no matter how much more ill she might become and the same goes for you Frank and Mattie. What I'm proposing, if it meets your approval at all, is this, my house has enough rooms to accommodate all of us, think quickly and decide what you think is best for you and for all of us together, whether we stay together and help each other or go our separate ways and take the chance we will not have another illness among us."

The plane touched down, Jack allowed Kane to do the honors of taking care of the group, getting them to the ground and to their two waiting vehicles. "I told him to stay inside, no need of his further exposure to us," Kane explained. "Now, Mattie, Frank, what have you decided?"

"Much as we want to go home," Frank replied. "It seems we must do our part in not exposing anyone else and while I'm not sure either of us will contribute much to the welfare of the group, we are going to accept Susan's hospitality...and I'll do what I can." Frank's words eased into silence, as Kane's eyes now rest on Barkley, seeing fear in the young man's features.

"Mother, I'll do all I can to help. I know Betsy needs a doctor but I've called and left a voice mail, if they'll just prescribe medication I can give it to her."

"Oh, Son," Susan's eyes filled with tears. "Betsy being pregnant, they will have few drugs to give to her."

"But Mother, we have to get the temperature down."

"Yes, you will, as soon as they tell you what she can take, but for now you must keep the cool compresses and we will rub her down with alcohol, which is supposed to help." She saw his disappointment. "Right now, let's go home."

The suitcases were loaded, Barkley and Betsy were in the lead vehicle as they filed out of the lot. Kane's vehicle had not moved but the older couple were in Susan's suburban.

She pulled up beside Kane. "Won't it start?"

He seemed surprised at her question. "Well, yes, I'm sure it will, I haven't tried, yet."

"Then come on, Alberson. Frank needs help with the luggage."

Mattie was laughing as Susan cleared the air strip drive. "I think you surprised him, Susan. I know Kane well enough that he wasn't certain what role he played in this little saga we got going here. Frankly, I don't either. Whatever Betsy has, I sure don't need it."

"What worries me," Frank added, "is if we should come down with it, then I won't be any help to you."

"Don't worry, Frank. Right now, we don't know anything except what Dr. Miller said. It may be different here at home. We will all help each other."

"I hope." Frank replied. "I can't believe we are quarantined. That being the case I know it's serious."

It as serious enough Susan called her daughters to tell them the situation and not to drop by. "We can't endanger you girls or the children," she said. It was then Sophia told her Emily had the virus. "We can stay in touch, Sophia, let's sit a time and try to call each day and if we miss one day not worry over it."

Chapter 9

"**S**USAN, I WOULD have loved to go home." Mattie was careful with the suitcase as she searched for the medicine bottle she had placed inside at last minute. "This isn't right, our being here."

"I understand, Mattie, but should either of you become ill; we can't help you if you aren't here."

"Well, I'm not worth much but I'll do my best and it is wonderful of you to take us in when we live practically across the field."

Susan laughed, "as the bird flies." She turned to the door. "Get some rest, Mattie and I'll call you when I get a bite on the table."

"Sounds good to me." Mattie sank onto the side of the bed. "Susan, I am so tired, it's not natural."

The next morning, Susan would remember those words. Somehow they had made it through the first day together and then the night. She hadn't slept for worrying over Barkley, knowing he was applying the cold compresses trying to help Betsy. Her doctor said it was all right to give her acetaminophen because it washed out of the body. She wasn't sure she slept but there were dreams. They were a strange mix and unusually thrown together. Now she wondered at the undertaking she had spoken so easily. Kane had been quiet and she realized she would have been under the circumstance. He was in Sophia's room, Mattie and Frank in Caroline Dawn's and of course Barkley had taken Betsy to his own. She thought she heard Betsy coughing throughout the night but she was so tired she didn't get up.

It was another day. She made herself rise. Finding a knit jogging suit in the closet, she dressed, a minimum of makeup and headed toward the kitchen to find Frank raiding the refrigerator. "Morning," she said as he turned to face her. "Oh, no," she saw his grave expression. "What do you need?

"I've got ice and borrowed a couple of your dish towels. Mattie's burning up with fever."

Barkley was coming down the hall. "Mother, Betsy has coughed all night. I mean heavy duty coughing to the point she up-chucked a few times and there's a lot of phlegm. I called the doctor again, but he said no, don't come in. He has to worry over the ones that haven't been around anyone with this."

"So, what are you doing for her, or, what did he prescribe for her cough?"

"He said if it's the flu it probably won't hurt the baby but cough medicine might and I ask him about her having fever and he wasn't going to tell me." Barkley seemed to be thinking over the doctor's words again. "Fever in pregnant women," he said, "Can cause birth defects. He said she should have gotten a flu shot. She didn't because she thought it would hurt the baby."

"What about chest rubs?" Frank had stood listening. "We didn't have a lot of over counter meds when Harriet had Frankie but she did use chest rubs and if Betsy's nose is stopped up there's a home-made nasal wash, and there's salt water for the throat."

"He's right," Susan agreed. "I know a woman's immune system is weaker while pregnant but we never counted on this. Let me see if Frank needs anything and then I'll come up to see Betsy."

"I'm fine, Susan. You go on and see what's happening with Betsy. I tell you, I don't know if Mattie can last through the coughing stage as she is already weak from those cancer treatments."

Barkley was waiting. "Mother, I don't think you should be around Betsy at this point. You might get the virus or flu whatever it is, too." Susan stopped and looked back at Barkley. "I'm not hiding anything, I just can't see how you can help and it could turn worse, the doctor said so."

Through the window Susan saw Kane, pacing across the yard and talking into his phone. "That's a worried man," Frank said behind her. "I overheard him talking to his father. Seems Tom is pretty ill, himself, and here's Kane been exposed to something we aren't even sure yet, how endangering it is."

"Had his father been out of Alberson?"

Frank's laugh was dry. "That's what I believe Kane is trying to get out of the old man. Seems Gina talked him into going somewhere with her and he found out later it was all a ruse to get certain papers from Tom that he has no idea the paper's where abouts."

"Who's Gina?" Barkley asked.

"Kane's ex-wife," Frank and Susan said together.

Barkley pinned an accusing eye on his mother. "How do you know?"

"I know because I have to be civil to the man when he is nothing but kindness and a gentleman around me." She saw that wasn't good enough. "In the course of doing business, I have learned or heard a few things." Silently she considered the girls daily calls. They were not as quick to condemn her as Barkley.

"Seems strange, him being in Dad's home."

Anger flashed in Susan's eyes. "Yes, I'm sure it does. But I live here, too, and you need to realize his being here might very well be an asset. If another person gets whatever this is that's moving in our midst, I may not be able to handle everything....I might need a little help,"

"Why can't he go home?"

"The very same doctor that warned you Betsy would be really sick also warned him that we as a group should quarantine ourselves away from the whole community and our family...and his father is elderly."

"Seems mighty convenient his coming here and he had all the clothes he needed with him. I find that strange."

"Barkley, did you want to go home to check on things? Son, we were on a trip and each of us had plenty of clothes. I'm in new territory, Son. If you have a better idea, please tell me."

Barkley's anger ran its course. "Mother, I'm just upset. Betsy's fever is raging. I'm bound to get this and I just want you to know I'm sorry it's putting more work on you." He was at a loss where to pin the blame. "It was that Doctor Miller said we must quarantine ourselves. I wonder about that…I guess we should."

Reminiscent of when he was a little boy, Barkley's head dropped, chin to his chest. Susan wanted to reach out and hug her son. Instead she tried clearing her throat. "I know, Barkley, you worry about me too much. Just take care of Betsy and if the doctor says to bring her to the hospital, then do it."

"Betsy's doctor Samuelson said they have a name for it now. It's a serious virus and people are dying from it. That's the reason for the quarantine. But, Mother if I take her to the hospital I can't stay with her and she won't accept that and the only other that could stay is her mother and she's sick." Barkley was thinking of the consequences. "The governor's making it mandatory people stay at home."

Frank spoke up. "What's the difference of demanding we are quarantined and a mandatory stay at home order?"

"If we are on the roads and the officials catch us, the mandatory order means they can stop us and who knows what they'll say or do? A ticket or a fine, but the order means well people must stay home, too."

"How far are we into this thing?" Frank lingered, trying to find something good come out of the information. "I don't recall the news mentioning it, before we left on the trip and I watch it every day."

"That's just it, Betsy's doctor said they'd kept it hushed so people wouldn't become alarmed, and now it's rampant and there's little they can do since it doesn't respond to the flue vaccine."

"Frank," Susan asked, "Could you start listening to the news again and give us a daily report? I don't even know how long it's supposed to last. For now, I will fix breakfast and Barkley you can come back for it. How's that?"

"I can tell you what Dr. Samuelson said about time, In some it's a light case but in others one to two weeks and then recovering another week." Barkley's countenance turned sad, "And many are dying." He turned toward the hall. "I better check on Betsy. I tell you I don't know what to do with myself."

"Nor do I," Kane entered the room. "Good morning, Susan, Frank." They smiled and replied. "It looks like I'll be quarantined in a different location, for this virus. Dad hasn't been to a doctor but like Betsy he's running a fever and on the phone admitted he is ill. I don't think it matters now. He probably has it."

"Could you wait for breakfast? I'm starting it right now, and Frank you can fix your and Mattie's plate in about fifteen minutes and take it to the room, if you like." She was tying an apron around her waist.

"Do you mind if I sit and watch you cook? I'll even help," Kane offered.

"Breakfast, for me, is the easiest meal to prepare, but come on in."

"More people in your home doesn't seem to bother you."

"With two daughters we were used to it. Barkley didn't bring people home to stay. But the girls…"she smiled, "and then married with children." She was quiet for a moment.

"I sense you are thinking of Hugh."

"Yeah, I admit, he was such a huge part of it all. Hugh was a hard worker, but he loved his children."

"I could tell, even from a distance. On the other hand, my life is kind of quiet; Dad and I don't get out much."

She couldn't resist. "Except for your wild years and wild women. Right?"

He groaned. "You had to bring that up." He rose as the oven bell beeped. "I believe the biscuits are ready." He set them on the stove top with platters of bacon and eggs and a bowl of gravy.

She removed the apron. "If you don't mind, serve your plate from the cooktop. It's warm and will keep the food for Frank and Barkley." She was pouring two cups of coffee. "There's crème on the table."

"Thank you for breakfast, Susan. You didn't have to."

"Well, I thought I should, after all it was sandwich and finger foods last night. Did you rest?"

"Let's say, you won't even have to change the sheets. I spent a couple hours on the phone returning calls until it was too late and then I did paper work from my computer and after that….I was too tired to sleep, so I just sit in the chair…and," he grinned. "By the way my neck feels, it's quite possible I dozed."

"Shall we ask blessing?" She asked. Kane bowed his head. "Father, we thank you for another day. We ask your blessing on this food and Lord, for all who are sick, we ask your comfort and healing and for that we thank you and ask this in your name." Amen.

"Religion is important to you?"

"Christianity is important to me, Kane. There are many religions that do not serve one God."

"I understand."

They ate in silence. "I'm enjoying being back in my own home. Peace and quiet."

"Well, not quite," he chuckled. "Why don't you come over to the Mausoleum someday and I'll show you a few of the antiquities J.T. installed for his Andrea."

"Mansion? You mean?" She was giving him a one raised eyebrow look. "I always heard it was beautiful and then at the tea, Sherry gave, I only saw the large room we were in that Sherry explained was to have been the party room, when Andrea invited in guests."

"Yeah, it was grand in their day but now it needs freshening and I don't know the first thing how to do it."

"What was that look I just saw on your face?" She paused, "Sadness, contemplation, what?"

"It was a fleeting thought. I found Andrea's's diary, or maybe it was just a journal, nothing secretive. In it she was ill and stated my grandfather built the house as she asked with room to grow children and a place large enough to dance. It is both, she said, but I have given him one son and I am unable to dance, still he loves me."

"That is a love story." Susan replied. "Thank you for sharing. It tells me she had such hopes and when they were not happening as planned, still she was happy and more important she knew he loved her."

Kane, with elbows on the table leaned forward to peer into her eyes. "Susan, you can be that woman if you wish. The offer stands. Do you remember the cabin?"

Susan blushed, letting her eyes drop to stare at her lap. "How could I forget," she asked.

They heard footsteps coming from the hall. Frank entered. "Did I time this right?" He lay a hand on Susan's shoulder as he passed by. "No, don't get up, I can fix two plates." His gaze held with Kane's. "I don't know how your Dad is handling this, but Mattie's is still running a fever.

Right now she thinks she can eat a bit….but I don't know." He sighed. "I guess we'll see."

Kane was folding his napkin. "I think I'll get on home, Frank. Tell Mattie I'll see her around."

"You don't think you'll be back?" Frank watched Kane rise from the table and thank Susan for breakfast.

"No, I'm breaking quarantine leaving but I must. Dad said he would see his friend, Dr. Ketterman, but he also mentioned he and Gina had a falling out. A lonely man is easily taken in by a woman, you know."

Susan was at a loss, trying to understand were there hidden meaning in Kane's words. He was out the door before she found a response. "That's Kane," she heard Frank comment. "He's out of here, his way."

"I thought Dr. Ketterman retired," she said, but her mind was on Kane. "I don't understand Kane at all."

"Don't try, Susan. He is complex but if he likes someone, he's loyal to them. I've seen that with Mattie."

Still, Kane's words stayed with her the rest of the day. Between that and hearing Betsy coughing, her concern grew. She was outside their door when Barkley rushed out. "Mother." There was desperation in his voice. "Do you think you could tell if the baby is still moving?"

"What does Betsy think?" She was staring at her son, did he seem more flushed, maybe feverish?

"She's worried, Mother. She can't tell. When she coughs it wracks her body."

"Maybe the poor little baby knows something's not right and has got quiet and listening."

Barkley was trying to determine if she was sincere. "What should I do? I have to listen and be sure Betsy's breathing and now this…she can't tell if the baby is all right. What should I do?"

"Sweetheart, I don't know. Have Betsy take a sip of cold water. Spit it out if she has to, but see if that helps with the coughing. Anything's worth a try and I don't know if there's anything to this but when I had the flu with you, you moved too much and the doctor knew it was wearing me out. He suggested we play music, hoping that would soothe you and keep you from getting in the wrong place in my cramped stomach." She was returning to the kitchen for a pitcher of ice water.

"Did it work?" He wiped a hand across his forehead. "Man, this is tough. Anyway, did it work?"

Susan laughed. "Barkley what is your favorite song?"

"Only You." He grinned. "I always wondered why. It's kind of strange when you're a little boy." He ran his fingers through his hair. "It's worth a try. My old stereo's still there and the record, too."

She watched him walk back down the hall. "Barkley?" He turned. "I love you." He dropped his head. She heard the door to his room open and shut. She was the mother. She had tried.

A short while later, the dishes were in the dishwasher and the table and stove cleared. She was thinking of checking around outside when she heard Frank calling. "Susan. Susan." She hurried down the hall.

"Frank?"

"Please, Susan, come tell me what to do or at least if I'm doing anything right."

She went into the room. Mattie was propped up in the center of the bed. Her face was pale but sweat was on her brow and as Susan looked at her friend, she saw the rash. "Is that what's upset you, Frank?"

"Honest to goodness, Susan, I hadn't noticed that. She didn't have it last night, because I bathed her." He looked ready to cry. "I don't know what to do, anymore. I called her oncologist and he said if I take her to the hospital, they're not letting anyone stay, no matter what the problem is and Mattie begged me," he caught a deep breath, "she made me promise not to leave her alone."

Susan was leaning into Mattie. "Mattie. Mattie. Can you hear me? What's going on, Mattie?"

Finally, Mattie's raspy voice replied, "I don't want to die alone."

"Die?" Susan repeated Mattie's word. "You aren't going to die. You're a tough old bird and you didn't go through those treatments for nothing. So get that out of your head. I have some medicine for those red spots. I know you don't have measles or chicken pox. We had those in sixth grade." She removed the damp cloth from Mattie's forehead and placed her hand there. "Frank, let's check her temp, again." He handed over the thermometer and Susan held it while it was in Mattie's mouth. "103." She read.

"That's what it's been since we arrived here and I know we should've gone home, Susan, to take the work off of you. But making her breathe… her breathing gets so low. Well, its comfort you're near."

"We're quarantined, Frank. You didn't do this and the other part is you are doing all the work. I'm going to make a call to Dr. Miller. He has been right on all that has happened this far, maybe he can help us."

Susan found a spot in the kitchen where the sun was trying to stream through the window. Somehow the sun was comforting. "Dr. Miller? Please forgive my disturbing your day, but this is Susan Preston, from the resort a few days back." She listened to Dr. Miller's pleasant voice. "I do appreciate your help. Here's our latest problem. Mattie, Frank who you spoke with quite a bit, his wife. Anyway, Sir, she has a rash now and running a temperature of one hundred and three consistently." Susan paused. "No, Sir, her husband is seeing to her care, but I did see the rash." Once more she listened. "What do you mean? Why are you concerned with Barkley?" Dr. Miller explained. "Oh," Susan felt a quietness claiming her. "I didn't know that." She reviewed Betsy's days of coughing non-stop as Dr. Miller offered his opinion.

They were down to the last bit of discussion when Barkley returned. "Mother, is it all right for me to use the thermometer Betsy's been using, if I clean it with alcohol?" Susan gave him one glance and realized what Dr.Miller warned might happen to Barkley was beginning. This was the sixth day, somehow Barkley had last one day longer than Dr. Miller thought, without a doubt, he was coming down with the same illness. She nodded, following Barkley down the hall.

"I'm coming with you. Maybe if we use the stethoscope we can hear the baby moving. What do you think?" Barkley just blew out a breath of air as though he were having difficulty with it all. Susan listened and just as she laid a hand on Betsy's stomach she felt the movement and heard through the steth. "I think everything's still moving in there." She watched her son cleaning the thermometer and then she brought her attention back to Betsy, trying to see if she had a rash and was pleasantly relieved when she found none but laying her hand on Betsy's forehead she saw the girl was still with fever.

"Barkley, I know you are coming down with whatever it is. We'll call it the flu. I know because Dr.Miller said there's no way you can escape it, staying all hours with Betsy and he advises you to go to bed early compared to your standard of time, rather than late so you will be over the virus quicker."

"Mother, I'm carrying Betsy to the bathroom. You can't carry her. I can't go to bed but I do have a temperature. It's only 102."

"It will increase." Just that morning Sophia called to check on them and told her Emily's fever spiked.

"Why do you think that? Betsy's hasn't."

"Barkley, aren't you giving her the acetomophen?' Her son hung his head, nodding.

"I forgot." Now he met her gaze. "You think its holding her fever in check."

"Yes, now get in the bed and when I need to help Betsy to the bathroom, you call me. Okay?" She left the door ajar. "I will listen for you. Now, try to rest. Dr. Miller said that is very important and open those drapes, Barkley before you get in bed. He said sunlight is good. I don't know if he means therapeutic or for the mind." She tried to chuckle but she was becoming more and more concerned. What if she came down with it? Who would care for the others and really, what should she do now?

In the next days she found Barkley had been concealing the severity of Betsy's symptoms. She saw his first hand. His temperature spiked at one hundred and four point five. Barkley moaned and she realized she had not heard that with Betsy with the door closed. Now Betsy was so quiet it was scary and it was up to Susan to keep the stereo going with the one lone record, but it seemed to soothe all three of them. Betsy was too weak to walk to the bathroom. Susan remembered Hugh's father had sent to their house a bed pan the hospital supplied when he came home from surgery and he had refused it saying, "Susan will need it for the kids." She left the house long enough to go to the shop and unlock an old trunk with a strange assortment of items she had saved thinking by some chance measuring one to a hundred might be needed one day and this was that day. Stuffed down inside was two cotton pads large enough to place under the pan to prevent accidents on the mattress and that made Susan smile. She glanced up and asked, "Are you taking care of my needs, Lord? Thank you."

"What's the worst thing, Barkley?" He was into the third day, huddled in a tight knot into the covers on the bed, he and Betsy couldn't stand to be touched and kept distance from each other. She was glad it was a king sized bed. "I mean is it the fever?"

"I hurt, Mother. It's like every bone hurts. My head is splitting with a head ache and I can't seem to get comfortable any way I try. I'm running temperature and sometimes I think I'm freezing to death."

In the room down the hall Mattie was struggling and Susan was impressed with Frank and thankful for his devotion to his wife. The rash hadn't left but Dr. Miller had checked back and it was his belief when the virus receded in Mattie so would the rash. "If she was up to telling you, I'd guess her throat's raw, too." She was thanking him when he asked, "how are you holding up, Mrs. Preston?" She didn't say she was bone weary. His next question was "how is Kane?" It came to her; they had not spoken since he left. Dr. Miller seemed understanding that Kane had gone home to his aging father. "I'll talk to you tomorrow," he reminded before breaking their connection. It did amaze her she received more information from Dr. Miller than from Mattie's oncologist or Betsy's doctor.

Two weeks passed, and nothing was easy. Susan was dead on her feet. She had washed bed sheets, everyone's laundry and struggled with changing bed linens. Frank was showing the wear of raising Mattie to breathe, at times thinking she had taken her last breath. "Please, love," Susan heard him pleading one morning as she was ready to open the door with their breakfast tray. "Mattie, let me take you to the hospital. I can't bear seeing you hurt so," and Mattie had replied in a voice barely audible, "You promised." Frank's crying disturbed Susan to the point she took the tray back down the hall and sit at the kitchen table praying. What else could she do? It was there, Frank found her.

His hand was shaking as he patted her shoulder. "I'm sorry, Susan. I thought I heard you at the door."

"Frank, you need not apologize. We are all in this together."

"And you do all the work."

"No, Frank. What you are doing, any Nurse would be proud to own. You are on duty twenty four hours a day but soon, dear friend, Mattie's fever should break. I have found information on the internet and Dr. Miller backs it up, the time is passing and we should see a difference soon."

"If she doesn't die," Frank replied. He wiped a weary hand across his eyes. "I've tried hard, Susan."

The fifteen days, Dr. Miller said they should observe passed. Frank, haggard and worn to the bone, asked, "Susan, if you think it's all right,

I'm taking Mattie home." A rasp of a tired laugh followed his words. "I forgot, you picked us up, didn't you? We don't have our own vehicle." As though that was the last straw, Frank collapsed into the brown recliner Hugh always sat in. "Isn't that the dickens?"

"Frank, I'll call Kane." Frank nodded.

Susan heard him mutter, "How do you suppose I didn't come down with this, Susan?" But she was already on the phone and Kane wasn't answering. The call went to voice mail and she left a message. When she turned to answer Frank he was shuffling down the hall.

A short time later there was a knock at the door. She found Kane standing there. He had opened his mouth to speak but seeing Susan looking ready to drop, he took a deep breath. "I won't come in," he was gaining control of the shock. "We never know if Dad had the same strain, or if I'm carrying it."

"No, we don't," she said quietly. "Thank you for coming for Frank and Mattie. He feels they are out of the woods and quarantine. I don't know what to think about anything these days."

"How are Betsy and Barkley?" It seemed too still, what he could see of the house from the open door.

"Betsy is almost over the cough and the baby is moving big time," for the first time a wan smile played around her lips. "I am guessing the baby is okay and Barkley is not far behind Betsy's progress."

"Then what?" Kane was studying her intently. "Do you have any of the symptoms?"

"No," she grasp the door facing for support. "Do you?"

"No, like I said." He saw Frank helping Mattie down the hall. "I can't believe that. She is tough." Mattie reached Susan and mouthed thank you and as she started down the first step from the kitchen, faltered. Kane caught her in time, slipping one arm around her shoulders and managing to pick her up and carry her to his truck. Frank said something to Susan and followed. It was all she could do to close the door.

Two days later Barkley rose up from the bed to find Betsy sitting in the rocking chair in the corner. She was wearing a loose fitting dress and looked almost well. Her smile was the best thing he'd seen in days. "You will feel better once you shower and change clothes," she said. "Trust me, I know."

They packed their suitcase once more, stripped the bed linens and left them in a heap on the floor. "I don't know what to do with them, Barkley. I'll ask your Mom." But they found Susan asleep with her head resting on folded arms on the kitchen table; stacks of folded laundry around her. "Maybe we shouldn't disturb her. I'll leave a note." Susan did not hear them leave, nor the sound of the truck. It was two o'clock in the afternoon when the doorbell rang but she was unable to stir from a deep sleep.

Kane found the key he'd seen her place under a heavy concrete pot on one side of the kitchen steps. Unlocking the door he went inside and stood for a minute shaking his head when he found Susan asleep at the table. A note was propped up against the counter that read ten o'clock. At least four hours, he counted and not moving. He bent down slid one arm under her legs, the other beneath her arms and picking her up, carried her to the rocker sitting beside the fire place.

It was four in the afternoon when the first clap of thunder sounded, outside the sky had darkened and rain was imminent. Susan stirred, her eyes opened as mysteriously surprised to see Kane's face above her as she was to realize she was on his lap in his arms, much as a child, being held. A throw from the back of the chair was draped across them and she it was possible she might move her body again.

"Hello," he said, as though it was nothing unusual his holding her, or his being there. "How are you?"

Her head against his shoulder, she wondered how she a grown woman could be so comfortable in this position and she wondered how could he be comfortable at all? A flush settled in her cheeks as she tried to straighten her body. "I'm fine," she managed. "You must be miserable. How did this happen and how long have you been here?" Suddenly she was struggling to her feet. "If Barkley should come in here…" She cast a worried eye toward the hall as Kane began to laugh.

"Barkley's truck is gone and if I'm not mistaken there's a note on the counter for you in the kitchen."

"Gone?" She hurried to find the note. "How…I mean, where was I when you found me?"

"Asleep with your head on your arms on the kitchen table," he grinned. "Does your neck have a crick in it? It should."

"Mother," she read, "Betsy and I thank you for taking care of us. We stripped the bed but didn't know if you wanted us to burn the mattress." A second note, reads, "Susan, you are the most wonderful of mother in laws and I love you. Thank you for caring about me like your own child. Betsy." There were tears in her eyes. "Isn't that sweet? I don't deserve such nice words."

"Yes, you do…and more. You have nearly killed yourself. Have you weighed lately? You are light as a feather."

"This says ten o'clock. I was folding clothes about then…I can't believe I went to sleep folding clothes."

Kane was getting up. Stretching all six and a half feet, he asked, "What's next? Burning the mattress?"

"No, we aren't burning a mattress…that would be two of them…if we did, but," the truth was setting in, "there has to be something. Let me call Dr. Miller and ask his advice?"

"I'll buy you new mattresses if you want to…the works, sheets…whatever." Kane was serious.

Susan made the call and placed the cell phone on speaker. When Dr. Miller answered, she said, "Good evening, Dr. Miller, Kane Alberson is here with me and we need information on how is best to clean the room my friends and my son and his wife used while having the virus?"

While Kane and the doctor exchanged pleasantries, Susan sat listening, her eyes traveling the length of her home. She felt with the heating and air units having run, germs could have traveled to every corner of the house. It was overwhelming and the spurt of energy was gone. She told herself, homes all over the state, the community and probably the nation were undergoing strict cleaning and now it was her turn, she certainly was not the only one, so quit feeling sorry for herself. She had a chip on her shoulder that was for sure. However, no amount of self castigation as to her moody person summoned energy, she felt deflated again. Whatever she experienced upon awakening seemed to have disappeared.

Kane finished the conversation and turned to tell her the doctor's advice. "What's wrong?"

"Did I say something was wrong?" She stood. "I'm fine."

"You appear by your expression to be unsettled or upset about something."

She turned away, biting her tongue in order to keep from saying something she'd regret.

He caught her by the arm. "Uh. Uh, uh. If I overstepped bounds, I meant well…is that it?"

"No." She hadn't meant to sound abrupt but the one word came out that way. "I…feel…overwhelmed. Maybe we should burn the mattresses…." She let the words drop. "It's me, Kane. I'm not good company. Go home."

He reeled her in, pressing her head against his shoulder. She tried to resist, but he kept her there. The tears came, unbidden and unwanted. She must have cried for twenty minutes. She quit because her nose was stopped up and she couldn't breathe. He reached behind to the table by Hugh's chair and found a box of tissue and sitting her down on the sofa hand them to her. "Now, what's wrong?"

"Other than I can't breathe, I don't know."

"Do your mattresses have any kind of protective covering?" He began to talk, giving her time. "If they do, Doctor Miller said if they are cloth, wash them, if plastic wipe them down and use a disinfectant spray for safe measure…leaving the bed open if possible a few days and to wipe down every hard item in the room and use disinfectant spray continually. Vacumn the floors if carpet and spray again, if other material, mop. The key word is disinfect everywhere you can in the house because it is thought the air or heating units in homes could spread the germ throughout. We are to wear protective eye covering, gloves and masks and it won't hurt to cover up our hair.

"In other words we need a hazmat suit?"

He glanced to see if she was serious. "Yeah, you could say that and it would have air, so you could breathe."

"Funny," she almost glared. "You are very funny."

"Susan, are we fighting?"

"You aren't, but I think I am." She slumped forward, her head hanging down as she stared at the floor. "You must think I'm awful."

"Yeah, you're awful something right now, but I think if you are trying to fight with me, that you feel comfortable enough to be yourself with me."

"You do have a way of holding me when I need it most," she countered. "Is that fair? I mean, I've built this case against you and you keep doing things that seem human and kind and I don't know," now she was wailing again, tears splashing on her hands, some even hitting the toes of her shoes. "I can't let you be nice to me, Kane. I'm so tired that I'm vulnerable now. Haven't you ever just wished someone would hold you?"

"Every time I'm with you." He replied softly, rolling up his shirt sleeves ready to work.. "I'll be in your son's bedroom trying to figure out whether to burn the mattress or maybe just the sheets."

"Roll your sleeves back down, I'm sure the doctor said to cover up bare skin. Right?"

She heard the washer going and finally summoned enough strength to follow down the hall to see what he was doing. The man seemed to have a sixth sense where things were because he had the utility bucket full of hot water and where he found it was a bag of rags. Wearing a mask, rubber gloves up to his elbows and protective glasses, Kane was wiping down the furniture and she was amazed.

"I never thought you to be a domesticated male. I suppose wonders will never cease."

He glanced her direction. "I wasn't always, but I've been through this with Dad's room, already. He was still too weak to do it and we couldn't risk the lady who comes to clean. She has an invalid husband."

"What's in the washer, sheets from here?"

"And the blanket. Is that all right?" He grinned. "It was the same color so I guessed…"

"All is well," she agreed. "So what about the mattress? You are washing the mattress cover?" He nodded. "Since you are in charge of this room, what do you want me to do?"

"Vacumn. Bending down, kills my back." He studied where he'd been. "I wiped down the walls but I wonder if spray with a disinfectant wouldn't suffice. It's a job, isn't it?"

She was unwinding the cord. "Yes, it has been all along. Have you checked on Mattie and Frank?"

He paused long enough to give her concern. "I did and it is as expected, Mattie is struggling."

By nine o'clock they had cleaned both bedrooms, disinfected the one he used and vacuumed and sprayed throughout the house. "All hard surfaces washed down. How're you holding up?" He asked.

She had finished cleaning both bathrooms and wiping down the shower had just about claimed her. "I'm hungry. I hate to feed you the same thing, but I was thinking scrambling eggs would be easy and I'm really low on energy… I thought I was better in the beginning with all those foolish tears…but according to what you said we couldn't leave it undone…are you in for breakfast for supper?"

"I tell you what, you are looking pretty limp, why don't you go freshen up and I'll cook for you?"

"Well that is the best offer I've had in weeks. Thank you. Just look and find what you want."

"That sentence is loaded," he replied and when she looked puzzled. "I'll explain later… Go.Go."

She felt saturated with something she couldn't see and had no idea its long lasting effect. Stepping into the shower, she let the water stream over her body, finally to shampoo and condition her hair, drying off all she could think was how wonderful the bed looked. Riffling through the drawers for underclothes, she questioned when she had last washed her own personal items? Dressed into a one piece jumper and sliding her feet into strapped slings she shook her hair one last time to free up the curls and feeling one hundred percent better joined Kane.

He had removed the long sleeved shirt down to an army green T and was sitting the food on the table. "Look at you, I bet you feel better." He grinned, and then bowed. "May I have the honor of inviting you to dine with me? Your food of course, but my brand of cooking."

"Looks delicious. What is that an omelet?"

"Eggs, crumbled bacon and cheese. Fluffy biscuits and tea. I didn't rummage too far into the cupboards.." He waited. She was lost to why. "Aren't you going to say the blessing?"

She laughed. "I am that tired. I guess I thought you would." Bowing his head, Kane listened as she prayed…."and Lord, bless our loved ones, we ask in your name. Amen." Immediately she dipped into the omelet. "Oh, Ohhh, I have died and gone to heaven." The clock struck eleven. "I can't believe we are still sitting at the table at this hour? After the busiest afternoon I've had in I don't know when…"

He was up stacking dishes, "I think you've had too many busy afternoons lately. That's why you are so tired…but I've got to check on

Dad. He seems to be doing well, but he is getting older." A few minutes later they were standing at the door.

"Thank you, Kane. I doubt you have ever done the work you've accomplished this afternoon for anyone else."

"You don't have to be so serious," he joked, "I'll live through it. Just don't tell it around, it might ruin my reputation."

She gave him a tired smile. "I can never thank you enough. The girls are barred from coming around and Barkley's still too sick to help…I don't know anyone that would have helped me. I think I dreaded the clean-up more than I should have…and it wasn't easy, it was intense." She was yawning. "Thank you."

"Yes, it was intense and you are welcome," he replied. Leaning in he kissed her forehead and was out the door leaving her surprised he had not pressed home the usual banter. Tired as she was, she could not focus on anything. Locking the door, Susan wandered back to her bedroom and slipping the slings from her feet lay across the bed and went sound to sleep.

Chapter 10

THE DAY AFTER cleaning the house, Susan awoke to the phone ringing. "Not, now," she moaned. "It's too early. I can't do this."

"Mother?" Sophia Raine was on the line, scolding. "Mother, are you asleep? I thought you'd be up hours by now."

"Sophia?" One eye open the other seeming to be stuck, Susan rolled to look at the clock. "You won't believe this, Sophia, but I slept cross ways of the bed all night. I have been so tired…."

"Mother, I'd come help you." Sophia sounded so forlorn, Susan sit up in the bed to comfort her daughter.

"Oh, darling. Neither of you girls can come here until the quarantine lifts. Pregnant…"

"Has Barkley not been able to help any, Mother?"

"Oh, no, Sophia. They have both been sick but they're home now and all the bed covers had to be washed…." Susan yawned. "I can't believe I'm still in this bed…." She yawned again. "I'm so sorry…" She closed her eyes and that was that….

Sophia chuckled and disconnected. Patting her stomach she said, "That is one tired woman."

Sun was streaming through the window. Susan felt it on her face. It was as if the winter that had hung on into spring's debut finally decided to leave. In that one moment as she opened her eyes, yesterday seemed a week away, the Seed show on the Beach was not a month past but was too far gone to remember…and then she did… dinner each evening, the surprise of who won the seed…she had won but not claimed it. Someone else got the prize. For a moment she felt the pain of losing. What was she doing that she forfeited such a windfall? Now it came to her, checking on Betsy; It was the beginning of a week of fever and coughing and wondering what would happen to her people quarantined in the house together, but finally Frank and Mattie went home, as did Barkley and Betsy, and that left her to clean the house, rid it of germs….

A smile teased its way across her lips. Glancing around the room, she remembered Kane working wonders while her body betrayed her, she was unable to make it move at first and then slowly she could function, not at top speed but her mind had snapped back to reality and she began to help Kane. Never would she have imagined Kane Alberson with a cloth in his hand wiping down walls. A laugh formed at the base of her stomach, rolled upward and spewed from her lips, as she rocked back and forth on the bed, it was almost too good to be true. Maybe it wasn't. Sliding off the bed, she hurried down the hall to the fragrance of disinfectant lingering in the air of the clean rooms, the hall, and back into her bedroom. This, this deserved some thinking…she lay on the bed again…her mind whirling but her body still refusing to return to its former self….time before the virus, she thought that had left her tired.

She needed vitamins. How could she participate in helping Barkley make a crop? Bert couldn't do everything. She glanced at the calendar. Time. It was time; Time for the rains to stop, as if she had anything to do with that. Time for the do-all to run across those encrusted rows they'd sit up last fall and then time for the seed to be planted and wait…wait for the seed to swell and come up…then they were on their way. She couldn't help but be excited. Excited or not, she was dragging her feet. Stretching, she had to get back on some sort of exercise regime. She had not fell to the flu, still she was victim to it. Now, she had to bring herself back to normal.

The more she thought of normal, the more she thought about Mattie. Mattie was important to her world. She had to see Mattie. How was she to handle seeing Mattie if Mattie had the virus, even though she had been around her from the start? Now that Mattie was home and she and Kane had rid the house of possible virus germs here, Mattie's home was a different matter. She called Doctor Miller and told him the situation.

"Mrs. Preston," the good doctor said, "If, as you say the time of quarantine passed and neither of your friends have the virus now, put a mask on and have her to wear one too, that protects you and I'm learning more about this virus every day, they tell me if you keep a safe distance six to eight feet from each other, that lessens the chance of getting it. Stories are circulating in our medical world how this virus has become so lethal and where it began but like every new strain we deal with year after year, I'm sure before long they will have named it and begin trying to find a vaccine. Right now, the best we can do, you or I, is be cautious and distance and mask are the only protection we have presently."

Susan called Mattie as soon as she finished speaking with Dr. Miller. "Mattie, do you have a mask?"

"Hello to you too, friend." Mattie was chuckling. "What do I need a mask for, Susan?"

"I need to see you, Mattie. I just finished talking to Dr. Miller and he said we would be protecting each other if we wore a mask. I haven't had the virus but if I happen to be coming down with it and don't know you don't want it again, do you?"

"Lord in heaven, no," Mattie exclaimed. "I thought I was going to die and Frank thought so, too. Come on over. We have masks they had Frank to wear when I was so ill from the radiation and my immune system was low. Do you have one?"

"Just the kind Hugh used when he was painting equipment but if we don't get real close, won't that do?"

"I want to hug you bigtime," Mattie replied. "But come on and I'll control myself and just say thank you for taking us in and keeping Frank fed."

"I'll be there in fifteen minutes."

"What's going on?" Mattie studied her friend. She could feel the vibes emanating from Susan. "Honey, you are in high gear and I want to know why."

"I don't know. We wiped down walls, laundered the bed linens, and in general germ proofed the house yesterday and I was so tired I slept a good sixteen hours and now I'm like someone on a high. My mind is going a million miles a minute and I just had to see you."

"Who is we that cleaned house yesterday? It can't be Barkley or Betsy, they had to be weak, like I was." She motioned for Susan to sit. "Surely the girls didn't come to help, being pregnant that wouldn't be wise." She was waiting for Susan to fill her in.

"It was Kane, Mattie. He came back to help me clean the rooms and I could never have done it without him, but…"she giggled. "I would never ever have imagined Kane Alberson would know how to clean. Mattie, he took charge. I was wasted and he seemed to know just what to do."

"You wouldn't be surprised if you had known his mother. They were very close and she taught him a lot of things, Susan. She was one in a million. I was around enough to see what they did together."

"I was shocked."

Mattie gave her a smile. "Why do I sense there's more to this story than you are telling?"

"No, that's it. I couldn't believe he came to help me and then took charge and really worked."

"Honey, is your head really stuck so deep in the sand you don't know how Kane feels about you?"

Dumb founded, Susan stared hard at her friend. "Why would you say that?"

"Susan, even Frank noticed. One reason Frank used to not have much good to say about Kane was the way if he wanted something, he walked in and made it his, but he handles you with kid gloves. He's a gentleman. By now, the old Kane would be sleeping with which ever woman he was trying to corral."

Susan blushed. "Corral, huh? What a description, Mattie." She put her hands to her face and massaged her temples. "I hoped no one noticed. It is embarrassing and for my family, oh, my goodness, Mattie."

"How do you feel about him?"

"I told him nothing can ever happen between us, the way Barkley feels would destroy us."

"Is that fair, Susan, to give up happiness for Barkley's sake. Not one of our children would honor us that way if the shoe were on the other foot."

"It's not like that," Susan began, but Mattie cut her off.

"Yes, it is. I see Kane has changed and I believe it's all because of you. Is there a better man for you?" Mattie fanned herself. "Susan, Hugh is gone. What, six years now and you aren't getting younger, but for whatever reason God left you here and we have suffered the loss of a great man, I realize Kane was a thorn in Hugh's side, possibly yours, too, but now what I'm seeing could be a blessing for you."

"Mattie, that morning when he and I sit down to have breakfast, he told me about finding J.T.'s wife's diary and how she felt about J.T. Alberson. I remarked that was a love story, she felt loved. And do you know what he said to me?" Mattie didn't answer, she waited. "He said, you could be that woman, Susan."

"In other words," Mattie said, softly. "Kane was asking you to marry him." They were silent for a while. Maybe Mattie was gathering her thoughts when eventually she spoke, "Susan, I loved Hugh Preston like a brother I never had, but he is gone. If you have any interest in Kane, don't linger. Some other woman will come along and like what she sees, and if you have shut the door on advancing your relationship, Kane will consider her attention because he is a lonely man and he won't be available anymore."

Susan rose to her feet. "I came hoping to go home feeling better, but I declare, Mattie, I believe I feel worse if that's possible but I will say one thing, I believe you are better. I was really worried over you."

"Darn, here I was wanting to hug you and then you tell me I've made you feel bad."

"Get over it." Susan was moving toward the door, "just for that I should tell Frank you actually told me you were going to die and you wanted me to take him under my wing and if it all went well, I was to marry him. Talk about sick." She couldn't hold in the laughter. "We are really terrible, aren't we? Is it all about men?"

"Sometimes," Mattie agreed. "I'm so glad you came over. I've really missed you."

They both turned as Frank came into the room. "Hey Susan, how are you? Got any symptoms of what Mattie had?" When she shook her head, Frank continued. "What do you hear about the new cotton gin going up on Geteman Acres?"

"Why, Frank, I'm stunned. I haven't heard a word. I had no idea. Does Kane know?"

"About his competition," Frank sank down into his old worn recliner. "I'm sure he does. The two have always compete for people's business, other men's wives, you name it scandal follows them both. To top it all off, Simon Geteman is pursuing Kane's ex."

"Gina?" Mattie and Susan said together. Mattie continued, "I don't know why we would be surprised. Gina has been after the whole estate J.T. left behind. It's as if Tom doesn't even exist but Kane does battle with her. She is no longer married to him so why does she feel entitled to the whole shebang?"

"This is interesting. I've been staying in so long I don't know what's happening in the surrounding area and you are telling me Geteman is building a new cotton gin and what you aren't saying is he will be offering more incentives for growers to sign on with him rather than Kane but can they do that?"

"The farmers are only tied to Alberson Gin Company if they rent ground from Alberson holdings or if they owe money personally to the Alberson's." Frank explained. "I rent ground belonging to the holdings. But I'm not interested in Geteman's gin, anyway. Word has it Geteman was after the Engle Brothers but while they have their own ground, they received funding from Kane this year, so they won't be straying."

"That's the brothers that one was hot headed, isn't it?" Mattie remembered having him in school.

"Yes, that's right and I don't think that problem has corrected its self."

"Well," Mattie gave Susan a knowing look, "I don't think Kane will be too worried over Gina. He has other fish to fry." She was waiting for Susan to take the bait but Susan was listening to Frank tell about the Engle brothers.

"That one, Larson is too easy to go off the deep end, while Sam is at least reasonable. He has a family to feed, but Larson can't hold his temper long enough to find a wife." Frank shook his head remembering things

Larson had done. "That one has a history," he finished. "For a long time he didn't like Kane."

"Is he dangerous, Frank?" She shrugged. "I mean, would he hurt someone? Maybe even Kane?"

"It wouldn't be to his best interest, considering Kane is windrowing their funding for the year. You know, don't you, growing up, Larson was kind of like an addled boy and he hung around J.T. a lot, kind of J.T.'s shoe shine boy…then they had a fallin' out, Larson's parents died and he became a rebel."

"Frank," Mattie chided, "You almost make it sound like bad fiction."

"No, bad truth," Frank replied, picking up the newspaper. "Have a good evening, Susan."

Susan waggled her fingers Mattie's direction and was out the door. She had to think on what Frank said. No doubt Geteman would be making the rounds to all the area farmers to see if they would change gin companies, her and Barkley included. She had come to Mattie to find rest for her busy mind but was leaving worse shape than when she arrived.

The third week of April the weather held for three days. The equipment rolled out of the shop and headed to the nearest field, a last minute effort to calibrate things, to check the equipment to be certain all was in working order and ready for planting. Some complained it was later than usual. Susan was the go-fer, whatever the men needed she brought. Barkley was on a tractor doing his part.

It was after work hours and the men had left when Bert asked, "did you hear Gina Alberson has opened a court case against Kane, stating she holds the deed to the land holdings under the Alberson name and title to everything else?" Bert was a bit worked up over the matter. "How could she do that right now at work time? We've got to get this crop planted and she's making a big splash on the public scene."

"Why would anyone pay attention to her, Bert? I plainly don't understand that."

"She's accused Kane of every sin under the sun and that he has stolen the papers from her desk saying she has legal right to it all. Yes, Sir, lock stock and barrel." Bert had a sixth sense that just maybe Kane liked Susan and he wasn't yet certain if she returned any feeling to him. "I just figure you need to stay abreast of the news, Susan. We're in a mess, as it is, and even if Kane has in the past done about everything she's accusing him of, he ain't doin' it anymore." Susan had shut down. He's seen it before, when she had her own thoughts she just plain quit talkin. "Guess I'll head on home," he said. "See you in the morning."

That night she couldn't sleep. Susan pulled a housecoat over her gown and went in to search the net. What Bert said was true; the newspaper in the next town carried the story. She wondered how did Kane handle such things? It had to be stressful. She wandered into the kitchen, maybe a glass of milk would help or a cup of decaf. She was reaching for the coffee when she heard a light tap at the back door. Startled she was rooted to the spot and then she heard a voice, "Susan, it's me. Kane." She glanced down at her housecoat. She was wearing more than most wore to the beach, she guessed it was all right to let him in.

"I saw your light."

"It's late, Kane. Why are you out?'

"Couldn't sleep," he shrugged, "started driving and wanted to drive by where you are."

"Are things that bad?"

"Yes."

"Nothing more, just yes?"

"I saw Mattie and Frank today. They said you were by a week or two ago and Frank told you there was a problem." He gave a sad smile, "Knowing you, I figure that you went to the Internet and looked to see if there was any truth to it."

"Just tonight, not before," she replied, truthful. "You want coffee?"

"Yeah, black." He was watching her expression. "So what do you think about what you read?"

"Is there truth in any of it?" She hand the cup of coffee to him.

"I used to be like that to some degree, maybe not as much as she wants everyone to believe." He took a sip. "She's building a case, against me to look good when she takes over." He grimaced. "Over my dead body."

She motioned he was to follow to where they usually sit in the rocking chairs by the fireplace. She turned the light off as they left the kitchen. "Where did you park?"

"As usual, like a thief, behind the shop."

She shook her head, eyes closed, "I'm sorry. I have a reputation." There was one light on in the room.

"I don't," he muttered. He waved his hand in the air. "Well, if anyone sees me here, they have x-ray vision. I can hardly see your face."

For once she laughed and that eased the tension. Kane began to relax, "I don't know why, being with you makes life easier and then when I leave and don't see you, the tension builds."

"You are in bad shape tonight," she consoled. "This will pass and things will be better."

"I don't know," he replied. "It all hinges on finding the papers J.T. drew up years ago."

"What about the ones she swears she has?"

"Fake, drawn up by a shister in cahoots with her and Geteman."

They talked for an hour, and when she yawned he rose up to leave. "Susan?" She stood to see him out.

She saw the longing in his eyes. "Kane, you are killing me?" He was pulling her close.

"Then why am I the one dying?" He stared down into her eyes. "Susan, they're trying to send me to prison?"

"For what? Claiming to be heir to your grandfather's estate?"

"Embezzlement, I moved all the money into accounts Gina can't access."

"They call that embezzlement? I truly don't understand what grounds she has to stand on."

"There's more." He pulled her so close she couldn't see his face. "Larson Engle has fallen in with them. He is willing to testify I threatened him and his brother concerning their land."

"That's ridiculous. You funded them, didn't you?" Susan's temper fired up. "For heaven's sake, Kane Alberson, you have been the ultimate of fair since your grandfather died. I don't know why you are so down tonight, yes, it looks bad, but you have a lawyer and I'm sure he's a good one, bring in Sherry and Mattie and Frank and dig up the older ones that care about you and let them stand against Gina. For heaven's sakes, this just makes me boil."

"Well," he blew out a built up breath of air, "I didn't mean to set you off…I was just talking it out and I guess what did it was I went out to eat and people were sitting at tables looking at me, making conversation. Do you like to be the butt of people's conversation?"

"I am sure I have been, when Hugh went to jail. Remember that?" Now she was angry for another reason. "Like your situation, it was plastered over every local and state newspaper…it was terrible…."

"I better go," Kane said, "for what it's worth, thank you for holding me."

"Was I holding you?"

"Yeah, you were, in an iron grip," he grinned, "But I liked it." He saw the look in her eyes. "Pardon me," he said, "While I slink out to my truck in the dark like a thief in the night."

He left. He had forgotten to ask her what she thought about the second gin being built in the area.

Susan went to bed. The whole thing was disturbing. She couldn't believe the mighty Kane Alberson was worried over an ex-wife, but then she had the papers if she could make a judge believe they were real.

She lay there thinking and then the phone rang. She knew it was him. "Hello Kane."

"I just wanted to hear that sleepy time voice. I know you are in bed. Thanks for listening, Susan."

"Good night, Kane, go to sleep."

He was smiling. "Good night, Susan, I will."

This was getting serious. Tonight she had felt his anger and hers rose in agreement. This wasn't good. She had to remain detached. She turned the light on, her eyes resting on Hugh's picture. "I love you, Hugh, but you are gone. What am I supposed to do? The other thing is, I take everything to God, just like we did together, but I'm not sure if Kane knows our heavenly father at all. There's so much here, Hugh and you're not here to share your opinion with me. You said Kane would want me. Yes, he does. You were right, but I don't know what to do about it. I'm dying of loneliness and yet you would say he is not the answer. And I'm talking to a man in a picture. I think I've gone off the deep end."

The weather held and planting was in effect for those living around Alberson Holdings. She didn't hear from Kane and wondered that he hadn't made his customary calls. But he would be busy at the office she decided. The following thought was to wonder how he was getting along with Gina and where did his father enter the picture? She and Barkley were doing fairly well and when it seemed things were about to get intense, Bert stepped in with one of his famous stories to let them cool off. Susan counted blessings and Bert was at the top.

As if that were not enough, The virus now had a name and the media was reporting thousands dying. It was almost unbelievable and yet, hadn't Dr. Miller warned them it was very serious. At that time when Mattie and Betsy had it there was no name. No wonder they were so ill, she thought now, looking back it was a wonder she, Frank and Kane had not succumbed. The last straw was when she and Barkley were called in to the bank. Their loan was supposed to have been ready by the first of March, the same as all the years in the past and now it was near the first of May and they had bills to meet. She had thus far paid out of her personal account, but it would not see them through the year.

Barkley was in good spirits. "It's about time," he said, when she told him they had a two o'clock appointment. Susan realized within the first five minutes something was not right, the President of the bank normally fell over himself in welcoming them, but this time he spoke through closed lips and his hand shake was limp. Barkley was still trying to figure it out when Aiden Quinn said, "Susan, Barkley, I'm afraid your loan has been rejected." Susan noticed his hand was on the desk phone. Was he expecting a reaction? "What do you mean turned down?" Barkley's voice rose. "You told us everything was in order, no problem whatever. We don't take kindly to your lying to us. It's a bit late to go elsewhere."

Aiden flushed. His hand came off the phone and up in the air. "Barkley, in view of the virus wreaking havoc with our world we don't have that kind of money."

Barkley jumped to his feet. "What do you mean you don't have money? You're a bank." He leaned forward, looking Aiden straight in the face. "My father signed for me to be able to borrow from your facility and he's not here to sign anywhere else, do you realize what a hardship I'm in?" Barkley turned toward the door. "Let's go, Mother."

Once they were in the truck driving onto the highway, Barkley turned to her. "Mother, I want you to take your money in your personal account out of that bank immediately. You can't trust a thing they say."

"Son, I don't have that much left. I've been paying monthly bills for the farm out of it. I thought soon we'd have our loan and I could easily pay back the expense."

Barkley beat his hands against the steering wheel. "We haven't even begun and now this."

Kane was driving into town when he saw Barkley and Susan coming out of the bank. The stop light turned red and gave him full view of Barkley's expression as he talked to his mother. It didn't look good. What he had been hearing was due to the virus and government mandatories and state shut down the banks were in a predicament same as the private sector. Everyone was suffering, including himself. But his was a different dilemma. The court date was fast approaching. Gina swore she had papers signed by J.T. leaving her everything. He knew they were fake but he had nothing to present himself, except the last years of overseeing the holdings…but no actual will or deed in his hands.

Now that Larson Engle was throwing in with Gina telling the media he had swindled them, making them sign over their farm in order to be funded the new crop year, more papers had surfaced to back Larson's story, and all Kane could think was whoever Gina's lawyers might be, they were busy printing papers that looked legitimate but were not. His father wasn't much help. He had lived his life in the shadow of J.T. Alberson. Kane had spent days tracking down evidence he was in charge of the operation, starting with the local government office, the assessor and J.T.'s own legal advisors. They knew Gina was wrong but she had papers and Kane did not.

"Kane, bring us a will or a paper that shows proof of ownership that reads the heirs of J.T. Alberson shall continue the business of J.T. Alberson land holdings. We don't care how it reads but your ex-wife has you over a barrel, she has papers showing J.T. left everything to her."

He had not talked with Susan since the night he stopped in. If Gina stripped him of everything, he had nothing to offer to make life better for

Susan, not that she led him to believe that could happen. He imagined Aiden Quinn's bank was suffering since he removed all accounts to another facility. He had to get them out of Gina's grasp and he didn't really trust Aiden. The new institution stood through the last epidemic of failing banks and he trust it would if this virus situation lengthened. There was more than one change. The government, according to the news media, issued a number of guidelines, wear a mask and keep a social distance. His business had received a right to stay open along with the medical teams touted as frontline helpers in the hospitals and nursing facilities Nationwide.

He understood, seeing Barkley pounding the steering wheel in frustration. But that young man had no use for him which was another hurdle to jump. Presently, the largest hurdle was keeping Alberson Holdings. He was doing business as usual out of the office but Gina had threatened to bring the police in and claim it. He had moved any important ledgers to Alberly and she would have a heck of a time getting them out of that vault. No doubt she and Geteman thought if they had the information on fall sign-ups for cotton being brought to Alberson Ginning Company, Geteman would begin to contact and woo those signers away from Alberson Gin. It was a dog eat dog world full of tricks and he knew because he had in his past used them all. Their plan was to bring him down and he was determined if he went down he would go down fighting. His only worry was that his Father would cave.

All the while Tom Alberson watched his son scrambling here and there looking for papers he had never seen and wasn't at all sure they exist except J.T. had often referred to them, saying "I left you boys the land and everything connected to it, but you'll have to find them. That'll bring the salt out in you." Tom knew whatever was to happen next would rock the whole community but he wasn't sure Kane believed it.

Barkley drove fast, trying to understand what had just happened. Finally, when he met a State Trooper and the trooper gestured, meaning slow down, Barkley realized his speed. "Mother, what will we do? We cannot make a crop without funding."

"I've heard of farmers who don't pay any on their debt until the crop is out and they collect money."

Barkley scoffed at that. "They either have a special friend or it's not true. What do you think would happen to us if we did that?" He pulled into the farm drive. "They'd be out here confiscating machinery, a tractor or two, and our name would be mud every year after that."

"We still have a lot to be thankful for, let's get through the rest of the day by staying busy and then sleep on it tonight."

"Isn't that just an old wives tale that sleeping on something helps?"

"Let's try it," she was climbing down. "I'll be in the house if you need me."

She spent the afternoon combing the books. If they were looking for another lender, there was always pertinent information needed. She wondered what was behind Aiden Quinn's remark, "We don't have that much money." Like Barkley, she assumed banks always had money, but evidently not on hand.

By eight o'clock she had enough numbers floating through her head to sink a ship. She glanced out at the farm shop; Bert was closing the big double doors. The other employees would come in as they finished appointed jobs for the day. She was mentally tired and if there had been hope now she wasn't so sure. After the fire, they had replaced several pieces of equipment but the Insurance money had not completed the payment. With the price of equipment it didn't take long to have a heavy debt load. She stepped outside as Barkley backed out of the farm drive and headed the direction of his home.

She locked the door, dropped the key in her pocket and walked the edge of the yard and kept on walking the turnrow next to the highway. Barkley always ask her not to walk by the highway, but she found a certain peace in reaching the first bridge where she and Hugh had taken the kids to fish, but now this time of day, like early mornings were the most lonely. Mornings, Hugh was always there preparing for the day, and they seemed to communicate without words; evenings he came home tired but never without a weary smile for her. Time had been precious and they thinking they appreciated it to the fullest had not known how dear it was. Now he was gone…physically absent from her life but still so very strong in memory. If she tilt her head just so and listened with her heart sometimes it was as though she felt his presence.

She remembered Mattie's words, and they hurt because they were true. Did anyone know how hurtful those words were, when someone reminded you the one you loved was gone? "Susan," Mattie said, "Hugh is gone and if you linger some other woman will gain Kane's attention. He's a very lonely man."

She walked on, coming to the bridge to the sound of water tripping over the rocks, just a low stream with the rippling sound of time. It was like nothing else she could imagine soothing and full of promise…and she thought of the scripture in the bible that said God could make streams in the desert. He could take this situation where their lender rejected their loan and bring something else into being. The scripture had come to mind out of nowhere. Surely it was meant to encourage but having looked at the numbers all afternoon she wore a skeptical heart. As on a note of its own, she wondered if Kane had ever had a personal relationship with the Lord. Her faith was real, it mattered whether he had or not.

She heard the vehicle pass on the bridge and then slow and back up. A man's step sure and firm was coming down the embankment, her heart skipped a beat as she remembered Barkley's request. Her hand in one pocket the keys clutched tight in her fist she turned and her heart tripped and started again.

"Susan?" Kane's puzzled expression said it all. He was as surprised to see her as she was him. "I saw something light colored and my mind went into a spin, asking was that a person or a figment of my imagination. I think I was scared something was wrong. Are you all right?"

She felt laughter bubbling in her chest but it came out frightfully near a half sob in her own ears. "I was startled that someone was coming down the path. I had stood here in my own world not comprehending another person was near and it did give me a moment of fear."

He glanced at his watch. "Have you got time to take a ride?" He held out his hand to start up the incline of the embankment. Dark was falling as he helped her into the truck. "I'm going to the cabin for one last look for papers J.T. just might have left there."

"I take it your search is not going well?"

His chin was set. "No, I can't say it is." They rode on in comfortable silence and thirty minutes later came to the cabin. He came around to the passenger side and opened the door. "It's a bit steep for you right here, hold tight to my hand." He flipped the flashlight on his cell phone and they hurried to the door. Once inside, he lit the lamps and began the search. "I should've come during daylight but I've exhausted myself looking everywhere feasible at the office, Amberly, the bank boxes and Lord knows where else. If anyone's watching I'm sure they think I've lost my mind."

"Do you suppose someone is watching?"

"Yeah, probably but they don't know about this place." Finally, convinced there was nothing hidden in the cabin, Kane slumped, defeated into the chair in front of the fireplace. "Do we have time for a fire? These evening turn cool and that's certainly not good for a cotton crop but I guess good for something."

She watched him rise again. The usual energetic movement of his body resembled a tired older man. "This has really burdened you."

"Yeah, it has. My ethics weren't always good, following J.T.'s lead, but I helped put Alberson Holdings together. I know the boundary lines of every piece of land, the names of the ditches that runs through it and the type of soil. I guess I have more to me than even I thought."

"How's your dad?" He gave her a strange look. "I mean, how is he holding up, considering he had the virus and has been quarantined with all this going on."

"He has recuperated and his appetite has returned." He gave a deep sigh. "You know what worries me?" She waited. "If I should happen to go to prison, even be incarcerated in the county jail, who will check on him. Your mother in law hasn't been around since he come down with the virus; do you see her much?"

"No, Kathryn has stayed away from us and she is not one to talk on a phone. I check with her once a week, that's about all she will allow. I thought you knew her…she is somewhat of a loner."

"Dad said he messed up. He calls her Kate. I pressed him for why he messed up and all he would say was when he went to Memphis with Gina, Kate told him that trip would come to no good and it didn't."

"What am I supposed to read between the lines, Kane? I don't know Gina or your Dad very well, either."

"I don't know." Kane's words were drawn out, almost a silent wail. "I think Gina tried her guiles on my Dad just like she did with J.T. Whatever she did it didn't work and he was frustrated and a bit angry when he returned, He said she drove him down there under false pretense and he insisted they come home. That's probably where he got the virus."

Kane chuckled. "That," Dad said, "Was when Kate got mad."

"I haven't seen my parents for six weeks now, but we talk on the phone. They're getting older."

"As we are, what about us, Susan?" Rising from the chair, Kane walked over to the old Victrola. "I'm told this thing is worth money now. It was Andrea's. J.T. brought it here when he would get away for a few days... and I think maybe he needed to spend time remembering the memories they made."

He finished loading a record and then took her hand as music began to play; Ray Charles singing in his mellow voice about a woman giving her hand to someone to say good bye and then walk away. He pulled her into his arms, "I think J.T. would have been a different man if his Andrea had lived." He was as natural at dancing as walking across a room.

"Have I asked you before, who taught you to dance?"

"My mother, and you?"

"A bunch of girls at a bunking party. We always danced."

"It's therapeutic," he said. The music changed and he looked down, searching her face for any clue. "I asked, what about us? I've told you how I feel but you hold back and as much as I need you, I need some tiny little bit of hope to keep going...." He was leading, gently leading in the center of the room.

She lay her head against his chest. Hadn't Mattie told her this moment was coming? "Oh, Kane, now? You need to know now? We've had a bit of disappointment today and I've spent the whole day crunching numbers...I don't know...about us." She felt him pull back to take her to the sofa, to sit.

"I don't know what happened. You can tell me if you want, but right now, Susan, I have so many things going on if there was one comfort it would be you telling me you care. That would be my one piece of hope. I have no encouragement coming from any place. My father is coming out from under the virus and for the time being he is lost, because I'm here and he is too weak to be helpful, he just leaves it up to me."

"Kane," she said, softly. "That is encouragement. It means he believes in you. For what its worth, I believe in you. You have been nothing but kind and a gentleman."

"Is that all? I'm asking you to be the woman in my life, my wife." He sounded tormented.

Her eyes filled with tears, her voice was almost raspy as she replied. "I don't take it lightly, Kane."

"But you still love Hugh." Suddenly he stood, pulling her up with him. "I'm here, Susan. I'm offering you my heart. Everything I have, well if we get this thing with Gina settled. We can grow old together, God willing. After what happened to Hugh, we don't know how long we would have but this has to be settled. Sometimes I don't sleep thinking of you and why you can't love me as I love you."

Her heart was breaking. This was the moment Mattie said would come and knowing Kane there would be no other. She thought to kiss him, as one would a child to soften the moment, but Kane took it farther. His was not the kiss one gives a child. Susan felt her knees grow weak. Could it be she cared? Was there room to love another man? Flashes of what if's were on overload, her emotions were overwhelming, her mind was swimming.

She pulled back, her hands over her ears, shaking her head as if to clear the cob webs.

Kane was laughing. "You felt something. You won't admit it, but you did."

"And you think it's funny?"

"I think let's try that again and I think it's about time!" He sat down in one of the rockers, taking her with him, onto his lap.

"Kane," she tried to reason. "This is not very ladylike and I want to tell you something. When I married Hugh I never planned to lose him and certainly I never had thoughts of another man.

"But along came Kane and he won't let up, will he? Come on, ease up, we can work through this. It's not as though we haven't been through this before. What else can you throw between us? I think you are ready to commit." The cloud had lifted. For the first time all day, he was feeling better. "I have to think of all the consequences, too, Susan. Your son doesn't like me, but if I can be fair and not judgmental, maybe in time he will. Surely there's a safe ground for the two of us."

"It…" She began but he cut her off. "Susan, how does it feel in your heart?"

She didn't look at the clock when they arrived home. He parked out front and walked her to the door. He didn't ask, he turned her toward him and kissed her, the kiss of a man claiming one to be his wife and she must have responded, letting herself in, going straight to her room, to fall across the bed. She didn't want to think. She thanked God for the day and shutting out all she could she fell asleep.

Kane drove home. He hadn't found papers to prove J.T. left anything to him and Tom but maybe God was smiling on him for a change. Several times he thought Susan was going to ask him about his relationship with God, but she was so unsettled thinking she could love another man she kept getting side tracked. The walk to his door was same as usual he stumped his toe on the rock and vowed once and for all, that rock was going to be dug out of the ground. Why would J.T. have left it there all these years?

Chapter 11

SUSAN HEARD THE sirens of the police car. She raised up to look at the clock. Three o'clock in the morning. It could be an ambulance, on the way to River Delta Hospital. They often used highway 610 because it was a secondary road not as busy and there were few stop signs. Immediately her mind was taking stock of where her children would be. At this hour, she decided all would be home. She pulled the covers around her body and prayed whoever was in need would find medical aid and comfort at this hour. Checking outside the back door, she saw there had been a light rain and she didn't want to get up at three, it made the day too long. She went back to bed and once warm fell asleep.

It was seven o'clock when she heard someone banging on the door. Abruptly awake, already pulling a house coat over her gown she hurried to the back door. Mattie practically fell into the room, Frank only steps behind her.

"I'm sorry, Susan. You were still asleep. I told her it was too early to drive over her but nothing do her."

Mattie was staring at Susan, her face as pale as porcelain. "You don't know, do you?"

"Know what?" Susan was motioning they sit at the kitchen table. She was turning on the coffee pot.

"Kane was arrested early this morning." Mattie's voice turned bitter as she said, "They came after him as though they'd never sit together at a table of cards, bellied up to a bar or took his money during an election."

"What do you mean, Mattie? I don't understand."

"They arrested Kane, this morning sometime around three to four o'clock, we know because he called us."

"What about his dad, Mattie? Where was he through all this happening?"

"Why he was there. When we arrived he was beside himself. He even cried when they took Kane out of the house in handcuffs."

"So Gina convinced the Sheriff and his men her papers showed ownership? I thought that's what a court trial decides."

"No, that's not it, Susan." Mattie's voice reached a high, her pale face framing those jet black flashing eyes. "Not papers, Susan. They arrested Kane on suspicious of committing murder. Gina Alberson was found dead. They think she died sometime between eight o'clock of the evening and midnight because she was seen with some man shortly before that. Someone has identified Kane."

"The Police came earlier, Susan," Frank explained, "and then the Sheriff and his men but Kane wasn't home and they decided he had run to keep from being taken in but they returned around the time Mattie said after searching the area around here, you might say between Alberson and Brighton but quit the search when it rained."

Susan's mind filled with dread. She and Kane were together during that time. He could never have been near Gina and if he had he wouldn't have been so worried over what she would do next. Someone was setting Kane up and everyone would abandon him. She would have to go to an attorney today.

"Did you come just to tell me or do you have something else in mind?" It came to her suddenly, they had not said how Gina died or had they and she was in her own private turmoil and it didn't register? "Frank was she physically abused….?

"It looked as though she was pushed, according to one of the deputies. I went to school with him or he wouldn't have told me. What's so strange about it, they found her body on the Engler farm. Someone tried to make it look like she was scouting the land, possibly for purchase, but there were signs of a scuffle and a man's footprint found a reasonable distance away."

Frank shook his head. "The Engler land joins a piece of ground belonging to Kane and Gina had threatened to take it. Another person they've questioned said the fight between the two was full of the usual words, over my dead body and such said by Kane, when Gina threatened him."

"I can almost hear him saying that," Susan murmured. She was studying Mattie. "Are you better?"

"You mean my coming out? I don't know, maybe. Or either it's an adrenalin rush. Kane is my friend." She took a deep breath. "There's more. Frank, you tell her."

"There's not a lot to tell but you can read whatever he sent you in this letter." Frank pulled the envelope from a back pocket and hand it to her. "They allowed him one phone call to Mattie and said we could come over and one of them that was a buddy let him write instructions down to give to an employee, except he wrote to you. So read it and see if there's anything more me and Mattie can do."

"For me? Why would he write anything to me?"

"Susan." Mattie's drawing out her name meant to chide her. "You know why he would write you."

"No, honestly, I don't." She was tearing the envelope and unfolding the sheet of paper inside. *Susan, I am in deep trouble. I cannot tell the deputies where I was this late evening when something happened to Gina. If they allow bail, here is the number to one of the accounts I moved from SIlverline Bank. I meant to tell you and forgot, I had to list someone on those accounts, other than myself and I used your name. IT was my intention if you or Barkley should need help with meeting funding for the new crop year that I could help you as I have heard Silverline is in a serious crunch, possibly to the point of closure and having once sit on the board I was aware that was where your operation made loan each year. Please forgive my knowing your business, I found your operation to be very astute in all that mattered. Now, if they allow bail into someone's custody will you please do that for me and if not will you ask Frank? There's enough to cover the bale and whatever, is needed, if your funding has not come through yet. Susan if you are reading this note from me a package should arrive in a few days. Read it and guard it and when you can, Go to the bank listed on back Affectionately, Kane*

"He ask if bail is possible, will I see it is done and if I would choose not to, to ask you to do it, Frank."

Frank was watching Mattie, all the while, and shook his head. "If you don't mind, Susan, I'll pass."

"Do you think there's a chance they will allow bail if it is a murder case?"

"I honestly don't know," he replied. "I've never had much dealing with court cases."

"Then we shall wait and see. Now, Miss Mattie, let's see how you really are." Susan led Mattie to one of the rockers in front of the fireplace, as she motioned Frank into the other, pulling an ottoman in front of Mattie, she sat down to study her friend. "Now, tell me, are you better or can you tell if it's the cancer or the treatment is the problem? You are losing more weight and I can tell you are nervous."

Mattie's hands were shaking and she was near tears. "I don't know, Susan. The virus really took me down and then the call tonight…shook me up, didn't it Frank?" Her eyes locked on Frank as if needing his undying support even in words spoken.

"She's a rock, Susan, but the virus almost got her in an already weakened body." He shook his head, staring hard at his wife. "We pray God lets us keep each other but times are trying right now and I'll have to tell you, I've always been skeptical of Kane but there's not one thing in me believes he killed Gina."

"What do you think happened, Frank?"

"There's not much I can speculate on Susan. The deputy said, her body was found on the road that runs between the Engle place and one of Kane's pieces of ground. That's a dead end road, except lots of people fish that ditch and some kid saw this dressed up woman slumped over the steering wheel of her car and when he touched her she fell over…then the Police go out and see where she was dragged a few feet and put into the car. They took pictures and everything…and that's about it…except then they began to look for Kane and couldn't find him."

"Why would they immediately look for Kane?"

Frank hated to say the words, "Someone saw them together, earlier, in Kane's truck."

"Does that someone have a name?"

"Larson Engle. Which don't make sense this happened on Engle ground and the Engle's, I don't think would have been doing business with Gina, except there's this new piece of gossip going around that Gina started saying Kane coerced the Engles into some kind of business deal, maybe buying their land."

"But that's not true," Mattie interrupted. "Kane told me he was funding the Engles because Silverline Bank tried to take their whole farm when they couldn't pay of all of last year's loan…that's where Kane comes in on being connected to the Engles but in the beginning, Larson did try to create trouble until his brother shut him down."

"How do you know this, Mattie. I mean why would Kane tell you?"

"He said you told him to talk to me and Frank and to quit letting her upset him all the time that we were friends and he needed to see who would stand by him. Did you tell him that?"

Under normal circumstance Susan might have smiled, but nothing was normal and she was trying to find her way in how she felt about all that was happening. "I did tell him something like that, Mattie, but I'm surprised he listened."

"He puts great store in you, Susan. Are you seeing him?"

"We see each other but we are not seeing as in the way you are inferring." Susan glanced at Frank. "Does that make sense?"

"I suspect a lot of what's happening doesn't make any sense, but you are saying you all talk but you're not a couple dating, right?"

"Yes." She felt a niggle of conflict in her own words, hadn't something changed tonight? "That's right."

"Will you help him, Susan?" Mattie was trying to hold her accountable. "I know Barkley will give you trouble over this but you are going to have to decide what you must do because with a murder charge hanging over his head, Kane is going to need his friends."

"Mattie, let's see what they decide. If he gets out on bail, Kane will take care of his own business."

"And that leaves you out," Mattie didn't seem happy with Susan's reply. "I think we need to go, Frank."

"Mattie." Susan lay a hand on Mattie's arm. There was no visible movement but Susan felt her friend's detachment. Somehow in Mattie's mind Susan was not willing to stand by Kane and Mattie didn't like it. She waste no time in going to the car, leaving Frank to deal with the two different opinions. "Just ignore that, Susan," Frank whispered as he went out the door. " Presently, I deal with it daily."

Kane had found himself in the back seat of a cruiser, one of his friends from the lower grade classes was driving and seemed to enjoy every description of life as he and Gina had known it, bickering for the most part. A safety mask hung on the visor. He was relieved when the interrogator finished interrogating.

"So you live a quiet and respectable life?" Marvin Camp, his friend said. "And my name is Houdini." The same friend said he was investigating whether any other person of interest might possibly have motive.

"Is that in the line of a deputy, or a friend and if the latter, why?"

"You don't remember third grade and little Billy Barber picked on me?" Kane shook his head wondering the relevance of that year. "You took up for me, Kane and I always liked you."

Kane was trying to grasp the meaning of Marvin's words. Did he actually have one friend?

They drove past Brighton City Hall. "We're not stopping here?" Kane asked.

"Nah, you're County material. You'll be spending a few weeks in the County jail if the big chief says so."

"It's already been decided?"

Marvin grinned, peering at Kane in the back by way of the visor mirror. "First we investigate to see if there's reasonable cause to charge you and there was, while you were hiding out, we looked into it."

"I wasn't hiding out. I was checking Alberson Holding farms to see what progress was made this week."

"Yeah, well, anyway now you've been arrested and going in to be booked at County Jail. They'll take your finger prints, and do a photo of you where they slash those pretty letters on front of it. Then, tomorrow you'll appear in court, where I do believe you will be charged with attempted murder."

"Is that the worst?"

"Bad enough," Marvin replied, "I'd say it's the most severe on the criminal system books. Now if it's also premeditated? That's even worse."

"I wish I knew who turned my name in; I haven't even seen anyone I think would do that."

"You want to know who said they saw you with Gina Alberson?" Marvin's face lit up. "Why, why didn't you ask? That would be Larson Engle."

"Larson Engle." Kane shook his head. "Where in the world did he come up with something like that?"

"Personally, I don't believe Larson's elevator runs all the way to the top, but in your case too many people will see him as a lesser person and they'll fall in with his way of thinking and prosecute you to the fullest degree for being a person that has more than they do?"

"I funded Larson and Sam's crop expenses this year. Why would Sam even allow Larson's accusations?"

"Maybe Sam's going to be the last to find out what his brother has done. Through the years, Larson has a regular diary kept by the County Sheriff's. They can't see putting away a man can't even think for himself. They say he'd be dead meat the first week he landed at a maximum security."

Marvin made a right turn and they were on the County Sheriff's parking lot.

"You seem to like your job," Kane said and Marvin, grinning ear to ear was shaking his head yes.

"I really do," he said. "I'm sorry I had to bring you in, Kane, but it's the Sheriff's orders."

It went exactly as Marvin had said. Kane was finger printed, his photo taken with big black numbers across his chest and told there would be an arraignment the next day. "I'm not certain you will qualify for bail," the sheriff's deputy said. "It all has to do with what's said of you and how lethal you are."

"Tell me the process, Marvin." He had been allowed his one phone call and made it to his attorney.

"Well, you'll be in the courtroom before a Judge, in this case Judge Rickman, and the charges will be read against you, then you will plead either guilty or not guilty. If you don't have a lawyer present you will be advised whether you need one and for murder, I can tell you, you need an attorney."

Kane spent a restless night. First of all he questioned why Larson would do such a thing and he concluded Gina had a hand in it. Sexual kitten that she represented, he would guess Gina made an advance on Larson to make him throw in with her…but he fully doubted Gina complied because she was a cold person, unless she wanted something. But who killed her? There were few who hadn't thought it, if in words only. He hadn't been around her since she threatened to take the office.

The bed wasn't long enough and one blanket on a cool night left much to be desired. For some reason his thoughts turned to Susan. Of course he was with her but if she acknowledged it, the whole world would know and that meant Barkley. Should she have to dip into the funds he set aside for the Preston farming operation, then she would have to state they were together. He had nothing to hide, and while Susan wasn't hiding, it was Barkley they were both trying to appease.

The next morning someone shoved a plate of food his way as Marvin stepped up by his side. "Word has it," he whispered, "You can ask for bail." Before Kane could ask what was in his favor, "It's based on Larson, like I told you, there's a record on him that goes back to his seventh grade, when Sam left him alone that time and he tried to burn down old man Johnson's shed."

The rest of the day was a blur. He remembered the Court saying, "Tell me your name," and after that the charges were stated and he was asked, "Sir, how do you plead?" It was then he fell into a state of disbelief. Bail was denied until the Judge studied the case further. When he glanced Marvin's way his grade school friend had hung his head and didn't look up.

Kane was in a state of shock. The bed was as hard and cold as the night before. For the life of him, Kane couldn't figure out if the arraignment went as it should or if there had been improvising circumstance on hand. One thing for certain there was no bail allowed and he felt numb all over.

This is it, he told himself, I'm being tried for murder of a woman I wasn't within fifty feet of that night.

Barkley heard the news. Bert remained uncommonly quiet on the subject and Barkley's conclusion was that his dad's long time employee knew something and wasn't about to share the information. "You all right, Bert?" Bert nodded. "I guess you heard Silverline Bank is not backing us, we are looking for funding."

"Yup."

"Guess you heard Kane Alberson has been jailed for killing his ex-wife?"

"Yup."

Kane's lawyer called Susan. "Mrs. Preston, I have a message from Kane Alberson. He request you check on his father. I will call tomorrow for that information. Thank you." The line clicked to a disconnect. Susan stood staring at the house phone in her hand. Was there a real person behind the voice? Of course, probably a high paid person that was very much in control of the conversation and he knew she would ask questions. She wondered how Mr. Alberson would receive her.

It was eight o'clock when Barkley called her. "Mom, do you think I should go with you or you can handle it?" He spoke of their appointments with other lenders to seek funding of the year's crop, something they thought settled in March with Silverline Bank. "I really need to stay on the planter," he said.

"Yes, I can do this," she spoke bravely but inside she shuddered. Lenders could be so cold. "I have three appointments lined up, hoping to cancel two immediately." What if Kane's package arrived?

"Okay, Mom, I'll let you go."

She dressed. It was a gray day, the only accent to her slacks and light jacket was a scarf of mingled colors, chartreus, yellow and blue. The first appointment, Harlan Gray came out to speak with her. "You have not been a client of ours, previously, have you Mrs. Preston? Was that your husband incarcerated, oh, let's see, was that nearly seven years ago? My how time flies." She knew the appointment was useless.

"I'm surprised you remembered," she murmured, as she rose to her feet and he bowed away.

The second appointment, Chandler Collier shook hands effusively, a gentleman waiting for her to be seated and then took his seat behind the room sized desk. "I understand your husband always signed the papers."

"Yes, he did but he is gone and we are carrying on. Women are taking their place in the work world."

"Too bad, a lot of mistakes could be prevented if they stayed home in their little house with the children."

"I don't particularly care for your attitude," she wanted to say, but she had to squash her words. "Yes, men seem to have that opinion." Susan was feeling apprehensive, mostly angry. "We only lack in physical strength," He ignored her as she finished, "this is a different century, you know."

"I would need to see the deed to your land, a complete list and estimate of your machinery and the amount of capital you have already spent plus future expectations. It will take a day or two to assimilate. Good day, Mrs. Preston, I will talk with you very soon. Please leave any of the above mentioned papers with our receptionist."

The third lender also welcomed her effusively. "Come right in to my office," he waved her into the empty chair in front of his desk. On the wall the small television was showing the Dow, "and it's a good day to make investment," he was saying. "I guess that's why you are here, right, Mrs. Preston?" He extend a hand, "I'm Mark Waterston, glad to meet you. I've heard a lot about your holdings. How, exactly can we help you?"

Susan took a deep breath and plunged in. Mark Waterston listened, seeming to appreciate the telling. "I am most definitely certain we can be of help to you, Mrs. Preston. If you will, please sign this form and we will begin the process to move funding into your hands to make this year's crop."

Hugh had stressed over and over, again and again, read the fine print. She paused to do so, and that was where Mark Waterston lost his cool. "My goodness, Mrs. Preston, surely you do not think I would lead you wrong?" Susan stared at him.

"I can't believe you would be so deceitful." She crumpled the form and dropped it into her purse. She was on her way to the door when he spoke.

"I'm afraid I can't let you take the paper with you, Mrs. Preston." Susan kept right on walking. "Mrs. Preston?" They were out his door and into the public area of the establishment. "Mrs. Preston."

She turned and gave her best smile. "Really, Mr. Waterston, are you following me? You have a good day." Those waiting, smiled warmly as she walked by and out the door. Once inside her vehicle, she couldn't get far enough away, fast enough. Keeping an eye on the rear view mirror, she muttered, "next stop, Alberson Gin Company."

Incensed over Mark Waterston's intention she sign papers that would have ruined them, Susan drove onto AGC premises. "Lord, please let this go well," she prayed quickly, "On my part and Mr. Alberson's."

There was no one sitting at the receptionist desk but the door to Mr. Alberson's office was open and she found him sitting at the desk, head down as he studied figures in an old time ledger. "Mr. ALberson?"

He looked up. "Yes. May I help you?"

She walked forward, "Mr. Tom, it's me, Hugh Preston's wife." She waited for him to grasp the moment. "I was in the area and thought to drop in and see how you are. I understand you also had the virus."

"You heard about Kane, didn't you?" His voice sounded tired. "I'll just bet you know he's in jail and he probably asked you to drop by and see if I'm all right. Is that about the gist of the story?"

She smiled. "Yes sir, you are right on." She offered her hand and he took it. "So how are you feeling?"

"Lonely." Tom replied. "We don't spend time together but I know he's there and he does check on me every day. I was wondering how he's doing?"

Thinking silently, Susan assumed he would be doing well, but then it was a jail. "I have no answer to that, Mr. Tom." She smiled. "How are you, really? Have you recouped from the virus?"

"Slowly." He stood to reach across where he had laid ledgers in the visitor's chair. "I don't believe I remember your given name."

"Susan. I am Star and Anson's daughter."

"Oh, yes. Star. We're the same age, started school together. She grew up to marry Anson. Good people." He was quiet for a bit as though collecting his thoughts. "I tried calling the jail and they wouldn't let me talk to Kane."

"No sir, I don't imagine they would."

"How about you, young lady? Could you find out what's going on?" She was hesitant. "Aren't you the one he spends hours playing piano and thinking about?"

"I don't know, Mr. Tom."

"Well, he does and you are so if you do learn anything about my son I hope you will tell me."

"Yes, sir. I can do that but it is highly unlikely I will hear anything. But you are all right, otherwise?"

"Tell my son, I'm all right and haven't found a thing to help us against Gina." He seemed so forlorn, Susan stopped.

"Mr. Tom, you look like you need a hug and I haven't had one either." She lay an arm around Tom's shoulder and hugged him. "Now, let's spend the rest of our day happy we have friends and for what its worth, we both know Kane will make friends wherever he is." She left him with tears in his eyes.

"That was very kind of you." Tom whispered. "Now to get Kane back home."

Arriving home, Susan found the package from Kane in the mail. In her mind that package labeled her as an accomplice.

"Didn't you know your sins were going to catch up with you one day?"

They were sitting in the outer yard of the County Jail. A twelve foot fence with barbed wire at the top surrounded the area. Kane heard the voice but wasn't aware the question was aimed at him, until someone kicked his foot and said, "He's talking to you."

Kane turned to look at a white haired old man with an equally white beard. "I said, didn't you know your sins were going to catch up with you one day?"

"I don't believe I caught your name," Kane replied. "If you're talking about my sins you must know me."

The old guy spit a distance, "Not necessarily know you, but heard a lot about you and your escapades."

Kane had an uneasy feeling the whole group was getting ready to pounce on him. He sat up straighter. "I'm not here to bother anyone, I'd appreciate if no one bothered me. I got my own problems."

"Yup, you have," the white beard fellow said. "I'm referring to all the down right mean and evil things you did in the employment of James

Terrill Alberson. You know, I owned a nice little farm until he decided he wanted to add it to his necklace. You know, like when we were kids we strung clover blooms together? Well, J.T. comes by to see me and says I'd like to buy your land. I say, it ain't for sale. He just laughs and drives on. Let's just say within the year he had my land at his price."

"Did you personally see me, concerning your land sale?"

"Nope. I didn't. I just heard down the road in the years to come you were his henchman. I figured when I saw you here last night, well, now ain't that justice. Here's the heir to the Alberson Holdings; Here to see what the rest of us go through, here to be punished for all the wrong doings he's helped to heap on his fellow man. Me included. And here to see what that good man went through that was blamed for every other Tom, Dick and Harry's wrong doing."

"I'll think on that one," Kane replied. "If it would make you happy I'll be glad to leave you fellows to your own resources. I can't say that I feel I should take the blame for every mistake my grandfather made."

"You just sit there, Sonny," the white beard said. "I just wanted you to know we are here."

"Is there a reason you are here, I mean like I'm blamed for a murder I didn't commit."

"Of course you didn't," White beard soothed. "I'm blamed for one I did commit."

"Do you have a name?"

"Rufus Cornelson."

"I'd like to say I'm happy to meet you but under these circumstances I'm afraid that's untrue."

"A word of warning, be careful in trusting any of the Sheriff's people. There's a mole in the works."

'Thank you for that. I'll try to be very careful." That left him to consider his friend from school. He was relieved when they were called back to their cell. His attorney was working on his release, but it wasn't happening very quick. He decided to lay down and think on what Rufus Cornelson told him.

The next day he was once more shuffled out into the open air yard. Rufus motioned he come sit by him. "How'd you sleep?"

Kane grinned, "if you have an iron slab under you, one thin blanket and your fist for a pillow, how did you sleep?"

"Welcome to my world. Been sleepin' like that nine months now. They can't afford pillows."

"Nine months, you tellin' me the truth?"

"If I'm not missin' my guess, they'll tie you up like that, too."

"Hope not. Man, what did you do?"

"I shot my son in law. Son of a Bitch didn't die though, just lived long enough to tell a pitiful story, said I hog whipped him. Truth is I caught him beatin' my daughter. She was layin in the floor turned purple and he just kept kickin her, raisin' her up slappin' her around. I told him to stop. He said he'd quit when he got good and ready and by then she'd be dead." Marvin wiped his eyes. "I thought she was already dead. I went out to my truck and got something to make things even. I warned him but he wouldn't quit."

"Why isn't he here and not you?"

"You don't know? I thought everyone heard my story. He's our fancy representatives boy."

"Owen Carol's son? Jesse?"

"Yup. My daughter's husband."

"How's your daughter now?"

"High blood pressure. Limps and she's only twenty nine, but he ain't in no shape to beat her presently."

"What did you do to him, besides shoot him?"

"It's not what, it's where I shot him. Let's just say he probably won't be producing more little Jesse's."

"Rufus, I believe I was at your daughter's wedding."

"Yup, you were. I remember you."

"Some Colonel Sander's looking guy gave her away."

"That was six, seven years ago, that was me."

They were having a laugh together when Marvin appeared. "Cornelson, Sheriff wants to see you. Pronto." Rufus shuffled away and Marvin sit down by Kane. "I wouldn't trust him, Kane. He'll sidewind you."

"How's that?"

"More ways than one." Marvin didn't elaborate and Kane got quiet, remembering Rufus warning.

Later when his attorney showed up, Kane said, "Have Owen Carol call me. Tell him where I am and then say, Kane wanted me to remind you of Dark Oak, Missouri." Kane's eyes narrowed on his attorney. "Go now, and make the call. It is imperative it's done, today."

Two hours later the Sheriff came looking for Kane. "Someone important must be on the phone, Alberson. I got orders from our Representatives office to let you talk when the call come through."

Kane followed respectfully ten steps behind the County Sheriff. Everyone backed away when Kane picked up the phone. "What do you want?" Owen Carol got right to the chase.

"Get me out of this hell hole and Rufus Cornelson comes with me." He heard the profanity. "You remember Dark Oak? That won't look too good on your billboard next time you run for office, will it?"

"You'll still have to stand trial. I'm no magician. You might walk now, but I doubt you will later."

"You let me worry about that. Remember who is going with me. Thanks for calling." Kane hung up and returned to sit by Rufus. "You might want to go to your cell and start packing. I'd say by noon we'll be out of here."

"Where do you reckon I'll go?" Rufus scratched his chin. "Marvin tells me they went in and riffled through my cabin, left the doors open and snakes everywhere and I shore can't go to my daughters."

"You trust me like that?" Kane was shocked. "I figured you'd give me trouble. "There's one of those portable buildings out by the gin we use when the fellows need a little sleep but can't go home. It's got a bed, a frig and a closet equipped with a toilet, sink, shower. You think you can make it there?"

"Has the bed got a pillow?" Rufus laughed and poked him. "A man needs a pillow," Rufus said, rising.

Five minutes til twelve, the Sheriff sent Marvin to collect Kane and Rufus. Both were sitting waiting. "I don't understand this," the Sheriff admitted, "but you are both free to go. Don't make us come after you." He handed Rufus a small bag and a flip phone.

Rufus grinned, "It ain't fancy but it works and it don't cost much."

"I believe you have my wallet and cell phone," Kane reminded the Sheriff.

"Interesting stuff you have on there, Alberson." He handed over Kane's possessions.

"Don't worry. I don't put anything on my phone I wouldn't want you seeing, Sheriff."

"Yeah." The Sheriff opened the door and watched them walk through. Marvin seemed to be pouting.

Kane was already calling Frank. "He will be here in about thirty minutes. Let's walk down the road."

"Man, they'll pick us up for loitering." Rufus lifted his small suitcase to emphasize.

"You don't think they might change their mind if we stay? I'm beginning to think the Sheriff's all right but Marvin makes me uneasy. The question is, who is he in with? It struck me he was waiting for someone." He turned to Rufus. "Did you ever see him hanging around with anyone in particular?"

"Only that guy who's building the new gin, your competitor. But he's nothing special. Is he?"

Kane scratched the two days growth of beard. "Geteman?" He blew out a breath of air. "I guess that depends on whoever is talking. Word has it he and my ex were getting pretty thick."

"Good Lord, man, you don't worry over a few bales of cotton going elsewhere, do you?"

"It's not cotton, Rufus, it's the whole Alberson Holdings they were after, anyway Gina was, and now that she's gone, I'm trying to figure out when the next shoe drops or where?"

Rufus whistled. "Either you're a man in deep shit or you're paranoid. I don't know if I'm safe walking down the road with you."

"On second thought, maybe we need not to be so visible. Something's making the hair on my neck bristle."

Rufus was eyeing him like he was crazy. "All right, what's the next step?" They were next to a drainage ditch with a deep drop and a bracken of trees. "You want we get off this road and wait it out there?"

"Let's do it. I'll call Frank and he can let us know when he gets close and then we'll come up." They made a scramble down the drop, up the bank and behind the trees. Standing there to get their breath it wasn't minutes later two black Suburban's passed, both with tinted windows and the first baring a logo on the driver's side that read **Geteman Realtors.**

"Nah," Rufus drawled, "You ain't paranoid. Whata ya bet, they turn into Court Yard Square." He shook his shaggy head. "You still thinkin the Sheriff is all right?"

"We like to think a man's innocent until proven guilty, don't we?" Kane's phone buzzed. "Frank's here." They retraced their steps back to the highway just as Frank came to a stop. Kane took the front and Rufus the rear. "Step on it, Frank. We got trouble on our tail. The guy back there is Rufus Cornelson."

Frank began to laugh. "I know who he is. We worked together a long time ago. How you doin, Rufus?"

"I think I was doin' better when I was in jail, Frank, but it wasn't near this excitin."

"Turn the first road ahead, Frank, we are running from trouble and I got a feeling it's ahead of us, too." Kane began to fill Frank in on what he thought, not what he could prove, "But I just want to get home fast and see if Dad is safe. I don't suppose you've heard from him the last few days."

Taking the back roads that crossed through Alberson Holdings Kane directed Frank to the mansion. "You all come in as you wish; I've got to see how he's doing before anything else." He found the back door swinging wide, his room had been turned upside down, no doubt someone looking for something. Kane raced on down the hall to his dad's room and found it just as scrambled. He went down the hall calling his father's name but didn't hear a reply and then he came to the dining room that led back to the kitchen and thought he heard a slight groan.

"Dad. Dad." There he was, Tom Alberson, tied to a high backed kitchen chair, his head hanging forward on his chest. Kane found a sharp knife and began to cut loose the extension cords they'd used to tie Tom to the chair. "Dad?" He was lifeless, if he'd groaned it must have been a miracle because his skin was a pasty gray and when Kane lifted his head, his eyes opened for a minute and then rolled back.

Frank and Rufus had arrived to see Kane bodily lift his father from the chair and head toward the sitting room to lay him on the sofa. "You better take him on to the hospital, Kane," Frank offered. "His chest is barely moving, if he's breathing at all."

Kane was on his phone. "Dr. Ketterman, this is Kane Alberson. I know you don't practice medicine anymore but Dad said he saw you last week, now there's another problem, I wonder would you come over and check on him right now?" Closing off the cell, he explained. "He lives just down the road. They used to be occasional fishing buddies until Dad just lost heart in everything and quit going. He will be here in five minutes."

Chapter 12

BARKLEY TURNED THE planting over to Bert and the new guy. Bert was slow but he wouldn't wrap the planter around a pole and Barkley had to find out how his mother's day went with the lenders. He had spent a number of hours on the phone yesterday speaking with lenders in the near-by towns, other than Brighton. On the way in, he saw the stacks of cotton seed that had been delivered. That was a blessing.

His face went from worried pale to flushed and red as Susan gave him the complete story of how they acted and pulled the paper from her purse from the last place. "If I hadn't read the fine print, we'd be in a heap of trouble if I had signed. But that's one thing your dad always stressed."

"Are they all just out to make another dollar, Mother. Is there no one with an understanding of our effort. I haven't built up to your and Dad's status, and I have to make a loan. You might have made it through if you hadn't been paying our bills this far." He buried his head in his hands staring down at the table top. "I feel really bad about that, Mother."

"You needn't, Barkley. You would have done the same." For a moment, Susan felt strangely nauseous.

"What are we going to do? Dad always said sell off something, and not go deeper. I can sell my truck but that's just a dip in the bucket. We need thousands. A million is more like it. We know we have to purchase supplies and do maintenance, then there's chemicals, fertilizer, fuel, salaries…I don't know how we'll make it. We can bluff saying we'll pay next month but I'm not good at that. Dad taught us to pay our bills and not lie about anything. You don't show your hand, he said, but neither do you lie."

"No, we didn't lie. We may have kept quiet a time or two." She was thinking about the time the woman made a pass at Hugh and he waited a bit late in telling her and she was angry he kept that tid bit to himself. She must have smiled. Then there were the times he would steal away by himself to the shop.

"What's funny?' Barkley asked.

"I was just remembering something about your dad. You know he would go out in that shed and pray."

"Times like this, yeah, I'm just not good like Dad, Mom." He took a deep breath. "I had them leave those old cypress boards when they repaired the damage from the fire. That was where he stretched his arms up and placed his hands as he prayed for us, or the crop or whatever injustice we faced." Barkley rose to his feet. "I'll go back and plant, Mom. Bert's good but he's slow. He's older than Dad would be." For the first time in months, Barkley turned to his mother and put his arms around her. "Mom, I'm sorry for all the pain I caused you. I just wish Dad was here right now to tell us it's going to be all right."

"Son," she forgot and called him by his father's special name. "Maybe you should touch those boards and ask God to help us through this troublesome time. It could be that's one thing your dad left you."

"Grown men don't cry, Mom and right now I'd like to bawl my head off."

She sit down at the table when he left. She couldn't tell him Kane Alberson offered a loan. She and Barkley had just passed a hurdle, no need making another. Would she be doing wrong if she made the loan and didn't tell him? In her heart she knew if he found out the rift in their relationship would not compare to the one they'd just come through. Either Barkley would leave or never speak to her again. Her mother's heart could not stand the absence of her son. Just as sudden as before she was nauseous.

Laying her head on her arms, Susan let the terrible truth slip into her conscious. She had kept everything to herself, not explaining Frank and Mattie's early arrival that morning because Barkley didn't ask. She cared that Kane was in jail, though when Barkley questioned did she know she'd barely nodded when in reality she couldn't get his being incarcerated out of her mind. It was almost more than she could handle. She must get up for something to control this nausea. To think Kane had seen something coming and moved the accounts and put one in her name was more than she would ever have imagined anyone doing. Could he care that much that he would overlook Barkley's hatred?

And where did that leave her? Ungrateful? No, no, she was never ungrateful but to acknowledge any feeling for Kane…even for his kindness… she groaned within her spirit. "Father in heaven," she whispered, "take this and make something good because I can't see beyond this moment how there's hope." She had to go on, let no one see the inner workings of her mind and most of all the condition of her heart. She wasn't even sure of that. What did she feel? Numb, that here was a situation she was helpless to fix. To think she had hugged Kane's father because he appeared frail and lonely. She knew the feeling. If she had to keep on feeling that deep longing to belong somewhere to someone again, she had rather die. Life alone was a hardship she had not adjusted to, yet. She was working on it.

There was no way to hear how he was, because then people would know there was something between them and usually people thought the worse. What was she to do? She worked in the house until every task was finished and still she fret. There was no one she could talk to and yet she was the only one could swear they were together at the time Gina was said to have died and hopefully clear Kane's name. What if they didn't believe her? There was no evidence they were together except her word.

By end of day she had worn herself thin. When a light rain began to fall, she saw the men leaving the shop. Watching Barkley turn toward his home, she closed the window blinds and settled in one of the rockers by the fireplace. Somewhere along the day's fretting she had begun to fill guilty. She didn't want to hear the news but the silence was deafening. Choosing the station that played the oldies she turned the volume low and settled down to think, When she purchased the rockers she hadn't taken into account the size was large for her, but when she added a cushion and a throw she could practically sleep in it. She had to clear her mind. She couldn't figure out why her body ached, stress she guessed. She was coming closer to knowing what she must do regardless of being seen with

Kane Alberson becoming the community's news. After this many years, she wondered, how many would remember the other side of Kane. Since his grandfather died Kane had turned over a new leaf.

Somewhere in all of the deep thinking and soothing music, Susan fell asleep. When she heard the tapping she thought Barkley had come back to check on her. "I'm all right, Son," she called. "Go home to Betsy." But the knocking continued. Slipping into her shoes she padded into the kitchen and opened the door."Kane?" Glancing at the clock she saw it was nine and pitch black outside. "Kane." Joy in seeing him spread throughout her body. "Oh, Kane, I'm so glad to see you." Her eyes were bright with tears.

She reached out to touch him but he, surprised by her reaction, gathered her into his arms, her head on his shoulder. This was home; this woman. "Susan." His voice broke. "I didn't realize I was scared, until this minute." She pulled back to look at him. "Not seeing you would break me."

She led him to the sofa. "I thought I was dreaming. Finding you standing at the door? When did this happen that you are out? I mean, was it all a mistake? Something's happened….. I feel it."

"When I arrived home I found Dad tied to a chair in the kitchen. I thought he was near death judging by the color of his skin. The house was a mess, someone was looking for something. The papers probably."

"How is your dad now? I thought of him today. I'm so sorry I didn't carry through with my thoughts to go see him."

"He is not good as gold health wise but he is stronger than I thought."

"Who would do such a thing?"

"I thought it was Gina and he isn't sure but what she was with them. They blindfolded him and slapped him around pretty much but no bones broken."

"He didn't see who it was?"

"That is the ruse, he didn't see the people because of the blindfold but before they broke in, from the window he saw the vehicles, two black suburban's and that is interesting as we saw two turn in to Courthouse Square today."

"I can't make the connection."

"Geteman Realtors." She was still at a loss for understanding. "Geteman that's building the new gin company, more importantly rumor has it he was seeing Gina. Don't ask me if that was important."

"What am I missing here?"

"Land grab or at least a take-over, it seems. " He rubbed his chin, it was tender from shaving off the beard. "We haven't had one of those in a hundred years in the United States."

"Who is with your Dad now?"

"Funny thing, I called old Dr. Ketterman and he insisted he stay over. He has no family. Tonight he's in the one room the vandals didn't touch. He and Dad are rekindling an old friendship, since they're both alone and," Kane smiled for the first time. "His house is being painted inside and he doesn't like it."

Susan pulled her hand free, "you were holding on so tight I think circulation stopped." She held up both hands. "Yep, they're goners…you were holding as though they were your…" He interrupted.

"Lifeline. You are my lifeline. I come to you when I'm so down I can hardly make it."

"Something seems different. What has changed?"

"I've had enough of this mess, Larson Engle turning me in when I'd bet he knows who was with Gina and he has either been threatened to tell it was me or he has been paid a sum of money. Threat or bribe, makes no difference to a man when he's losing everything."

"They have picked you up once, and will again, so how do you accomplish what you're thinking, without someone killing you?" Susan gasped. "I can't believe I said that…?" She shook her head, "this is very serious. But I'm sure you came to get the package."

"No, Susan, I came to see you and to be sure you are all right. If you will, hang on to what's in it until this mess is closed, and I either go to prison for something I didn't do or I'm cleared. The other thing I've been thinking about is what about Gina's funeral. Doesn't it seem strange to you we haven't heard?"

"I didn't know Gina, Kane; where she was from or if she was from a nearby community. Is it possible her family has taken charge?" His expression changed. "Are you thinking it was a fake set up."

"No, she wasn't a local girl and a brother in Chicago would be all the family. I actually wondered if she died, but the Sheriff's deputy, Marvin, said they found her on one of the farms that borders the Engle place." He started to rise. "I must go back and check on Dad. He hasn't recovered from the virus one hundred percent. I was afraid you would have it by now and my concern is Dad having it again."

She walked with him to the door. It was there he took her in his arms, held her for a spell, saying nothing and then kissed her good bye. She listened to the rumble of the truck motor coming to life and then the tires crunching on the drive way as he left.

There was definitely something different in Kane tonight. He was determined to find who was lying and why and she suspected he would pull out all the stops to find that person. If he had felt beat down before, now he was back on his feet. She shuddered as a combination of fear and anxiety owned her. He was making no apologies. Kane was back in his element. She went to bed with her mind full. By Monday bills were due with no funding available. If she revealed a source of funding would Barkley walk away? And then it hit her, Kane had not taken back the package, it was still in her care.

Kane drove home to check on his father and finding him and Dr. Ketterman sleeping, tried to settle down but found himself restless. He had a desire to find Larson Engle and beat the words out of him that said he had lied, in an attempt to bring the matter of their land being sold to Alberson Holdings. It was that bothered him most when he had made a deal with Sam that he would make their loan if they in turn brought their cotton to Alberson Company. No way had he been near Gina that evening.

He was out early the next morning, driving the ditch bank road to the farm where Larson Engle said he was with Gina. He had to have a look at the spot. He was surprised to see a tractor going the same direction just ahead of him but evidently there was a problem. He stopped behind the equipment, a planter reduced to road size width but heavy on the ditch bank was attached to the tractor and then he saw the reason the driver had stopped. Due to the many rains erosion had set in, but either the weight of the tractor and planter or a natural occurrence had left a gaping hole in the bank. All the while the back tires were vibrating from the sudden stop and dirt was sliding away. The driver couldn't see whether to go forward or stay and let someone come shore up the front erosioned hole but there was still the sliding dirt happening between the tractors back wheels and the attached planter.

Kane walked to the front of the tractor. The windshield was tinted and he couldn't see the driver but If the driver could turn the wheels to the right, there was a solid piece of earth a wheel's width without the top sliding away, if he'd follow Kane's instructions, there might be a chance of getting the equipment out before the rest of the dirt slid in and the equipment ended up sideways in the big drainage ditch. Kane spread his arms to show here's the dirt. The driver nodded…and the process began, inching forward on the wheel's width of earth, foot by foot, following instruction as this went on for half an hour with dirt sliding beneath the equipment into the bottom of the drainage ditch.

As the equipment reached safety, Kane realized he had to move fast to use the same path to recover his truck. Waving to the driver he hurried back to where he'd left it, climbed in and gave one last glance before he backed away. Now the hole had become a deep chasm. The road through the field wouldn't be used for a while and he wasn't certain that much erosion could be filled in. Ditch bank roads were a shortcut for the farmers but this one was now a hazard and out of use.

Kane found a second field road that came within a quarter of a mile of the Engle brothers homes. He knew Sam had a small welding shop on the side but Larson was anyone's guess. He pulled into Sam's drive. Sam came to the door and seeing Kane stepped out to talk with him. "What's going on? I heard you were in jail."

"Who told you?"

"That deputy told me when he came looking for Larson. Is that a problem?"

"Did he also tell you Larson told the Sheriff that he saw me with Gina?"

Sam scratched the scraggly beard on his chin. "I'm afraid he failed to mention that part. Is that why you went to jail?"

"Something like that. Don't guess you know the rest of the story?"

Sam motioned for him to follow inside. Once inside he motioned to two old planter seats welded to a three foot stand, comfortable as chairs at a table. "Thanks," Kane said. This works."

Sam leaned forward. "Tell me whatever you know. I haven't seen Larson in three days, It's what he does when he's been into something he shouldn't be involved in. How bad is it? Tell me?"

"How's someone dying, for starters?" Sam looked startled. "How about lying and saying he saw me with someone that I wasn't around and it's the farthest from the truth? You really don't know any of this, do you?"

"Nah, I guess I don't. I've been workin' the field nearly by myself with Larson missing."

"Man." It was Kane's turn to shake his head. "I tell you, if it happened according to Larson right down where our acreage connects, he said I was there with Gina but I haven't seen Gina since she came to the office and told me to get out."

"I bet that didn't go well. Why would she expect you to leave?"

"She decided she would take over."

"But she can't without legal documents, can she?" Sam was thinking about his brother's last threat. "I just have to tell you, something got into Larson a week or two ago, he wanted the deed to this place Mam and Pap left us together and I told him to sell both parties have to agree and no one wanted to buy anyway, so why didn't he settle down and quit disturbin our lives?"

Kane's mind was whirling, it sound like Gina behind the Engle's case, too. "Did Larson ever mention a woman, Sam?"

"Larson always had a romantic interest if it weren't no one but little Miss Georgia down on the corner. But to answer, yes he ask a lot of foolish questions about where did you get the license to marry and if he married would I feel bad if they lived in Mam and Pap's old house instead his little one bedroom house?" Sam stubbed a toe at the shops dirt floor. "I may have to sell for sure," Larson said, but he wouldn't say why; I just chalked it up to his usual yap. I've listened to it for years." Sam stared hard at Kane. 'You tell me, now, what woman would put up with Larson's way of thinkin?"

"A greedy woman who has plans of taking him out of the picture and own half of your parents land," Kane replied. "Well, thank you, Sam, I don't know if any of this can be explained without Larson."

"So...," Sam was thinking, "Whoever is doing this, behind Larson's back, would soon root me out, wouldn't they?" He scratched his head;

this was almost more than he could figure. "But if it's Gina, you said she's dead and whether Larson had anything to do with it, we don't know. Do I need a lawyer?"

Kane drove away wondering that Sam, as smart as he was didn't have a computer or a cell phone, and was patient to receive today's news a week later. He may not know where his brother was but Sam knew enough to make a man worry. His brother could end up signing away the farm Sam had worked hard to keep and Larson would do it on a whim and have no guilt. They were both in a fix, all because of Larson. The other thing was, where did Geteman come into the picture if Gina was dead? He wanted to know why no one was talking funeral arrangements but then he hadn't been around anyone to hear.

He stopped by the gin, driving around to the portable building where he'd left Rufus. Rufus heard him drive up and came bustling down the three stairs. Slipping the flip phone in the front bib pocket of his overalls he said, "Man the wires are hot about the Sheriff lettin' you outa jail. Said you must know someone can pull strings. I had a laugh, me knowin it's our sterling Owen Carol. Nah, I didn't tell."

"What else did you hear?"

'That they cremated your ex."

"Who did?"

"Geteman. Paul Geteman." Rufus was waiting for Kane's reaction. All he saw was Kane's chin set and his eyes narrow. "My source said either they were planning marriage or got married. I didn't get that clear."

"What?" Kane's head jerked up. "If she married Geteman and he found those fake papers, then he will think he would come in on her estate, the Alberson Holdings." Kane's eyes closed as he thought over this piece of news. "What next?" To answer Sam Engle's question. "Looks like we need another lawyer."

"Thought you had one, already." Rufus face was a ruffled question.

"You can never have too many lawyers, they're like a maggot in mud, circling the meat." He blew out a hot breath of air. "I don't think a small town one will do. We will have to call in the big guns."

"That bad, huh?"

"Yeah, I believe it is." He was returning to warn Sam and then he needed to see Susan; needed to bad.

Chapter 13

BARKLEY SAW THE sky turning blue. They'd had enough rain to see them through May. What was important right now was finishing the field. Another rain and they could kiss this one good bye. They had no choice but to try planting the field, if they wanted cotton. The window was closing on planting dates. Mid evening and there was not much else they could do if it rained.

He was still wrapped up in what happened early morning. He wouldn't have thought Kane Alberson would have helped him, but he did. It didn't appear he was even interested in the cab. Barkley knew it was impossible to see through the tinted windows, other than a form. He had come within an inch of losing tractor and Planter down the embankment after the soil started slipping out from under the tires. Erosion was worse than any he'd ever seen. The ditch board would have to bring in rock this time. It would take truck loads to fill that gaping hole.

They had history, him and Kane Alberson. All the way back to when Barkley tripped him at the ball game and made him fall. He still shivered in remembering. And what had Alberson said, "I admire your spunk, boy." Completely disrespectful he'd replied, "I'm not your boy." And today, the same man he always thought of as a family enemy had saved him from being hurt and from losing an expensive tractor and planter. The whole thing made him feel ashamed. He'd messed up plenty already this year.

The rain held off and he finished the field by eight. There was a small plot Bert had hit with the duall that was ready for planting, with an eye on the clouds Barkley pulled into the field with the lights on. If he was lucky, by nine he would finish and it would be a good feeling to know at least the fields around the home place were planted. By nine he had started the last round as lightening hit the ground in front of him. He finished out the through and hurried to the shop, hopping down and running in as huge drops of rain pelted around him. All the men had left an hour earlier and one lone light shone on the windows. He flipped the switch and the building went dark. He thought he heard a rumble but with thunder rolling he wasn't certain what would make that noise, anyway. He locked the door and after seeing his mother's house was pitch black, headed home. He guessed she had either gone to bed early or had run to Mattie's. Tomorrow they would talk about how to survive without a loan.

Susan heard the last tractor coming in to the shop and she believed it was Barkley with the planter. She had only seen him briefly today and he seemed quiet, that surreal quiet where you wonder what the other person is thinking. She knew he was worried over the farm loan because she was.

She hadn't had the best day. Worry, knowing bills would be coming in and the fact her account didn't have enough to pay everything, she couldn't concentrate on the books and the books revolved around bills paid. The other thing was she felt unsettled over Kane's situation. She was between a rock and a hard place. There was no one she could talk with. It wasn't fair to Kane that she couldn't go to the officials and tell them she was with him the very evening they said Gina died. Mattie's words rang in her head, "Susan, someone else will be happy to be interested in Kane. He is a very lonely man now that he's trying to change. She finally closed the books, laid them on the desk and went outside. She had avoided the yard and now it was time to pay. That had been her day, weeding and pulling grass in the wrong places and moving divided plants to other spots. If they couldn't manage the cotton fields due to the rain maybe she could at least manage the yard; but her bones ached and she was so tired when night fell she wondered if she could get her shower and find the bed. On top of that she had a tickle in her throat that the cough she was experiencing wasn't stopping. She found the cough syrup in the bedside night stand and drank a big swallow. In time it seemed to slow the cough and made her sleepy.

She heard the knocking on the door and for a moment wasn't aware if it was the same day or a new one. A look at the clock said she had been asleep an hour. It couldn't be Kane. He was there the night before. It would be Barkley. She couldn't go through the guessing game. "Just a minute," she called as she did a quick dress and walked through the rooms noticing she had left all the lights on, something she seldom did upon going to bed for the night. Evidently she wasn't thinking either. She opened the door to Kane. For some reason the walk to the door had been a task or maybe dressing too hastily.

"You are up. I saw the lights." His worried expression changed to a smile.

"You came for the package." She turned to go get it but his hand was on her arm, turning her around.

"No, I came to talk to you about what I heard today and see what you think. Maybe I found soemthing."

"Please forgive me, I was asleep. I've been out side trying to clear this yard that's so behind due to the rains." She felt of her face, her cheeks were on fire and he was staring at her with a strange look.

"Oh," he touched her cheek. "You are sunburned."

"I feel baked. I thought because the sun was hidden I had it made… even my throats dry." She coughed.

His chuckle came, "I'm afraid you will feel it tomorrow."

She sighed. "I feel it now." They sat on the sofa. "Tell me," she said taking a deep breath as he began.

"Come here." He saw her tiredness and pulled her into the curve of his arm. "Now," he finished, "tell me what you make of that? Rufus said either they are married or were going to be married."

"I'm like you, when was the funeral. I don't believe Gina would have consented to cremation, if she was truly the person you and your father saw her to be." A new thought entered her mind. "Or not dead."

"Yeah, I thought of that, too. But what would that benefit them?" And then it struck him. "She always said when she come into money she was moving to Italy."

"Why Italy?" Susan was trying to suppress a cough. "I apologize, I must have gotten into weeds. Why Italy?"

"Some romantic dream she had and believe me, Gina's achievements always hinged on her dreams."

"What you are saying, is that Gina needed a catalyst or incentive to keep going, a challenge of sorts."

"Tomorrow, I'll have my attorney check for a marriage license, a trip out of the country, to Italy, of course. Honestly, I've been so worried I didn't even think of that. See? I need you to help me."

"You are on overtime," Susan coughed. "I think I got too much sun. I meant to say, all you've been through is catching up with you…was anything missing when your home was vandalized? Whose cleaning up the mess?" Susan got up to move a distance as she coughed. "Where did I get this cough?"

They heard the back door open and footsteps coming toward them. Kane froze and kept his seat, Susan was trying to put an end to the coughing as Barkley came into the room.

"Mother?" Barkley stopped, dead still seeing Kane Alberson on the sofa. "Why is he here?"

"Why…are you here, Barkley?" She could barely talk for coughing. "Is something wrong?"

"I came back to the shop for my phone and saw a vehicle here and wanted to be sure you're all right." His eyes blazing, he turned to Kane, "I wouldn't have bothered if I'd known it was him."

Kane stood to full height. "I'd think you would use a more respectful tone to your mother."

"What would you know about it?" Barkley spit the words out. "You kill your ex and then I find you here in my mother's house? She must be out of her mind. Get out."

"Barkley." Susan stretched out her hand but she was having trouble breathing. She thought as she crumbled to the floor Barkley was leaving. Watching the back side of her son…she tried to rise but fell.

Kane caught Barkley by the collar of his shirt. "You apologize to your mother." There was a scramble between the two and then they heard her gasping. "Don't you leave." Kane rushed to where she lay on the floor, starting to pick her up but was hesitant. "Susan. Are you choking?" She managed to shake her head, no. "Is it the coughing?" He glanced around the room. "Barkley, turn on the ceiling fan and if you know where there's a portable bring it and turn it on your mother. Let's try to get air to her. She's burning up and for some reason she's been coughing the last few minutes."

Barkley had fallen on his knees beside her but when Kane said she was coughing the last few minutes he drew back. "It's the Virus. I should have known." He was up, doing what Kane ask, running to the garage to bring in a portable fan." Susan's coughing became sporadic, but it did not end.

"Pharmacies are closed," Kane was busy putting a sofa cushion under her head. He was on his cell punching in a number. "Dr. Miller, this is Kane Alberson. Yes, yes, from the Orange Beach convention. No, Sir, that's what I called about. Everything's closed this time of night here, but it's Susan. Yes, yes, the boy's mother. We called you before. I can tell she has a high fever but it's the cough. She started coughing a few minutes ago and she can't stop. Barkley's here and his opinion is it's the virus."

Barkley had the good sense to swallow his anger along with his pride. This was his mother. He waited for the phone call to end. Kane was writing something on an envelope. "He says he can have this here in the morning. There's an overnight courier passes by here on the Interstate on the way to St. Louis University, but if you will meet him at midnight, she will have it quicker. What time is it now?"

Barkley checked his phone. "It's eleven fifteen. Tell me where and how I'll know the vehicle."

Kane shot the text Dr. Miller had sent. "Let him know, so he will tell the driver." Kane met Barkley's glare. "You needn't look so hostile. I'm going to take your mother to my home. Dad isn't well and Dr. Ketterman is there watching over him. If your mother needs him, he's there. Now, if you'll go get a few things you think your mother will need, she will be with me and you can bring the prescription later."

Kane was picking Susan up out of the floor. "If we take her to the hospital, we can't be with her or know exactly how she is. You can't take her home with you. Don't fight me on this. Just open the door and help me get her inside the truck. Don't forget her things and lock up. By then it will be time for you to meet the courier." He was climbing into the cab. "Oh, and come to the back to bring the prescription."

Kane drove out of the drive with Barkley staring at the truck as though one of them was crazy. Kane wondered if he'd remember to get her things or go meet the courier. He turned loose one situation for another. Dr. Kettermen was in the guest room. That left Kane's room. What else could he do? He carried Susan in, laid her on his bed and pulled the sheet up to her shoulders. He remembered Susan placing cold wash cloths on her daughter in law's forehead and went to the kitchen for a deep pan and cold ice water. By the time he sent the washcloth through a few times it was getting tepid. Susan coughed, dozed and pushed the sheet away. After an hour he was dead on his feet and slumped by the bed side in an arm chair. Barkley found him there, shaking his shoulder to wake him up.

"Man. You still got your jacket on. Take it off and your shoes. So, here's the prescription." He listened to his mother's breathing. "This could go on all night. Betsy's did. Where's a glass of water?"

Kane tried to come awake. "She can't swallow water right now. We'll have to mash those pills up in something."

"Applesauce," Barkely said. "My gramma uses applesauce."

Kane mumbled, "where's applesauce?" He was getting a grip on himself. "In the kitchen. I'm going."

"Wait, it says don't break the pills." Barkley was standing over his mother. "Mom. Mom. Wake up."

"She just went to sleep. She wore herself out coughing." Kane was exasperated. "Let her sleep."

"I can't. We have to get this medicine in her. I talked to the doctor. And we have to keep her hydrated." He looked around. "Where's the water?"

"I apologize." Kane grimaced. "She refused water when she was coughing so bad so I put it back."

"You have to have an insulated glass. Don't you have anything?" Barkley glanced around the room. "This is pretty austere." Saying it out loud sounded like an insult. "Sorry, but it is. I expected a refrigerator or something cool." Susan groaned. Barkley touched her forehead. "She's burnin' up."

"I know she's burning up. I'm a fifty year old male, Barkley, not some drooling kid."

Barkley was dipping the wash cloth in the water and applying it to Susan's forehead. "What's with the rock. I like to fell over it in the dark." Kane didn't answer. "I'd dig that thing out. It's dangerous."

"Don't you have a wife waiting for you at home?" Kane watched him bathe Susan's face.

"I called her. She went to her parents." He gave Kane a scathing look. "At least I didn't kill her."

"Do you really think I killed my ex-wife?" Kane was becoming more awake by the minute. "Well, do you?" Kane wouldn't drop his gaze. Finally Barkley paid attention to the cloth in his hand.

"Not physically but probably some other way." It was his turn to stare at Kane. "Where is she?"

Kane snorted. "As you say probably in ten buck two or Italy." He stepped to the bed. "Go home. I'll do this. I won't hurt her or kill her. But I can do it and the doctor will come in and check on her in a while."

"I'd just like to know one thing. Why were you at my mother's house?"

"I guess this is the moment of reckoning, either you'll take the information like a man or you'll tuck your tail and run like a little boy." Kane studied Susan's son for a minute before continuing. "Before you say a word, I want to remind you, there have been people who will cut off their nose to spite their face, you understand that saying?" Barkley was mute. "Do you?" He nodded. "All right then, I was there because I heard Silverline and a few others turned down making a loan for your operation and I came to offer that service if you want the loan. I was on Silverline's board but I moved my accounts because they were not doing loans for farmers. I did this for the Engle's, not that Larson appreciated the fact but Sam handled it well."

"Why?" Barkley's eyes tightened. "There has to be something in it for you."

"We handled it like any lender, Barkley. Other than that, they will bring their cotton to Alberson, but in your case you already have in the past and I'm assuming that won't change."

"That's it?"

"Yes, it is. Think on it. Give me an answer tomorrow, but right now go home and get a few hours sleep."

"Are you crazy? I can't leave my mother with you."

"Not yet," Kane replied. "But I am tired. Crazy is next. I didn't sleep night before and now…."

"Are you trying to humor me at a time like this?"

Barkley reminded Kane of a young bull trying to make a point. "I'm trying to get us both through a trying situation. You have a wife. I don't. I thought your mother needed someone to watch over her through the night. I couldn't stay there with my father sick here, so chalk it up to my mistake, Barkley. Now that you've told me your wife is at her parents, feel free to make yourself at home here. We will watch over your mother together the rest of the night."

"Where did the doctor come in on this story? I'm very suspicious of you. Your reputation is not the best. How do I even know there's a doctor in this house, just because you say so?"

Kane in his stagnant tired mind was thinking of the young bull ready to charge. "Barkley, someone entered our home and roughed up my dad. When I found him he wasn't' breathing well and since they are friends and the doctor lives down the road I ask him here…but the thing is if your mother needs a doctor he is in the next room. Now if she is admitted to a hospital, I learned to day they are on lock down and a patient's family cannot stay in the room with them."

"Yeah?" Barkley was watching his mother intently. "I can tell, her temp is higher than its been."

"Don't you listen to the radio or anything?" Kane was shaking his head. "If you did, you would know this. Now there's a name for the virus and all kinds of rules being set for society to conform to." Susan was groaning. Kane watched Barkley laid his hand on her forehead again. The boy was truly worried. "They always say a high temperature is part of the symptoms and chills. Do we need to wake the doctor?"

"Do you have any alcohol, the rubbing kind?" Kane nodded. "Then get it. We are going to get this temperature down. Mother put it in the water and a few ice cubes to stay cool. She said not to use it alone it will cool down the body too rapidly and fever is what's killing the infection. Anyway something like that. It seemed to work on Betsy." Kane shook his head, he was dubious but if Susan did….well. He left to find the item and returned to hand it to Barkley. The boy did love his mother. He certainly had loved his daddy. Kane didn't forget. He dumped a cup full of ice cubes in the water and waited.

"The thing now," Barkley was saying, "is to keep mother modest. She will have our heads if we don't." Kane privately rolled his eyes. The question was how to do that if they carried out Barkley's intention. "All right. She's got on loose fitting pants. Just roll them up to her knees and I'll do the same with the sleeves of the blouse she has on."

"You think maybe we should call some woman to do this?"

Barkley snorted. "Who do you know would come do this at 2:30 in the morning? On second thought we need a towel each to protect your bedding where we do the sponging." Kane hurried to the bathroom and returned with towels. Barkley showed him how to fold the towel and lay beneath where they were applying the mix. Barkley began. Kane was hesitant but with Barkley eyeing him with a beady eye, he rolled Susan's pant leg to the knee and began. They must have been effective after thirty minutes whether the sponging or their effort to bring down the fever, something worked. Susan eased into sleep without groaning or coughing. Finished they sat down in the chairs and closed their eyes. It was time for a two hour nap.

Susan awakened to sun streaming through the windows. She lay there staring at the ceiling when all of a sudden it hit her. Where was she? A moment of panic rushed through her veins. Where was she? Trying not to move a muscle she tried to look around and there at the foot of the bed, someone's bed she'd never seen before, there sit Barkley, asleep, his chin on his chest and drool at one corner of his mouth. Was she in a hospital? No, hospitals didn't have four poster beds. Her glance rounded the room. Then it stopped, where the pillows ended on the head of the bed, there sit Kane. Shocked to the point her breath caught, Susan started to sit up but for some reason was too weak to accomplish the feat. "What is wrong with me..." She sputtered, feeling the commotion when the two jumped to their feet. "Why are my pants and blouse sleeves rolled up. What have you two done?"

Barkley was laughing. But his mother was glaring at him. "We brought your fever down and you stopped coughing. We think you have the virus."

Susan was trying to get out of bed. "I do not have a virus. Barkley James Preston, you take me home." She rounded on Kane, "And you…I never would have thought…did you bring me here, Kane Alberson?"

"Something like that. Does it matter? We were concerned when you fainted or whatever that was happened and you couldn't get up. There's a doctor in the next room. He can check you."

"What am I being checked for." Susan felt very hostile. She tried to hide a cough behind her hand. "I got in a patch of weed, I'm probably allergic too."

"And that explains the high fever?" Barkley didn't give. "Mother you have been out of it all night. Don't tell us something didn't go wrong."

"Barkley James," her eyes were bright and she didn't know whether she was angry or embarrassed. "I don't know why I'm here, but what in the world would the neighbors say?"

Barkley shrugged. "Who's going to tell them? Beside that, didn't we learn we don't care what they think?"

Kane listened to one, then the other. "And you," he heard, snapping back to attention. "Did you mean me?" Her hair was damp around her forehead and tiny little curls escaped where the other was pulled back. He shrugged as his hand went up, "Don't worry about your reputation no one knows you are here."

She had exhausted herself and in doing so stirred the coughing which was happening full force now. She lay back on the pillow, breathing heavily. "I….I….suddenly it's as though I have a block on my chest." She lay her hand across the top of her breast. "I can't breathe any deeper than this."

Kane stepped out of the room. Just as he knocked on Dr. Ketterman's door it opened. "I hear the noise," the doctor informed him. "Where is the patient?"

"In the next room, Sir." Just follow the coughing, Kane thought but he did not say.

Dr. Ketterman went directly to Susan, with a stethoscope in his hand which he placed just above her breasts while he listened, then her side, "now the back. Breathe deep. Again. Thank you." He peered into Susan's face. "You sound like you have pneumonia. Lungs aren't good. When did this happen?"

She was stunned. "I have a bit difficulty breathing but that's all." She cast a worried glance his way."

"Young lady, you rest a few days, three or four and maybe you are one of those who will get off lightly." He was listening to her heart now, "You are not to be alone. In case the lungs start to fail. Now is not your worse time that is yet to come."

"I thought last night was it. They…" she pointed an accusing finger her son and Kane's way. "I don't even remember being brought here. Yes, I think last night was the bad night. What should I do?"

"You stay in this bed. Let others do for you. If you were in a hospital, that's what would happen. It can happen here. Right, Kane?" The doctor looked around the room. "The others must keep to their own room, no more gathering in here except whoever waits on the miss."

Susan was dismayed, glancing down at what she was wearing. "Oh, my, may I go home first?"

"You take shower and change clothes and back to the bed, four days settles it and then we'll check to see how you are." Her head dropped, chin to chest, as big tears splashed down onto her hands. "Now, now," Dr. Ketterman crooned. "I believe you will be fine. The fact you try to sit up attests to that." He waddled from the room, saying, "call me if you need me."

"I brought things, Mother." Sinking deeper in the pillow, Susan stared at her son. "I didn't know what you would need, but Mr. Alberson said bring them." Barkley was as uncertain as when he was a boy. "I didn't know what to do, Mom." She would have tousled his hair and pulled him close if they were home. "I," Barkley came to the bed and sank down beside her. "I love you, Mom. I'm sorry you have this virus and I want you to take care of yourself so you will live through it."

She reached out. "It's fine, Son. You've done good. Thank you for taking care of me all night. I didn't know I was sick." She felt the coughing trying to stir again. "The coughing tires me down, otherwise I think I'm as the doctor says, going to be up in four days. You go ahead to work and don't worry."

Barkley squeezed her hand. "I'll be back to check on how you are, tonight."

"Ask the doctor what your chances are of having this the second time, Barkley. You have a crop to get in and then take care of, so I don't want you putting yourself on the line to come down sick again." She tried to smile, but her eyes filled with tears. "I love you, Son."

"Love you, too, Mother." Barkley stood and leaned over to kiss her cheek. "I'll check with the doctor."

There was silence in the room, Kane waiting for whatever she wanted to blame him, as she listened to Barkley going down the hall, a door shut and then a sound she didn't recognize at all. "Barkley?"

Kane couldn't suppress a chuckle. "He stumped his toe on that old rock. It's right outside the door and he asked me last night what's with the rock and I told him nothing. Then he says, I'd dig it up."

"Has it always been there?" She was tired again and she had no control over drifting off to sleep.

After making the necessary call to his attorney, Kane checked on his father, spoke with Dr. Ketterman and returned to his room. He was at a loss what to do. He hadn't thought through his action of bringing Susan to his home. It was a rash but caring moment when she needed attention or someone to stay with her and he wasn't certain Barkley would. Now he realized old wounds had somewhat healed and trust was returning between the two. The next thing would be whether Barkley accepted the loan. Barkley's concern over the rock was amusing. But then, the boy was right. He had intended to dig it out since he'd returned home. While he waited for news from his attorney, perhaps it was a good time to see to that task. It appeared Susan would sleep most of the day. Barkley had given her the medicine Dr. Miller prescribed and Dr. Ketterman agreed with, all he could do was keep watch on her.

After finding something in the frig, Kane found a shovel, rolled up his sleeves and went to work, digging out the rock. It was no easy task, two hours later as he sat by Susan's bed, he pondered why it was left there in the first place and why Andrea's journal never mentioned it. Was it possible it was buried there after she died as a memorial? The whole idea seemed foolish on his part, but his curiosity grew with each foot of earth he dug from around it.

Susan's temperature held on a lower number but Dr. Ketterman checked her lungs and her breathing and said, "she is not out of the woods. If she was, I'd be surprised. With the virus you tell me Betsy and Barkley had, no one can waltz through without some effects, and that means the pneumonia. But many people have pneumonia and never know."

Kane checked in at the office by phone and rerouted any calls to his cell. The day had become a challenge. It was getting dark when Barkley stopped by. He was amazed the amount of dirt that was piled up where the path to the door was obscured by the rock and now it appeared Mr. Alberson was trying to dig it out.

"Looks like you have a job."

Kane paused with the shovel handle straight up. "You might say that. I think its growing, wider down where you can't see it."

"Yeah, well I'll check on Mom and be out of the way. Has she slept?" Kane nodded. "If you remember Betsy and I did that and even missed more meals than we ate. It's okay if she does."

Barkley returned a short time later. "She's sleeping, deep it seems, and her forehead is warm and she's sweating. I notice she's in the same clothes."

Kane stopped to stare at Susan's son. "And how do you expect me to handle that?"

"When she wakens, Mother will let you know she's got to get out of those clothes. Just shut the door and let her do what she wants, but be sure she gets back in the bed because she's bound to be weak."

Kane shook his head in wonder that now Susan's son who supposedly hated him was giving him orders.

"Don't worry," he responded, "I'll take good care of your mother with great care to her morality."

"Her morals are fine," Barkley stated, "It's yours I worry about." He gave Kane a dirty look and walked away.

It angered Kane that the boy would use that tone with him and he had to agree his character wasn't always considered chaste. He didn't bother to reply. The statement made him angry enough he bent to the digging of the rock with new stamina, and he saw it would take equipment to move the rock out of the path, due to its size. He had to check on Susan once more before settling on how to handle the removal.

He was so tired he nearly fell into the chair, making it scrape across the wood floor. Unknown to him Susan opened her eyes. This time she knew where she was but she didn't know if it was the same day or the next as she let her eyes come round to where he sit. He seemed tired and she wondered if he slept in the chair overnight and forgot to wake in a new morning. She heard his breathing and realized he was asleep. His cell phone was laying on the foot of the bed. If she could reach it she would know what day it was.

She slid from the bed on her hands and knees crawling to the phone. The second day, then this was the same day the doctor said she had Pnuemonia. No wonder she thought a block was sitting on her chest and she was hot, burning up. If she could shower, that would help. Her small suitcase was sitting by the door that led into what she supposed was the bathroom. It was a wonder her bladder hadn't burst but then again no fluids or food had gone through her system. She tried to rise but was too weak. Again on her hands and knees she crawled, resting ever so many feet to crawl again til she reached the room and pushed the door. How in the world was she going to get up and onto the commode? There was a handrail on the wall. She managed a task she had done a million times before with great effort, thankful in the past she had accomplished it with ease but the effort had set her body on fire. Easing the door open again she pulled the suitcase inside to see what Barkley had packed.

If it hadn't been so dismal or she felt better, she would have laughed at her son's effort. The cosmetic bag made that part easy. Underwear in three sets of bra and panties, a gown and "Lord help us all," she whispered. He had found the drawer where her outside yard work clothes were kept. Two pair of faded denim capris, three oversized pullovers and one matching set that might save her dignity. At the bottom was a housecoat and a pair of slippers she could slide her feet into and a small cosmetic bag with her name on it, a gift from Hugh with her favorite perfume. "Not bad, Barkely, I will look like Mr. Alberson's poor cousin but at least I have a change of clean clothes and I'll smell good."

Now she studied the shower. She could crawl into it but how to stand up and shower when she was so weak. The glass was a dense smoky hue that she couldn't see through, perhaps there were handrails if there was one by the commode. She tried to stand but her knees buckled. Again she crawled, there were no handrails but there was a seat in one corner with a formed hand rail built into the shower above it, if she could manage that. She turned the water on and let it build to the right temperature. Evidently the height of the man who normally used it caused the projection of water to come to the corner and wash down her body. If ever she had felt the freshness as much as this moment she couldn't remember. "In all things give thanks", she whispered.

Clean towels and washcloths by the shower, body wash inside, her perfume, what more could she want? When it was time to get out, she sit huddled with the towel around her, weak as a starved kitten. "This too, shall pass," she prayed, "Lord, you will have to give me strength." And he did.

Now for clothes. She chose a pair of the denims and an oversized pullover and the next chore was to get back onto the bed. But she was too weak and succumbed to the floor just outside the bathroom to curl up in a fetal position and went to sleep. It was eight o'clock.

Kane came awake abruptly. Whatever he was dreaming had brought him around with a jolt. Passing one hand over his mouth he turned to see Susan lying on the pillows, except, she wasn't there. His heart did a quick dip and leveled; where was she? He rose up to pat the covers. Who could lose a sick person? Evidently he could. He was near panic when he stumbled past the bed toward the door and there she was lying on the floor, sleeping. She was sleeping; A folded person on the floor, her knees drawn to her body, her head resting on her arm. Instant relief flooded his mind, as he stooped to pick her up.

"Susan." He sat back down in the chair, Susan on his lap, startled from sleep, her eyes a deep solemn hue. He just gathered her closer. "Don't scare me like that."

"How did I scare you? I just took a shower. I feel much better and I think it took down my fever."

He shuddered. "I can't believe I went to sleep."

She was silent, too weak to talk and talking created the coughing, so she would remain quiet. Besides, it felt good close to his body. She had drift off to sleep, aware she was cold, perhaps chilled as she was shaking but sleepy and once she went to sleep it didn't matter. She yawned, her hand over her mouth. "I hope you don't get this."

"Why?" His voice was husky. "Are you afraid you couldn't hold me on your lap?" He laughed when she failed at trying to poke him. "You are weak, aren't you?"

"What have you been doing?" She was hesitant but added, "You have an earthy smell."

He really laughed. "You are saying I stink? Well, I earned it. I've tried to dig out that big rock."

"Why?"

"It seemed the thing to do, I've meant to for years now, but Barkley seemed to think I should."

She would have smiled but she was yawning. "It never sounds as if you and Barkley would agree on anything."

"Taking care of you appeals to both of us." He stared down at her. "Your son does love you."

"He wouldn't like my sitting here in your arms."

"That's not what matters. Do you like sitting here in my arms?"

"Yes." Her smile was sad, the sadness reflected in her eyes. "I'm beginning to get used to you thinking you would like to take care of me. You do things on such a grand scale."

"You say that and I'm scared I won't be around if I don't find those papers to prove Gina wrong." His shoulders slumped in defeat.

Trying to bring him out of the dark spirit, she said, "Maybe today you will show me the place where you are digging. It sounds interesting."

He shook his head, yawning, "I guess. I can't figure out why it was left there but I do know Andrea loved gardening and according to her journal she used, shall we say, oddities often to accent the plants and the rock would be an oddity. Perhaps she planned it as a backdrop or something. Who knows. Shall we go to the kitchen ? I'll find something for breakfast?"

"What about your Dad and the doctor, if I'm contagious?"

"I will ask them. That's their decision and you still don't think you have it do you?"

"We need to ask the doctor what heat stroke is and if that could be my problem."

Kane was setting the table when Dr. Ketterman brought his father in a wheelchair to the table.

"How are you, young lady?" Mr. Alberson asked. "If, you have the virus, as I did I imagine you feel a bit spaced out right now. How about the fever and body aches?"

"I feel feverish and the body aches are painful. Your description about says it, spacey," she repeated. "You must wonder why I'm here and to tell you the truth I wondered. too." She tried to smile.

"It was a complete blur, wasn't it." Mr. Alberson nodded, "Kit, here, came down and picked me up out of the floor. He's been here more than he's been home since someone tried to rough me up."

"They did rough you up," Dr. Ketterman replied drily. "So, young lady, you live near here and I don't know you?"

"Please, call me Susan." Kane was sitting bowls of scrambled eggs, sausage and canned biscuits on the table as he brought the coffee pot too. "No, Sir, I don't remember us meeting before." She glanced up to Kane, "I wish I could help you. This makes me feel downright lazy."

"You wouldn't last five minutes. We'd be picking you up off the floor." To the gentlemen he said, "She keeps fainting."

"Are you pregnant, Susan?" Dr. Ketterman asked. He glanced from her to Kane.

"I uh, I think I'm past that age, Dr. Ketterman." She was caught off guard and embarrassed to the hilt. "My husband has been gone almost seven years." Her face turned beet red. "That's embarrassing, I'm sorry. You didn't ask for my personal history, did you?" She was mumbling.

Dr. Ketterman was laughing while Mr. Alberson was trying to figure out the joke. "No, I didn't," Dr. Ketterman replied but you answered any misconceptions completely, not Kane's usual style."

Kane took that moment to ask her to say the blessing. She gave him an I can't believe you'd ask at this moment look and bowed her head.

"Father in Heaven, we thank you that we can share this meal together. We ask your blessing on the food and each who enjoys it. Bless our day Lord and help us to bless each other. In your Holy name, amen."

The bowls of food went round, but Susan suddenly felt she shouldn't eat, her stomach was rolling and that feeling was in her throat. She tried to hide what she was experiencing, taking a tiny bite of the eggs, a nibble from the biscuit and ignoring the piece of bacon in her plate altogether. Kane seemed not to notice and ate generously, acting as their host and very careful with the two elderly gentlemen his father and doctor friend. She was relieved when he rose from the table. "Kane," her voice rose just enough for him to hear. "Would you mind, please, take me back to the bed."

Alarmed, he scooped her up and was down the hall, laying Susan on the bed in seconds. He found a small container and placed beside her. "I can tell you are sick to your stomach, aren't you?" She nodded. "Do you want the sunshine or pull the shades? The latter? Okay." The room became darker. Susan curled into the fetal positon that seemed to comfort her body. He was saying, "you hardly ate."

"I'm sorry," she whispered. "If you don't mind, I'll just sleep." Sleep came instantly as did the temperature. She felt the wet compresses on her forehead but was too weak to say thank you. When she was stronger she would….

Sometimes she heard voices, not discerning the words or meaning, but for the most part she slept, responded to *take this or let me do this for you*; otherwise she slept. She heard Barkley's voice and with a flash of trying to reason wondered why they were in her room.

She awoke, yawning and feeling better than she could remember. The last five days she had responded to voices, acted according to instructions and performed robotically to get through whatever had attacked her body. Those times she questioned where she was, the questions were always soothed away and then there was the tap tap tapping she heard that resembled hammering and her mind was curious. She sensed someone standing near the bed and opened her eyes. Barkley grinned. "Hi, Mom."

"You're smiling. Does that mean you and Kane came to an agreement?"

"Heck no, maybe to not bash each other's head in while you are here sick but I think you're better." In the background while Barkley talked Susan could hear the progress of Kane digging around the rock.

"Strange as that sounds I think so, too." She started to move but found her body weak for that simple task. "Well, I thought, maybe I'm just weak. What do I do next, Barkley?" Her eyes fixed on her son, she waited. "There has to be something I can do but I need you to tell me what you think."

Barkley came to sit on the edge of the bed. "This has been strange, Mom, someone like Kane Alberson picking you up and bringing you here, he said because I didn't step up to the plate and say I'd keep an eye on you." Barkley bowed his head. "I'm sorry, Mom. Part of me was lost with the fact I resented him. I always thought he mistreated Dad because of all the things that happened."

"You were a little boy, Barkley and that would have been his grandfather who actually owned the land they farmed. Your dad would come back to help those whose name was on the list, if he could. Let's face it, he was a champion for the underdog." They laughed. "I think, Barkley sometimes you just need to talk about Dad. That's like reliving life with him. I do the same."

"Really, Mom? I miss him so much and when I saw Mr. Alberson with you I thought you had forgotten Dad."

"Barkley, I could never forget Dad. We loved each other too much. Kane is a completely different person. I have tried to dissuade him but he doesn't give up and those days I am so down, feeling alone he seems to show up and at least make me smile. I have given him a hard time and no encouragement."

"Does he want to marry you, Mom?"

"Yes, he does say that but I've not had even one date with him." She reached for Barkley's hand. "I don't know what he sees in me or why he continues to be there. He's like a protector. I don't get it."

"You're a good person, Mom. Do you think he has changed? Bert says he believes he has." Barkley blew out a breath of air. "He asked me again if we were taking the loan, in case they take him back to jail."

"It's up to you, Son. I can't tell you we will find funding other places but we can certainly try."

"Mom, if you're feeling better can't you go home? I don't want to leave you here with him."

Susan laughed. "Son, do you realize you chose my gardening clothes and that's what I've been wearing the last few days, was that part of your plan?"

Surprise registered on Barkley's face. "No, I didn't know." Suddenly he grinned. "That was a good move."

"As to your question, I am ready to go home. Let me see Dr. Ketterman once more and then we'll know."

"Mom, I think you had the virus, you had all the symptoms Betsy and I had, so you will have to be careful." His eyes strayed to the door. "The hammering has quit, what does that mean?" He squeezed her hand. "I'm going to see."

"Barkley?" Susan was trying to get out of the bed. "Hold my arm and let me go with you."

Chapter 14

"WOW!" BARKLEY EXCLAIMED at the pile of dirt. He had entered through the front door since the Doctor had moved his car and it blocked the driveway. "Two days since I last saw where you were digging and now this. Impressive." He pulled the iron bench closer for his mother.

"I'm surprised to see you," Kane's eyes were on Susan. "I guess I thought your sleeping late would hold." He glanced to Barkley. "Is this about the loan?"

"It's about me ready to go home." She replied, instead. "You've worked so hard on the digging and then there was no noise….I haven't seen your work. I'm impressed with such a big rock."

Kane wiped away the sweat. "I will need a tractor or an excavator to pull it away."

"Looks like a two man job." Barkley whistled. "That rock was placed there, it's not natural. I'll help you, if you want. I have a chain in the back of my truck and if there's nothing to damage, I can come across the back to get to your yard…it's up to you."

"I'd like that. I'm about sick of this rock. Go. Get your truck and see what you can do. I'm all for it."

He shook his head, his eyes now on Susan, as Barkley left. "I didn't expect that offer." He sit opposite her. "Did you check with the doctor whether you're ready to be in your home now? Alone?"

"I will but I want to thank you for watching over me...even," she grinned, "even if it's not natural to find yourself picked up off the floor a number of times and sit on a man's Lap when you are a grown woman. That has been an unusual experience for me."

"Funny, I've never done that before...but with you it seemed the thing to do. I don't know if I was comforting myself or you."

"It was shocking at first, then I was embarrassed and now I know it just happens and it doesn't carry the sting."

"I embarrassed you? I never intended that...I apologize." Suddenly he grinned. "I have done a lot of things I am rather shocked about, myself, but you want to know what's the most remarkable? I've felt happy and I don't recall being this happy in years."

"What about when you first married Gina?"

"She burst that bubble quickly. It was all about the money, which I didn't have and once she realized J.T. was in charge of it all, she switched horses in mid-stream. She became his right hand girl." He stood as Barkley backed across the lawn. "I'm not sure why your son decided to help me but I appreciate it."

"I could be wrong but I would guess he has thought it over and will discuss the loan with you. It isn't his nature to be other than courteous and respectful. To do otherwise worries him more than anything."

She watched as the chain was wrapped to secure and move the rock from its present location. Barkley eased forward, the rock trembled and finally moved an inch in the hole. He backed up, eased forward again and the rock moved a foot. A number of times Barkley tried the same process, but the rock would not go beyond where Kane had dug. He could stand at the edge and look down into the hole where it sit all those years. He had dug out enough dirt the space would hide a car, but it was deeper.

Kane gathered the chain and put it in the back of Barkley's truck and waved him on. "It's going to take a cat," he said, resigned it was the thing to do. Susan joined him. His arm went around her for support. "If you fell in there I might not could get you out but I'd die trying."

Barley returned. "Sir, I'm ready to discuss what you expect in return of our taking a loan for the farm."

"I tell you what, Barkley, since your mother is going home. Let's get her things together and go there before it gets any later and then we'll discuss business."

It was then, Susan realized the papers were still at her house. Kane had remembered but didn't expound. She expected Barkley to help with her one suitcase but he was standing gaping into the hole. "Sir," he called, "There's something down there. Man, I hate to say it but it appears to be a coffin."

"Oh, Lord, don't even think that." If Kane had mentioned being tired, this news served to energize him. "What do I need to dig out whatever it is? I have a hoe but the handle's not long enough."

"There's enough room for one of us to go down the side on a ladder, we can pull the top loose and if there's anything worth bringing up, bring it up the side. I'm thinner."

Kane turned to Susan. "What do you think? I'm blown away he would do this for me. I never knew why this rock was here all these years but now I'm questioning, what if J.T. buried the papers? Why would he?"

"His dreams died when your grandmother died, Kane. I can see that."

Barkley was leaning down the side, head first when Kane called to him. "Stop. You might fall and that's a terrible position, head first. Let me find a lad…" At that moment Barkley lost his grip and started down. Kane ran…grabbed his feet and pulled….Barkley's weight and gravity were against him but Kane dug in one foot against the sidewalk the other a small sapling and pulled. Barkley was pushing with his hands and then he was free of the dirt. "Man," Kane was trying to regain his breath, "I thought what else?"

"It's my fault. I thought I could tell more about that object that looks like a coffin but I dropped my phone. Long story short, I couldn't reach it." He looked ashamed. "It's still down there."

"We'll get it tomorrow."

"Listen, you two." She yawned, "I don't think I'm as well as I thought. I really need to get back to the bed if someone will help me." Kane took her arm. Barkley was waiting. "I love you, Son. Go home." Barkley was uncertain. Susan knew his thoughts. "Don't worry, Son. I'll be fine." Kane stopped and stared at Barkley.

"Barkley, spend the night."

"You know I can't. I have Betsy to consider." He turned and stalked away. "Good night, Mother."

"There goes a young man who loves his mother and has such a fear he is losing her. Is he?"

They walked the path to the house and through the hall to the room where she slept. "Where are you sleeping, Kane?"

"In the den on the sofa. Where else? Dr. Ketterman is in the room next to you and then there's Dad. Yu are surrounded by men, no wonder Barkley is concerned."

"I don't think he's taken all that into consideration," Susan said quietly, "but this is the first my brain has functioned to realize these many days you gave up your room for me and I know you aren't resting well." She stifled a yawn, as she sank onto the bed. "I don't want food or water, my body craves sleep. This whole thing is surreal, not as bad as a nightmare but almost out of this world in an odd way."

"I think I've caused your feeling of let-down. I've been too vocal. It's just that thought of losing everything the family has worked to create to Gina or whoever is behind the incarceration, the claim to have papers, put it all together, I'm sure I've talked to you too much of things that don't concern you. And I realize now you feel insulted when I just reach down and pick you up, since you told me it has a big bearing on my mind. You've lost so much weight it worries me and yet I know the reason…I just can't seem to absorb it all."

"You feel Gina is alive and they have faked her death? Really, inside of you, what do you feel."

"Yes, that she's still alive. For all I know the Sheriff may be in on this. I hope not but I don't know."

"You've hid your worries well."

"Have I? I'm afraid not. Sometimes I shake in my boots to think…but you've been through this with Hugh."

"Would you feel remorse if she was dead?"

"I think if I truly thought she was dead I would feel sorrow, as for remorse Gina is tough and hands out as much as the next person…I guess her tying in with my grandfather…the old two against one idiom was in play. I resented both of them, I had to do the dirty work…let me rephrase that I was so set on showing them nothing mattered I did the dirty work."

"What about now?" Susan asked but when her eyes closed she didn't hear the answer.

"I need to find the papers to save Alberson Land Holdings or lose everything and I am working on a lot of important things in my private life." His words died off. She was asleep.

Susan awoke to the quiet of the house. It was almost as though no one was there. She lay thinking about what had brought her to Kane's home. She had been really sick that evening. It was decided she could not be alone. Barkley had Betsy to consider. She couldn't' go to her parents, neither they or her daughters families could not be exposed. It was a mess and now she was in the last days of recovery, or so she thought. Being out of bed yesterday had ended in a terrible weakness. Reviewing also brought Barkley and Kane's response to each other. Once, only, once they agreed. She wasn't sure they would ever come together as friends. Barkley's response was that of a boy's excitement and the challenge of the moment, not an expression of changing his mind over their situation.

It was five; the house would come alive any minute. Susan made up her mind. She showered and dressed in the most decent of garments Barkley packed and placed all others in the sack to take home. She was wondering what to do about changing the bed when Kane knocked on the door. When she bid him to come in he stood before entering taking in she was dressed and the bag Barkley had brought was setting by the door.

"I see you've decided to go home." Disappointment was written on his face. "I'll help you with anything that's too strenuous presently."

She sighed. "I was just now trying to think if I'm strong enough to change the bed sheets."

"Don't worry about that. Dad just informed me our housekeeper is ready to come back."

"Kane, thank you for all you have done for me. I would have been so beat down, alone with no one."

"Why the misery in your voice?" He studied her with troubled eyes. "Why do I sense this is good bye?"

"You read me well, Kane. I never thought anyone would, again. I'm sorry that especially now with a court case pending and your complete situation of being blamed for Gina's death when she may very well be alive, that I can't be with you."

"Why can you not be with me, Susan? Get over this virus completely and let's get married." He dropped down onto one knee. "Susan, I'm asking you to marry me. To make me the happiest man in the world. If you don't love me now, I promise I'll do everything to make you happy and I truly believe in time you will love me." To her surprise, he pulled a small velvet box out of his pocket. "This was my mother's, she would be pleased to know you, Susan." He slipped the ring on her finger, an oval ruby with diamonds around the outer edge.

"Oh," her breath caught. "I can't. I mean it's beautiful, but it's your mother's it has such meaning you must keep it. Do you know what a ruby stands for?"

"Yeah," He was standing. "I remember mother saying love and I thought there was more so I looked it up. It's a stone of love and passion." He took her hand and rubbed the tips of her fingers. "I know we have that passion but you won't allow it. If you walk away, Susan, you will remember this and regret. I know you will. Why won't you commit to us?"

She closed her eyes as she removed the ring from her finger and gave it back, but he surprised her, sliding it back on her hand. "I want you to have this. Please wear it." With that said he walked out the door. "I'll wait for you, where the rock is. I'm thinking of a way to reach Barkley's phone."

She said goodbye to Mr. Alberson and Dr. Ketterman, thanking them for everything and joined Kane. He had a long pole taped to a flat board and to that piece was taped a sticky item. He was able to navigate the depth of the hole and bring up Barkley's phone on the fifth try. "Guess I haven't lost it all, yet. Can still think out a small problem, but the large ones throw me."

The ride home was completely silent. Neither could think of anything to say. When they reached her house she thought to slide out of the truck and go inside quickly, but he followed at a leisurely pace, carrying the bag with her clothes.

Completely saddened by the thought of losing contact with Kane, she was at a loss how to say goodbye. The tears were building and she dare not look at him. She tried, she said a quick prayer and without turning she was able to say, "Thank you, Kane. This is very hard. If you don't mind, just leave me now."

His hands on her shoulders, gently he turned her into his arms and pulled her against his body. They stood there, each lost in thought or no thought at all, Susan would think later, except for that final moment.

"I love you, Susan. I've saved those words being said directly to you so many times thinking eventually they would be returned, but it hasn't happened, so I have to say them now and whatever the future holds always remember, I love you." When she tilt her head to look up into his face, he bent his head and kissed her. He felt her grip and then the softness of yielding and in that moment he knew he could have taken her, but if it was gratitude that he helped her, he would help her again, if he knew she loved him still he would have waited. She was that kind of woman; too good to be taken, she had been ill. She was vulnerable. His voice was husky when he said, "If you find in your heart life would be happier with a man who loves you, come looking for me."

She heard the door close and in that second she thought her heart would break, that life had dealt this blow, so much offered but so much refused. It was she who mothered Barkley from a love no one could doubt. Now, she was offered love again, but no one could be that blessed. She must tend to her family.

She settled into her old life. Mattie called. "How are you, Susan?"

"The question is, how are you, Mattie? I've lost a week of my life, like the rest of you. How's Frank?"

"You sound down," Mattie replied. "Any particular reason?"

"I've been sick, remember that terrible feeling you ache all over, your temperature runs rampant and all you want to do is sleep. I'm still in that sleep mode…what do I do about it?"

Mattie laughed. "You sleep and when that period of lingering side effect is over you will feel better."

"Mattie, are you really better? Or is it just your voice that's stronger?"

"I think I'm better, Susan. The doctor says I'm a wonder, but we knew that, didn't we?"

Susan listened to Mattie's laughter and it warmed her. "I miss you, Mattie."

"Miss you, too." Mattie's laughter was gentler. "Keep praying for me, Susan."

Barkley brought papers to sign the heading read Alberson Land Holdings. "He was decent enough," Barkley said. "He said you have to sign too, because of your interest in owning part of the land we farm." He frowned as she was hesitant. "Mom, we have no other place to turn. This is it and we need it now."

"I know." She signed a dozen places on the papers. "Did you say thank you?"

"I did." He fold the papers together, patted his shirt pocket where his phone was and turned toward the door holding up the loan papers. "He wouldn't have loaned to us if he hadn't known you. As Dad said, sometimes you have to have friends but I'm still not keen on him. I doubt that ever wears off." He was out the door when he called back, "Mom, it's time for the baby. I'd appreciate if you'd start praying everything goes all right. Right now, our world feels pretty good and full of expectation."

"Barkley, I've been praying all along." Susan wished her world would return to normal…but it hadn't been since Hugh died and now that one small pleasure that someone knew she was alive and cared was gone.

Two weeks passed and Susan went to the hospital to be tested. "You must have had a light case," the health worker remarked, "to be able to stay home. You're clear, test shows negative."

"Yes." She replied. "Fever and sleep." These days she wished she could sleep and forget what was missing.

The call came in the middle of the night. "Mom, Betsy's in labor and we are headed to the hospital."

Eight hours later a nine pound boy was staring at them from behind the glassed walls of the hospital nursery. "I can't believe he's that big,"

Barkley said, "and Betsy so small. But look how long he is." Susan thought of Hugh and then without realizing it she remembered Kane was also a very tall man.

Sophia and Caroline Dawn came to see the new baby, leaving their children with the daddy's as the virus was gaining momentum. "We have to wear masks," Sophia and Caroline agreed. "Now, it's all the media talks about and there's a special task force has been formed. Actually, Mother, I think the three of you were in the first hot spot and that's how you got it."

"It's no fun," Susan replied. "I pray neither of you comes in contact with it and certainly not the children."

"Caroline will be in the high risk group, having had Leukemia." Sophia hugged her sister. "I've missed everyone. But," she whispered, watching Susan going into the kitchen, "Mother seems really quiet. What's that about?"

Caroline shrugged. "I don't know. Ask her?" At the same time they said together, "Barkley would know."

"Mother are you all right? I mean is there anything you need to tell us?"

It was an afternoon of warmth in being together but Susan felt the interrogation got out of hand when the girls kept asking questions. It was the only time she remembered being relieved when they went home. The first hours had been wonderful, but the last two had left her spent. It was four o'clock and she went to bed.

It became her custom she didn't go to town, except to shop for groceries and that was early of the morning when most people were still asleep. Church was halted and she didn't have to associate with anyone. Mattie called weekly and seemed to be growing stronger. Susan was thankful for her friend but when Mattie asked, "Have you seen Kane?" She knew Mattie was hunting for something. "Did you know he found proof Alberson Holdings was to be passed on down to the heirs? Yes, by a document written in nineteen fifty. It seems when Kane's grandmother died, James Tomas was so distraught, he drew up a very well worded will. The poor man was contemplating leaving this area for good but his son, Tom was to be considered. Oh, well, you know the rest of the story."

Susan was thinking of the huge rock Kane said he always stumped his toe on. "I wonder where he found the papers."

Mattie was quick to reply. "You won't believe this, he didn't tell me either, but I heard under a rock."

For the first time, Susan smiled.

"What's the rest of the story, concerning Gina Alberson's death?"

Mattie's intake of air was audible over the phone, "Susan, surely you don't believe that. Is that why you never say Kane's name? You know Kane couldn't kill anyone. Yes, she's still missing but if she's dead it would be her boyfriend or someone else did the murder. I'd stake my life on Kane Alberson."

"Mattie, I didn't mean to offend you. I know you and Kane have been friends a long time."

"Since first grade," Mattie huffed.

"You are a loyal friend."

"Well, if someone doesn't come forward to help him out, Kane's going to prison."

Susan welcomed working with Bert and Barkley. It kept her mind off what was happening to Kane and whether she should go to the Judge or whoever was in charge and tell them she was with Kane that day and late to the evening but he had told her not to. The weeks passed and then it was September and the harvest was upon them. A dribble of rain on a Friday night touched on the melancholy of being alone. She couldn't stand it any longer and picked up the phone.

The phone was answered by a woman, breathless and happy sounding. She sound young if one could determine by laughter. Susan hung up the phone and checked to be sure she'd called the right number. Mattie's words rang in her head, "He's a handsome man, Susan, and he wants you but if you aren't interested there's a hundred others that are. Kane's a lonely man, don't linger too long."

She pulled the cover over her head and willed herself to sleep. Barkley found her there. "Mother, are you sick? It's five o'clock. We brought the baby to see you." He was laughing again. "Mother, he's so funny. Dad would have been so proud."

"Yes, he would," she agreed, joining the three, hopeful nothing was said about her being in bed. That night she prayed that God would give her peace, not to worry over Kane and to enjoy family and be an example to them. "I've never been in this predicament, Lord," she added, "and frankly, I don't know what predicament I'm in but it was nice having a friend. It's just as a mother I don't like keeping secrets from my children. Now, Lord, I want to put this to rest and be able to pray for others."

"Kane," Alexanria Worth called to Kane in the kitchen, "I'm afraid my call to New York was cut off and when the phone rang, thinking it was John calling back I answered, evidently I was wrong the person hung up."

"It happens," he replied. "Our rural lines are not like your big city servers."

"I don't know how you accomplish anything business wise, I rely on my phones."

"Patience," he motioned for her to sit. "There's tea or coffee. Now tell me how John's doing."

"He would have loved to come with me but he has a Federal case coming up and will be going to Washington tomorrow."

"I can't imagine how your children will grow up with two lawyer parents."

"Smart, I hope." She smiled. "Now, let's go over your case. Who is Larson Engle and what is his part in this?"

"He's the one said to have turned my name in, that he personally saw me kill Gina, the only problem is, since that report was made no one has seen Larson or Gina and there's no record of her burial."

"Who is Marvin Camp?"

"The Deputy Sheriff they sent out after me due to the fact the Sheriff was picking up a convict that escaped the nearby prison."

"You have a prison near you?" She shook her head. "Do you trust this Deputy Camp, or for that matter the Sheriff?" She twirled the pencil between her fingers. "I've read this report and honestly, something doesn't set right."

"Here's part of the story but I don't know if there's a connection." He began with the day Marvin Camp arrested him and ended with seeing the black suburbans turn in to the Sheriff's Courthouse Square the day he was released. It was twelve o'clock when Alexandria said, "I think we should let this gel over night and in the morning I may have one or two questions before we go to court. If you'll show me to the room I'm staying in, I'll say good night."

"I hope you don't mind. I've given you my room and I'll be next door."

"Kane, I'm so used to trips such as this and a different place every week, I could sleep in the bath tub."

The next morning, Kane was dressed, had breakfast ready and coffee to pour when she came into the kitchen. "I have a question. I forgot my make-up bag but I found one in your bathroom after a bit of scavaging, who is Susan? I like that woman. She had exactly the make-up I wear and that is very unusual." She smiled. "Take a sniff. I love that perfume; it's Pure heaven." She waved a wrist in front of his face. "Did you catch it?" Kane was quiet. "Oh, yeah, you caught it and it brought back memories. Fill me in. Who is she?"

"I think you should enjoy your breakfast while it's hot," he replied, "especially if we are going by the Engles."

"Mother," Barkley was on the phone. "Would you please go out to the shop and look in the corner where Dad's board is nailed to the wall of the office, there's wooden bins where we keep certain parts and when you get there I'll describe the part we need. We can't bring the equipment back to the shop, it's a do or die job right here in the field if you find the part. I'll be removing this one while you look. If you don't reach me quickly, here's a number to look for. Take your phone and record it."

Susan picked up her phone and punched record for the numbers as a noise came from the shop. Sometimes animals went inside and couldn't get out when the men closed the door or the air compressor kicked on acting up again. Barkley said they needed a new one. She glanced inside the office. Hugh's chair, looked a bit more used by the years, the second they'd brought in for Barkley better. Going on to the bins she had the strangest feeling she was being watched and turned to see, but no one was there. Still there was a lingering fragrance of some kind of food. She must be really hungry.

The first two bins were empty, the third had a door that let down with a small latch to keep it from falling open. She turned the latch and let the door fall to the floor. Sudden movement scared the daylights out of her as a man unwrapped himself from a cover and tried to scramble out onto the concrete floor. "Who are you?" She was screaming and the man seemed terrified.

"Lar-Lar-Larson Eng-Eng-Engle," he responded. "I ain't stole nothing, I'm just hidin out from my brother."

Susan heard the name and made an immediate connection. She had to get control of herself and she had to get something from him, legal or not. "Oh," she said, fumbling as she pressed the button on her phone; smiling as though they were at church greeting each other before services began she extended a hand. "I declare I'm glad to meet you, Mr. Engle. You are the one connected with Gina Alberson, aren't you? Wasn't that a fiasco? That girl does know how to charm a gentleman."

"I didn't push her. She fell down but that fellow that came after her, he said I'd be held responsible if she died and then I'd lose the farm for sure. I knew Sam wouldn't be happy with me at all."

"Gina should never have been down in that field, Mr. Engle. Do you need something to drink or are you hungry? I'll have to admit, you are a brave man to stay out here in this shed. I guess Barkley or Bert have no idea you're sleeping in. That's so funny. You pulled one over on them, for sure. I tell you, I've heard stories that you are a genius. It must be true."

"I am smart," Larson agreed, "but the only one ever knew it was Momma."

"Larson, I've forgotten the color of that vehicle that picked up Gina. Do you remember?"

"There were two, black. Two. Getteman never travels alone. He kept saying you'll be all right Baby and I just thought, If you knew what she just propositioned me with you wouldn't be talkin sweet to her."

"Gina was knows for risqué ways, Larson. She'd promise a man the moon."

"But her price was high," he complained. "She wanted my farm." He stumped his toe on the floor, "Well, it's mine and my brother Sam's farm. She said if we married it had to be in her name."

"I'm sure she was tempting."

Larson was mad all of a sudden. "I said Sam won't be happy and she laughed. He don't matter she said. It's just you and me. Let's get this over with. I didn't like how she said it. All of a sudden she says 'lets get this over like it's a job.' Before she was flirty and pretty and fun then she was mean."

"I understand that's when you pushed her but don't you doubt she died? They're hiding something."

"She slapped me when I called her a name and then I pushed her away, I didn't know there was an old concrete block there. It had a number on it. I remember that." Larson began to shake. "I didn't hurt her. She was coming after me screaming she'd plow up the whole damn field if she had to, then she stumbled and tried to regain her footing, instead she fell and hit her head on that block."

"Are you scared Larson?"

"That's why I've been in this shop for days and I steal from the men's lunch. They don't seem to miss it. If I didn't I'd starve to death."

"What made you think she was dead?"

"I didn't see her anymore and he told me she was dead."

"Who's he?"

"Geteman. He wants to marry Gina but when she's not mad she wants me. But Sam won't be happy."

"What do you need now, Larson?"

"I'm just tired and it's hot in that box, especially when I have to cover up so they won't see me."

"What do you think you should do, Larson?"

"Go home to Sam. He'll be mad but he'll take care of me. Pap told him too."

"Well come with me and I'll take you to Sam." Barkley would have to wait.

She watched Larson buckle the seat belt. He seemed satisfied. She drove through Alberson as though she and Larson took a drive every day together and then turned down the ditch bank road towards Sam Engle's home. Larson was practically asleep when she pulled into Sam's drive. Sam came out immediately. His worry outweighed his anger. Susan saw the love, as he unbuckled his brother and helped him down.

"Brother, I've not seen you in ages. You all right?"

Once she was a good distance from the Engles, Susan took the cell phone out of her pocket and listened. What she feared was that the cloth of her jeans might make it sound garbled; she had taped Larson's admittance to being with Gina and he'd not mentioned Kane once. She went home and sent the taping to Kane. "I don't know what you will do with this, maybe it's illegal and maybe it was wrong to do."

Kane and Alexandria were at the Courthouse when the text from Susan came in. Kane reached across to allow Alexandria to read Susan's words. Her eyes widened. "What?" She motioned he lean in close. "Taking him home may be a problem for your friend. Let me listen to it again, when the Judge is with his next case and then I'll ask the court to bring Larson Engle in. I can question him and if he answers a second time as this first, then we have a lot of hope this will end soon."

That evening Alexandria flew back to New York to take care of her family in the beginning of the city under attack by the Virus. Kane tried to call Susan. She didn't answer, There was no reason to; Mattie had warned her.

Harvest was underway. The Media carried stories that the curfews and various rules were being dismissed. The Government did not have the right to curtail their assembling with others, or closing business. Susan felt what they had done was a good thing, but now opinion was divided and she was unsure what was right or wrong in the matter. Saving lives should be everyone's goal, she thought. The family had a talk and decided to do all in their power to ward off a family member coming down ill.

There were days the harvest demanded she work alongside the employees. Other days she was free to work in the home. If she was able to keep her body busy her mind was less likely to stray but that which was capable of keeping her busy was an employee's job and the employee needed to work.

She drove over to Mattie's. "I came to see how you look and decide if you're telling me the truth when you say your doctor says you are better."

"Did you now?" Mattie laughed. "Well, here I am." She gave a slow twirl around the room. "What do you think?"

"I hope you aren't burning your candle at both ends because…"

"Because that's what you are doing," Mattie replied. "Come sit and tell me what's really going on." When Susan was quiet, Mattie said, "Kane said you sent him a text that had helpful information."

"So he received it. Good. I didn't know if it would be helpful and whether it was legitimate."

"Why didn't you talk to him, Susan?"

"There's nothing to say."

"Because of Barkley?" Mattie shook her head. "Barkley won't be there when you feel sad, or happy, Susan. He's started his family and you know families demand attention. He can't see to your needs."

"Kane and I decided our situation can't go anywhere, Mattie."

"You mean you decided."

Susan rose up. "I love you Mattie but this conversation is useless. Yes, it's to do with Barkley. He's my son. I had him. He's a piece of me."

"But you don't have to side with him in something that will destroy you, Susan. Look at you. How much weight have you lost? You were worried about me but I'd guess you're not eating or sleeping."

"On the contrary, all I want to do is sleep."

"And tune out the world. Depression. Susan, don't you see it? You are depressed."

"Don't worry, If I am I'm not going to commit harry-carry. I have family to live for, beautiful babies on the way."

"I've always told you like it is. We've been friends many years."

"You are a lovely friend and you tell me as you see it, but Mattie, how do I keep my family together if I agree to marry Kane?"

Mattie sighed. "I'll back off, Susan. I just hate to see your world turned upside down. You've been through a lot."

"Everyone has, Mattie. It's not always visible. I wish I could have kept it a secret…let's talk about something else. So how are you and how is Frank?

Kane intended to drop in on Mattie but he saw Susan there and for her sake drove the other way. Susan had made her decision and evidently intended to live by it. Barkley had been respectful when he dropped by to sign papers for the loan. It was all business right down to the last hand shake leaving.

Glancing at the papers he would have shone Mattie, the taping of Larson had been helpful, the papers under the rock had stated the heirs of James Tomas Alberson would forever inherit the home estate and the land holdings but to find the box number where final proof lay, Kane needed numbers that would open the box in order to produce the deed for the Judge viewing. He was on his way to the Engle's field where Larson said Gina fell and hit her head on a concrete block with numbers imprinted in it. With every detail, he wondered at his grandfather's reasoning and concluded it was grief acting in a man who had lost the love of his life and was finding it hard to go on.

James Tomas Alberson seemed to trust no one after his wife died; similar to Kane's own distrust of Gina. How could Gina know the need to have numbers to open the box for the deed? Only J.T. could have mentioned the proceeding he had gone through years past and left forgotten. It was even possible nature or an innocent person had removed them not knowing what they were. He stepped out on to Engle property, glancing each way before beginning the search. The block could be anywhere but if they were looking over the property it stood to reason the block was on the end of the rows by the ditch. He walked a quarter of a mile each direction, and as he gave up and started to cross the ditch to his truck sitting on the side of the road, there it was, an old time surveyors mark imbedded in the dirt that never would have last except for that fact and why it was almost in the ditch. He knew beneath that block a surveyors spike was attached and went down into the ground a possible three feet to keep it firm. Times had not changed that much but the day James Tomas lived in had its peculiararities.

He jotted down the number and went to the bank. Jed Lawson explained, "in the day when your grandfather left the deed for safe keeping in this bank, the boxes were unlike other banks. Those boxes had a dial system similar to some of today's vaults. You had to hit the number just right for it to open. Come with me and I'll show you the old boxes. Chances are one of them will be your grandfather's. Dad's not here. He would know." They tried the boxes. "I'll bet the numbers go by the same formula, start with the first number and turn right four times, the next number left three, and so on. It will be interesting to see. Of course now in today's world, you merely need a key. It was a very long and drawn out procedure." They were down to the last box. "We aren't allowed to rid ourselves of these boxes. J.T. laid down a life time payment in case he died. It will probably last as long as you."

Kane did as he said and on the fourth round he missed a number by a fraction and had to start over. His heart was pounding and sweat rolled off his forehead to sting his eyes. He tried again and heard a click. So near and yet so far he thought but the door sprung open. There were the papers. What he received from beneath the rock verified who the owner was but it had been useless until he had the deed in his hand. Geteman and Gina could claim all they wanted but they would lose. Finding Gina was the next item on the list. The Judge would not agree to calling either Geteman or Gina. His words were, "Sometimes people who have erred and committed a crime go free because they are on the outer fringe, there's no law mandates they come before the court because the law they have broken remains their secret as in this case. Prove they've done wrong and we'll reconsider."

Kane wondered what happened to the legal jargon of probable cause? How could he prove they had done wrong when no one had seen Gina and there was no body? Why were they on Engle ground, what was their motive? Everything fit together except one piece to the puzzle was missing. And then when he had given up and was taking a shower it hit him why they were talking to Larson and why Gina had made Larson think she was going to marry him. They didn't know where the numbers were either, but J.T. had in a weak moment mentioned the numbers were in the Engle field, because he had owned the piece of ground at one time. It was pure luck the brother's daddy had won the ground in a poker game. J.T. knew where the numbers were and he still owned the ground next to what he lost.

Kane remembered the story now. As children, J.T. and old Jess Engle were best friends. J.T. prospered, Jess didn't but Jess was the only friend J.T.

claimed. When Jess died, it was a whole new ball game. Kane and Gina were marriehe time, further reason to wonder why J.T. confided the whole situation to Gina. Larson had said Gina would plow up the whole field if she had to. Now he understood why. She was looking for the concrete block with the numbers on it to match to the box at the bank and then she would own all of Alberson Holdings. She never suspected the block of concrete could be on the end of the field, she was thinking farther out where no one would find it.

Gina must be hurting right now. She was alive. He felt it in his bones. She was probably pitching one fit after another or ready to kill Larson. They had checked documents with her last name as Alberson. It was time to be creative and use Geteman or maybe her maiden name. For the angst she had caused him, he wanted her in court before the Judge.

Chapter 15

"LOOK WHO'SE HERE." Susan hugged Mattie. "Are you feeling better?"

Mattie followed her into the living room. "I came to ride with you, today. That's about the only way I'll get to see you, isn't it? What's the plan?"

Grinning, Susan motioned, "Sit there. I think we're good but if Barkley or Bert calls and say I must go for parts we'll ride over to Brighton and pick them up and celebrate with an ice cream cone."

"Yay." Mattie clapped her hands. "We haven't changed much have we; when we were chasing boys we went to Brighton and drove around that old Swirly Top and about all we could afford was an ice cream cone." They laughed together.

"What's up?" Susan studied her friend. "I know you have an ulterior motive. Is it your health report?"

"No."

Alarmed, Susan asked, "Frank's all right?" Mattie nodded. "Whew, that's relief. So tell me. No theatrics."

"Me?" Mattie faked a gasp. "I would never do that. Okay, they found Gina Alberson."

Susan felt her stomach turn. "Dead?"

"Very much…alive in Italy. Kane always said she'd go there if there was a good enough reason." Mattie clapped her hands again. This time she sparkled with joy.

"Surely you of all people didn't think he was guilty."

"No." Mattie was indignant. "But now, in the eyes of the people this clears Kane. There's no charge to send him to prison. He did nothing wrong, in case you needed validation. He's a good man." Mattie was watching Susan closely. "Does any of this affect you, at all? Gina has to come back and make a statement or she can never set foot on American soil."

"Ever?" Susan's expression was dubious. "Can they make her come back?"

"I suspect if you wear one of those black Judge robes you can make people do what you want. The Judge had kind of run over Kane because he thought he was guilty but it's election year and he needs to look good so…there you go. Kane does have to take care of our little community's business, you know."

Susan's phone buzzed. "Yes, Barkley, I'll pick up the parts. I'm ready to go." She turned to Mattie. "Ready to ride?"

Mattie faked feebleness, "do you care if I don't tag along?"

"Mattie, you just came to tell me about Kane, didn't you?" Susan joined Mattie, laughing out the door.

Susan arrived at the parts place in Brighton to see Kane's truck parked in front. She was already parked but backed out and drove down the street. She had seen him through the window and her heart had that strange mix of feeling joy and sadness. It made her want to cry but she couldn't. When she returned thirty minutes later, he was gone. She went inside for the part and returned to the home field where Barkley was waiting. "Something wrong, Mom?"

"No, is it the right part?"

"Yes, it is, but you looked sad and I wondered."

"I'm fine, Barkley." She turned toward the truck, knowing he had raised up from under the machine and was staring at her, trying to figure out if there was a problem. "I'll see you later," she called back.

Where they'd had a wet spring the fall weather held and the crop was out the week before Thanksgiving. The family decided they had been apart long enough. Caroline and Oliver would come in for one night and Oliver's family was coming again with everyone looking forward to a day of being together. Susan thought about Kane and his father being alone and her heart ached..

"You seem down," Betsy said on Wednesday when she came to help sit up tables and make salads for the next day. "Is there anything else I can do to make our getting together easier on you?"

Susan smiled and shook her head. "Thank you for asking. Hughie is still sleeping. Will he sleep tonight?"

Betsy leaned in to kiss Susan's cheek as she replied. "He will probably sleep until about midnight and then up for an hour and back to bed." Betsy's laughter lightened Susan's spirits. "Wait until next Christmas. He will be crawling and pull the ornaments off the tree but tomorrow, he will sleep just like today, no problem." For some reason she reached over to hug Susan. "Holidays are hard when loved ones are missing, aren't they?"

Betsy left soon after and Caroline and Oliver arrived with Hope and Ollie. "Oliver's Mom and Dad decided to drive up and stay at the motel. They won't be out until dinner tomorrow, is that all right?"

"Of course." Susan was lost in the wonder of how her grandchild had grown. 'We are going to have so much fun," she said, but her words had no punch to them. Somehow she wished she could make her heart believe her words. Caroline caught the absence, too and was puzzled. Susan heard her name called but went on inside carrying one of the suitcases as though she didn't hear.

It was three o'clock when the doorbell rang and Susan answered. By then, Betsy and Barkley with Hughie had arrived and all were sitting talking. "These are for Miss Susan Preston." The delivery guy handed her a beautiful flower arrangement. Her family leaned forward, as she searched for the card.

"Are they from you?" She asked but no one made claim. She sit them in the center of the dining room table. "This looks like something your parents would do, Oliver. They are perfect."

Sophia and Thorn arrived with Shane, Sophia's maternity top was tight across her belly. "I am so ready to have this baby, Mother." She was hugging her sister first and then all the rest. "Yeah, they say it's a girl but if that's right she's a tom-boy because she moves more than Shane did."

If the night before Thanksgiving was busy, Susan knew Thursday would be lively. Around nine Barkly and Sophia took their families home, saying it wasn't long until tomorrow's dinner and Caroline Dawn put her children to bed. However, Susan could hear the cell phones when the house became quiet and she had a good idea they were talking about her. She was the fifth wheel on the wagon. They didn't know what to think, she was very quiet. She said her prayers and ask the Lord to give them a good day tomorrow and to bless Kane and his father but then she remembered the woman's lilting voice on the phone and considered maybe there was no need to call on the Lord to bless Kane. No doubt he was happy. She had invited Mattie and Frank and Bert and Leonie but Mattie had pled off, saying, she wasn't up to a large crowd. Kathryn Preston ignored the phone calls until Sophia called her but she still refused to join the family. "I think I will have dinner with Tom and Kane," she declared. "They're alone."

Chapter 16

KANE WAS RESTLESS. He left the gin company early to join his father and friend for a light dinner, of all people cooking Dr. Ketterman had done the honors, outside on a grill. "Fish makes such a smell in a house," he explained, "and it has been such a beautiful day. I tried to get Tom out with me but he was watching some documentary on television."

The meal was simple, fish and hush puppies and a salad. "There's French fries, Kane, if you will bring them over. Now tomorrow, Kathryn Preston will be in the kitchen with me. I think she and Tom are a twosome, aren't you?" Tom sputtered denial, "She won't even consider it so if you're thinking of moving forward with your own que go ahead. This will be interesting to watch."

"Why isn't she having dinner with her family?" Kane inquired. "I was by and noticed a Tennessee tagged car there. I assumed the family would be coming together to celebrate Thanksgiving."

"She's upset with her daughter in law about something. You have to know Kathryn. She's a lovely person," his father replied, "but she also thinks what she thinks is law and she's always right."

"Is it a serious rift?"

"She thinks Susan has found someone to replace the son of Kathryn's that died."

"Really?" Kane made eye contact with Dr. Ketterman and to diffuse the subject said, "The fish is wonderful, Dr. Ketterman. My hat's off to you and to think you stood out in the heat to cook this."

"Enjoy, Boys," the doctor raised his glass. "My house is nearly painted throughout inside. I'll be leaving."

When they finished eating the two older men sat watching Kane clear the table and load the dishwasher. "Kane, what happened to you and that little lady you brought here? She was a keeper."

"I don't know, Sir. Seems like she still loves the husband she lost and I don't know how to compete." After his father and the doctor retired to their separate rooms, he stood at the window staring out into the night. How did one compete with a dead man? Life had never been easy but without seeing Susan the days were becoming increasingly harder to bear. He was a man without hope and he didn't like it. To think tomorrow, for Heaven's sake, the man's mother would sit at his dinner table.

Kane wondered about Susan's mother in law. What would she know to tie the two together? He had seen Susan the day she pulled into the parts store and evidently she had seen him through the window. She backed out and drove down the street. He felt the disappointment, even now. Next week checks for cotton sold would be going out and then either Barkley or Susan would come in to pay off the loan. Sam had already called. It seemed Larson was ashamed and embarrassed. "We have him on medication, now," Sam had said.

Kane had tried once to call Susan and thank her for sharing the recording of Larson. Maybe it was illegal to tape but it was truth because Larson told the story to the Judge same as it was on tape and the Judge believed him. It wasn't long after that an ultimatum was issued for Gina to appear before the Court.

Finally, he sit at the piano, and now the keys rippled beneath his fingers. He longed to play the piano with Shane but he had never before considered the turmoil his own son would feel toward him if he suddenly joined rank. Possibly the boy would hate him for disrupting peace within the family. They would be tempted to keep Shane away from him. They all would have to make an adjustment. That was what Susan was facing. There was no way. She recognized immediately what he was beginning to see. How could he have been so blind? Even though he had worked hard at changing his work ethics and the stigma his grandfather had cast on their name, no one really knew that deep within his heart he longed for a better life, a family with ties that bound them together in simpler times that had meaning.

He went to bed more depressed than he had ever been in his life. It had all started with his infatuation with Susan. No, it was more than that, he felt something special the first time he talked with her. Maybe he didn't consider she was another man's wife, but she made him understand that. He loved her. And he knew in his heart she cared for him, he felt it. Please, God, he whispered, help us find a way to be together. No quicker had he said the prayer than he realized he was talking to God for the first time in years. Not even when he thought he was going to prison had he prayed.

He awoke the next morning not quite understanding what he felt; another day to get through, perhaps.

Leonie had baked a ham, made the side dishes to accompany it and all Kane had to do was put the ham in the over at ten and the dishes at eleven thirty and she promised they would have a good dinner; add Kathryn Preston to the lot, and surely the meal would exceed expectations. A grim smile claimed him, he was morose to say the least.

He was standing in the middle of the kitchen when his cell rang. "What are you doing?" Rufus voice boomed over the line.

"I'm trying to figure out if I know how to properly warm food a lady fixed for our dinner." He always grinned when he talked to Rufus. "What are you doing?"

"Thought I better tell you, if you come by looking for me, I'll be gone. Me and the old lady are going to Arkansas and spend the night then tomorrow we're going to get hitched. We got divorced about three year ago, but that ain't worked out no better than the marriage so we're goin to tie the knot again. Ain't no waitin in Arkansas. You take your birth certificate and driver's license and boom you are public record."

"Are you pulling my leg, Rufus?"

"If I'm lyin I'm dyin. Thanks for the loan of the pillow. I'll shore be seein you around. You don't reckon I'll burn in hell if we celebrate our honeymoon the night before the weddin, do you."

He heard Rufus cackle of laughter as the phone went dead. Kane stared at the cell. "That rascal hung up on me. I bet he's lyin."

At ten thirty he followed Leonie's instructions for the ham, at eleven thirty he slid the side dishes on the second shelf of the oven. And then he removed the extra table cloth she had spread over an already laid table, the silver ware gleaming on sides of the china plates, the crystal goblets ready for the drink of choice and from the second refrigerator on the side porch he brought in the bouquet of sunflowers he'd chosen for the center of the table. At fifteen til twelve the doorbell rang as he was putting the rolls in the oven and he heard his father welcoming Miss Kathryn. The doctor appeared from his room as if on cue.

"May I help you, Kane?" He was studying the table, his head tilted just so as he said, "Really, Kane, your talents are wasted. You would make some woman a good husband. She wouldn't have to do a thing." They were laughing when Tom ushered Kathryn in to the table. Acknowledging each other, they watched Kane put the finishing touch to the side dishes, and the ham was placed to one side of the bouquet. A crystal butter dish was brought to rest by the hot rolls and dinner was served.

"Dad will you say the blessing, please?"

When they raised their heads and food bowls began to be passed, Kathryn spoke, "Kane, would I be interfering with your lovely dinner if I tell you I brought a dessert? I hope you don't mind?"

"Why, Miss Kathryn, we are delighted." The men all nodded in agreement. "That would be our blessing."

"It's nearly a sin, I'm telling you. It has a chocolate filling on sweet crust and it is filled with whipped crème, pecans…oh, my, it is heavenly. I just hope you like it."

"Dear lady," the doctor inquired, "how could we not and tell us how are we blessed to have you at Kane and Tom's table. Do you not have family in this area?"

Kathryn sniffed. "I do, but there are so many of them and I desire a quieter atmosphere. I was very happy when Tom asked me to dine with the three of you. They won't even realize I'm not there." It was at that moment her phone rang and as embarrassed as she was, she asked, "Do you mind?" Taking her cell out of her pocket, they heard her say, "Oh, Sophia, you will do just fine without me. Of course I'm all right. I'll see you the next holiday. Christmas? Of course. Goodbye now." Shaking her head she said, "My granddaughter."

"Apparently someone missed you," the good doctor said. Mrs. Preston only gave him a nod.

"It was a wonderful day," they all agreed three hours later.

Kathryn was leaving and the doctor stood patiently waiting by his car for her to back out of the drive. Tom headed to his room for a nap and Kane finished clearing the kitchen of all reminders. No doubt Leonie would tell him how the dinner went at Susan's. Five o'clock. Six o'clock and then seven and night was drawing in. Kane could contain himself no longer. He grabbed his sport coat, stopped a moment in his bedroom to splash a bit of aftershave on his face, hoping if there were any remains of the dinner clinging to his body that would camouflage it.

He made himself steer clear of the road that ran by Susan's home. The only place he could think to go in this holiday-after-hour-day was filled with memories he wanted to bring to life again. Still, he drove on to Brighton, to find nothing was open except the gas stations. He found a group of truckers sitting at one table, the smoke so thick the room was a haze of gray and he didn't want to run the risk of the virus hanging on in that group, though he reasoned the smoke alone should kill it. If there was a bus out of Brighton he believed he would gladly take it; a train going to nowhere, he would embrace, an airplane going to Hawaii, he would consider…though that would be leaving his dad behind and he'd tried diligently to take care of Tom. He slapped his hands against the steering wheel. He was as melancholy as he had ever been. "Dear God in heaven," he said out loud, "help me." Taking a back road in, he pulled into the lane and stopped. Arms on the steering wheel, his face hid in his hands he prayed for understanding.

It truly was a full house. Susan glanced at the room full of people, teasing and talking, children sitting playing in the floor, oh, how Hugh would have loved it. She closed her eyes to visualize his face and his eyes were sad. Babe, she heard his voice in her mind as clear as a bell, Babe, you are brittle, you need to get away. I know you loved me and you love these people but you are only going through the motion of being alive. I want better for you.

"Mom," Sophia's voice broke into her thoughts. "Mom, are you all right?"

Susan replied. "Yes, of course. I was just communicating with your father. He would love this."

"Can you do that?" Sophia's voice hit a serious tone. "I mean, I didn't know you did, but I like it."

"It's just that this house is …" Susan was at a loss, "you know how he loved family being together."

"Yeah, he did. I miss him." Caroline joined them. "Mom's telling me she communicates with Dad."

"Really, well I could use a bit of that, myself." Caroline took time to study the two of them. "We have been worried about you Mom and then you spring something like this on us and we see you in a different light."

"Why are you worried?" They glanced at each other, neither speaking. "Have I done something bad?"

"You've been so withdrawn and you've lost weight and that's not an easy feat for us Preston ladies."

"What's going on?" Cecily and Charlemaine joined them. "Can we do anything?"

"Mom?" Sophia had a hand on Susan. "What did Dad say?"

"He said I need to get away." To Charlemaine she asked, "Do you understand?"

Charlemaine was listening. Her usually happy face was full of concern. "Yes, I think I do." Charlemaine had reached for her hand and was squeezing it. "We have all been there, or we will one day."

It was that moment they would all share and never forget. The others backed up a step. This was Charlemaine's line of work. "Honey, from what I heard, you never stopped to grieve, you just kept going taking care of family and working with your son on the farm. Then you had a bout of sickness that you didn't let slow you down. Take a trip, go where you want as soon as this national epidemic stops, and if you can't go far, go somewhere nearby that you have time to yourself. Eat when you want, rest. Read a book or do nothing. Take time for you because when you do that time will give back tenfold when you need it. You hear me girls?" She took them all in. "This happens to us, sometimes often or with some once in a life time but when it does, you have to work it out. God gave us one body and we can't burn our candle at both ends. We have to take care of ourself in order to be good for others. Now, Susan, after today, you take a week or two for you and I'll advise the rest of you, let her have that time. She loves you, now it's time to give back. Love her."

Later, Susan found Charlemaine alone. "Thank you for the advice and understanding and thank you for the lovely flowers."

Charlemaine looked puzzled. "What flowers?" Susan was pointing to the bouquet on the table. "No, Honey, we didn't send the flowers but they are beautiful. I noticed them immediately, a bright spot."

Everyone had left by four thirty and Susan felt like a wet rag, drained. Sophia and Caroline had seen to the kitchen being completely in order. She went in to shower and then to bed but it was early and tired as she was she couldn't sleep. It was a brisk evening and she never drove off the property after dark but tonight she didn't know if it was Charlemaine's advice or if she just needed to go farther than her boundaries. It was fool hardy but if she took a drive she could be home by eight. In case she met someone she knew, hurriedly she dabbed on makeup, a quick spray of perfume and before she was out the door temptation hit; did she dare wear the ring one hour, perhaps to pretend her world was good?

She came to the end of the lane, left or right? She turned to the right and prayed as she drove. In the background music was playing, she heard the phrase *you are the reason, but her mind was on higher powers.* "Father in heaven, Thank you for a day of family blessing. Forgive me Lord, but here I am, again, needing you to keep me safe as I don't seem to know where I'm going. It's not my family, Lord. It's me. I am so lonely. That dear man asked me to share his life and I not knowing what I should do waited too long and now there's someone else. I am regretful and my heart is broken. With years of differences it seemed out of our realm, we could not be together because it would cause so much friction in our family. Help me to find peace. Thank you that Kane thought he loved me and though it hurts me I'm asking you to help him to find love with the other woman." It was an extension of time and habit as she communicated with her Lord and Susan prayed for peace.

Kane pulled up to the back of the cabin, walked fifty feet to the back door and keyed the lock. It was still light; he didn't flip a switch, he had come to rethink the times he and Susan were there. It had been the beginning of trusting each other. He wanted to sit on the sofa and let the memories roll gently through his mind. He could feel her, the touch of her skin, the way she laughed. And that gave him pause. They yearned for happiness together in the little things; he knew she wanted that as much as he did but she had considered more; Betsy's brother, his biological son would be hurt. Barkley refused to give him space and the daughters, Caroline Dawn and Sophia…what would they think if their mother said she was interested in him? And then there was Kathryn Preston, rigid and unbending. What would she say?

He hadn't slept a wink last night, worrying over the dinner Leonie had made simple but his dad had thrown Kathryn into the mix. Relief over the Judge releasing all evidence against him should have made him sleep like a baby but then there was Susan. He assumed Susan had resolved much of the bittersweet mix of their not seeing each other and she would sleep no matter what happened. The clock on the wall ticked a constant message of sadness and a half-hearted need to accept loss. He listened, the sound as profound as a drip of water in a bucket and as his eyes closed he slept.

She prayed the key was where he left it. As though someone was listening she closed the vehicle door quietly and walked up the path to the house. Yes, it was there. She placed the key in the lock and turned while the door opened to a crack and she pushed on in. Darkness had closed over the cabin. She should set the alarm on her watch. She wouldn't last long, the dark would hide anything crawling and she couldn't handle that. She knew the location of the sofa and started that way, her hand on various objects for balance.

Suddenly she stumbled, in the process of falling, when a strong hand gained her own and she was righted. Her scream was muffled by the same hand over the mouth and then a voice in alarm saying her name. "Susan?" She melt down to a frightened heap of mortality. "What are you doing here?"

"Kane?"

"You okay?"

"Yeah, are you?"

He gave a low chuckle. "I'm not the one that nearly fell."

"My penance for breaking and entering I guess." She sit down beside him. "Actually, I remembered where the key was. I'm surprised you didn't hear me."

"I'll admit, I was asleep."

"What are you worrying about now?"

"You."

"Me? It's time you turned loose of me. You have other projects, other people to think about now."

"If that's true, what do you suppose brought me here…and why are you here, of all places?"

"I…I…wanted to think about the other times we were here. Closure is so hard, giving up good things."

He reached for her, pulled her into the curve of his arm. "What are you giving up, Susan?"

"That's not fair." Her voice caught. "Why isn't she with you?"

"Who? I've never been good with riddles. What are you talking about?" He flipped the battery powered light on the end table. In the dabble of shadow she looked bad. He probably did, too.

"The woman who answered your phone before you went back to court."

He had to think fast. Victoria was the only woman he had seen the last few weekends." She was my attorney," he said finally. I don't have much to say about that. She will be glad to hear you noticed her." His chuckle eased the tension building between them. "So you thought I had another woman?" He was turning her to face him. "And it bothered you?"

"Considerably," she admitted. He was tilting her head to peer into her eyes. He began by kissing her just above the ear, because that was closest to him, and then her forehead, the other cheek and then her lips; gentle at first, and then demanding. He had to know this time for sure, did she care? God had allowed them to be here, a time and place no one scheduled and he was wired for worry. "Susan. Susan." He folded her to his body. "What are you doing to me? I came here to try to work it out to forget you but I can't. Tell me, what's the answer…. to this….problem?"

"I wish I knew." With her fingers she traced the worry lines at the corners of his eyes. "I could hardly concentrate on my guests, let alone my family. One of them said I need time alone to find myself."

"Our dinner was horrible, the food Leonie made was delicious but we were a mismatched group. Your mother in law, included." He tried to smile but it was a wasted effort. "Does she ever bend?"

"She did when her husband was alive but alone she feels deprived and mostly resentful of me."

"That's not fair," he whispered. "I wish it were winter and we could build a fire."

"It's getting cooler outside. Your wish will be here before we know it." She shivered thinking about it. "I won't be here long enough to build a fire. Will you?" She moved away from him.

"No," he groaned. "I've been messed up today and had to suppress how I really felt that I don't know what to do with myself. Very few people have seen me like that." His voice low, he asked, "Why are you here?" This was so unlike her, he wondered what made her drive to this secluded place…

"It upset me that you have someone already and really it is none of my business."

"But I don't and it is your business. I told you that is the attorney. Her husband couldn't come with her. We all three met in college." He pulled her across the sofa into his arms. "I'm glad you care. Now what do you think we should do?" She was quiet a long while. "Say it. I know you love me. Say it, Susan. I *Love you.*"

"I can't."

"Can't or won't?" He glanced down to where he had dropped his cell phone when he pulled her across the sofa. In the process, a picture of Rufus and a woman showed on the screen. He bent to pick it up.

"To say you love someone is a commitment." She saw him staring at the cell. "Who is that?"

"Rufus. Let me tell you his story." The words were no more out of his mouth and he had an idea. "Did you say someone told your family you needed to get away for a few days?" She nodded. "What if…you and I, unknown to anyone, took a little trip and spent a few days together?"

"I can't do that. It's against my Christian belief."

"We can be married, secretly, if that's what you want." He raised his eyebrows and tilt his head, comically."

"Are you serious?"

"I am. We would be legally wed and that would mean we aren't breaking God's commandments and it gives you and I time to try to convince the family we care about each other and if God allows us being together why won't they?"

"They will ha…I mean they would have my head."

He was laughing. "Don't you ever give in? I'm beginning to think Kathryn Preston influenced you more than you will ever know." He was smiling with such joy, he couldn't believe it himself. He had started out to take a drive one of the most down in spirit people he had known and now he had hope. "Don't rip this feeling of happiness away from me Susan. Think about it, you came out here. This is a scary remote place and yet you were troubled enough or perhaps wanted to relive a good moment and you made the effort and just now you almost conceded." His eyes became pleading, "Marry me, Susan. I promise I'll make you happy and you won't ever regret it."

"Kane, if my family holds this against us, we will both have regrets… and they will."

"Do I sense you and I are getting married tomorrow?"

"Tomorrow?" She was stunned by his words. "How do we do that?"

"Meet me here, tomorrow morning around nine and I'll have everything ready." He was so happy he couldn't contain the smile. "I noticed you are wearing the ring. I guess I'll have to wear a lock washer won't I?"

"Maybe we better go slow on this. We are both having second thoughts."

He dropped down on one knee. "Susan, I've asked you before but I'm asking you again, will you marry me?" The silence was deafening. He didn't move, he stayed there, still, waiting, wondering, hoping.…

For the longest moment it was as though they were locked in time. It was a heady feeling. "I will," she said. They agreed to be man and wife. If their kiss before had made them want to build a life together they could only imagine what according to God's command would do for them. They would have no shame, no guilt, only a life time to love each other and count blessings. When Kane thought Susan had forgotten something important, she asked, "Kane, do you know the Lord?"

"I do, Susan, and it is He who brought you here today. I prayed he would make a way for us."

"We are going to need Him, Kane. I cannot tell you how we are going to need the Lord."

"We'll face that when the time comes," he said, "together." He was on his feet, pulling her up. "WE have to go home. You have to pack a small suitcase and smuggle it to your vehicle, as I DO, also. Remember, be here at nine in the morning." He pulled her close and kissed her. "I love to kiss you."

They stepped close to the battery powered light and he saw she had actually wore make up and she smelled of roses and a woman's powder all in one and he knew without even knowing Susan had wanted to find him…in a place where they had been but not discussed returning too. She had wanted to see him. "You are beautiful," he said. "Beautiful inside out. I think God does reward people such as you but myself, I've done so many things wrong in life and yet, when I began to want to do right, I felt his presence. Thank you for tonight. It tells me our future will be blessed from this moment on."

"Thank you for being here," she replied. "I didn't know where I was going, but I prayed and I ended up here. I don't know if it is good or bad for my children or your child but for us, for me, I feel it will be wonderful. I can't wait and yet," she sounded wistful, "I will."

They left, separate ways as they had arrived. She was almost in a state of shock. Never in her wildest dreams had she prepared herself to say yes on this day to Kane Alberson. Today was almost over but it was Thanksgiving and she praised the Lord that he had been with her. "Please, God," she prayed again, "Put a spirit of love for me in my children so strong they will not wish either of us any harm. Let us have peace and let it begin in me."

The next morning, Susan left early. Before Barkley arrived at the shop she left the drive. A note lay on the table saying she was taking Charlemaine's advice. If he didn't understand Betsy would explain. Always lock the house when you leave, the note read, and Barkley, wish me well. I love you kids. Mom

She was not expecting Kane to be there ahead of her, but he came smiling to open the door and lift her down. "Hello, Gorgeous," he said, bending to kiss her and take her hand. "We can leave early. Do you have your driver's license and birth certificate?" She nodded. "Then we are good. Where's your suitcase?" She pointed to the front passenger side. "Whoa," he laughed, "It may be small but it's loaded."

She heard the vehicle coming down the path and turned to see the owner of the Shack in the Woods restaurant. "Is that Andrew?" Kane nodded, "But what is he doing here?"

"Andrew is going to take your vehicle and put it in his garage at home until we return and no one will know where it is. How does that sound? Better than leaving it in the woods for someone to find?"

"I was suspicious you had a plan." She hugged Andrew and thanked him.

"We are going," Kane said, pumping Andrew's hand. "Take care, Brother." Andrew was a man of a few words he smiled and waved.

Kane helped her up into his truck. "Well, Susan, within two hours I plan to make you my wife. IF you have any concerns over that, please speak now...."

She giggled. "I'm nervous, but I'm ready, Kane. It's been over five years you have been trying to convince me to marry you, so don't start trying to talk me out of it now. I'm so tired of loneliness and being the third wheel."

Kane couldn't wait to see the surprise on her face when they arrived at the courthouse in Arkansas. He turned the radio low and hummed along with the songs. Susan couldn't help but think, yesterday she was worried how life was going to end and today she prayed it never did.

They pulled into the parking lot of a magnificent Arkansas Courthouse. In a matter of minutes Kane was holding the necessary document. As Rufus had said, they were ready to become a public record.

Inside in one of the private chambers, his friend, Judge Jared Worth was waiting. Victoria had flown in for the ceremony and John was with her. White lilies lined the mahogany wall where the Judge would stand, a small keyboard was hidden behind a bank of fresh flowers and Victoria would be playing it as she sang. She was holding the small bouquet of flowers Kane had ordered for Susan. Kane led her into Jared's private chamber. She was overwhelmed by the beauty and simplicity of the white flowers against the mahogany backdrop. He saw her eyes dampen with tears.

"Susan, this is Victoria and her husband John. I've told you about them." Victoria kissed her cheek and John followed suit. Then it was Jared's turn. He was a handsome man, as tall as Kane and he seemed extremely nice. "Congratulations, to both of you," he said. "Now, let's do the ceremony. Victoria?" She smiled as she began to play the refrain of the Reason.

The bride and groom listened to the words. She thought she had never seen Kane so handsome. Kane was completely captured by this woman. He had pursued her these many years, wondering if she would one day agree to live in his world. What lay ahead would be interesting until the day they could share.

Love set its spell upon them. Jared saved the day with his wit and caring for their ceremony. God bless he said when Victoria finished. And in time he asked, "Do you Susan take this man to be your lawfully wedded husband? Kane, do you take this woman to be your lawfully wedded wife in sickness and health, in good times and bad, til death you shall part, so help you God? And then those words that bound them together… "By the authority invested in me through the state of Arkansas, I pronounce you man and wife. Whatsoever God hath joined together, let no man put asunder." He grinned. "Kane, you may kiss your bride."

They kissed and Kane glanced up as to say, Thank You. He smiled at Susan. "Hello, Mrs. Alberson. Do you hear it? Do you hear my heart? I am so happy when my heart sings….and it is singing for you."

She was breathless and she was truly happy for the first time in months. The worries of the past were at rest today. She had fought long and hard in an effort to keep Hugh's memory alive but she almost lost herself in the process. People thinking the wrong thoughts over the most mundane matter could not be helped. And she realized if Barkley loved her at all, she would bear the brunt of his wrath again and wait for him to find his way. He was his father's son and they both were blessed in the memory of a good man. As a family they would go forward. Whatever it takes with God's blessing, she believed, the future is in His hands.

The End

www.ingramcontent.com/pod-product-compliance
Lightning Source LLC
LaVergne TN
LVHW040051080526
838202LV00045B/3586